FARRAR
STRAUS
GIROUX

Call Me by Your Name

Call Me by Your Name

ANDRÉ ACIMAN

FARRAR, STRAUS AND GIROUX

NEW YORK

Farrar, Straus and Giroux
19 Union Square West, New York 10003

Copyright © 2007 by André Aciman
All rights reserved
Distributed in Canada by Douglas & McIntyre Ltd.
Printed in the United States of America
First edition, 2007

Library of Congress Cataloging-in-Publication Data
Aciman, André.
Call me by your name / André Aciman.— 1st ed.
p. cm.
ISBN-13: 978-0-374-29921-7 (alk. paper)
ISBN-10: 0-374-29921-8 (alk. paper)
1. Teenage boys—Fiction. 2. Gay teenagers—Fiction.
3. Authors—Fiction. 4. Italy—Fiction. I. Title.

PS3601.C525 C35 2007
813'.6—dc22   2006011720

www.fsgbooks.com

13 14 15 16 17 18 19 20

For Albio,
Alma de mi vida

PART 1

If Not Later, When?

"*Later!*" The word, the voice, the attitude.

I'd never heard anyone use "later" to say goodbye before. It sounded harsh, curt, and dismissive, spoken with the veiled indifference of people who may not care to see or hear from you again.

It is the first thing I remember about him, and I can hear it still today. *Later!*

I shut my eyes, say the word, and I'm back in Italy, so many years ago, walking down the tree-lined driveway, watching him step out of the cab, billowy blue shirt, wide-open collar, sunglasses, straw hat, skin everywhere. Suddenly he's shaking my hand, handing me his backpack, removing his suitcase from the trunk of the cab, asking if my father is home.

It might have started right there and then: the shirt, the rolled-up sleeves, the rounded balls of his heels slipping in and out of his frayed espadrilles, eager to test the hot gravel path that led to our house, every stride already asking, *Which way to the beach?*

This summer's houseguest. Another bore.

Then, almost without thinking, and with his back already turned to the car, he waves the back of his free hand and utters a careless *Later!* to another passenger in the car who has probably split the fare from the station. No name added, no jest to smooth out the ruffled leave-taking, nothing. His one-word send-off: brisk, bold, and blunted—take your pick, he couldn't be bothered which.

You watch, I thought, this is how he'll say goodbye to us when the time comes. With a gruff, slapdash *Later!*

Meanwhile, we'd have to put up with him for six long weeks. I was thoroughly intimidated. The unapproachable sort.

I could grow to like him, though. From rounded chin to rounded heel. Then, within days, I would learn to hate him.

This, the very person whose photo on the application form months earlier had leapt out with promises of instant affinities.

Taking in summer guests was my parents' way of helping young academics revise a manuscript before publication. For six weeks each summer I'd have to vacate my bedroom and move one room down the corridor into a much smaller room that had once belonged to my grandfather. During the winter months, when we were away in the city, it became a part-time toolshed, storage room, and attic where rumor had it my grandfather, my namesake, still ground his teeth in his eternal sleep. Summer residents didn't have to pay anything, were given the full run of the house, and could basically do anything they pleased, provided they spent an hour or so a day helping my father with his correspondence and assorted paperwork. They became part of the family, and after about fifteen years of doing this, we had gotten used to a shower of postcards and gift packages not only around Christmastime but all year long from people who were now totally devoted to our family and would go out of their way when they were in Europe to drop by B. for a day or two with their family and take a nostalgic tour of their old digs.

At meals there were frequently two or three other guests, sometimes neighbors or relatives, sometimes colleagues, lawyers, doctors, the rich and famous who'd drop by to see my father on their way to their own summer houses. Sometimes we'd even open our dining room to the occasional tourist couple who'd heard of the old villa and simply wanted to come by and take a peek and were totally enchanted when asked to eat with us and tell us all about themselves, while Mafalda, informed at the last minute, dished out her usual fare. My father, who was reserved and shy in private, loved nothing better than to have some precocious rising expert in a field keep the conversation going in a few languages while the hot summer sun, after a few glasses of *rosatello*, ushered in the unavoidable afternoon torpor. We named the task *dinner drudgery*—and, after a while, so did most of our six-week guests.

Maybe it started soon after his arrival during one of those grinding lunches when he sat next to me and it finally dawned on me that, despite a light tan acquired during his brief stay in Sicily earlier that summer, the color on the palms of his hands was the same as the pale, soft skin of his soles, of his throat, of the bottom of his forearms, which hadn't really been exposed to much sun. Almost a light pink, as glistening and smooth as the underside of a lizard's belly. Private, chaste, unfledged, like a blush on an athlete's face or an instance of dawn on a stormy night. It told me things about him I never knew to ask.

It may have started during those endless hours after lunch when everybody lounged about in bathing suits inside and outside the house, bodies sprawled everywhere, killing time before someone finally suggested we head down to the rocks for a swim. Relatives, cousins, neighbors, friends, friends of friends, colleagues, or just about anyone who cared to knock at our gate and ask if they could use our tennis court—everyone was welcome to lounge and swim and eat and, if they stayed long enough, use the guesthouse.

Or perhaps it started on the beach. Or at the tennis court. Or during our first walk together on his very first day when I was asked to show him the house and its surrounding area and, one thing leading to the other, managed to take him past the very old forged-iron metal gate as far back as the endless empty lot in the hinterland toward the abandoned train tracks that used to connect B. to N. "Is there an abandoned station house somewhere?" he asked, looking through the trees under the scalding sun, probably trying to ask the right question of the owner's son. "No, there was never a station house. The train simply stopped when you asked." He was curious about the train; the rails seemed so narrow. It was a two-wagon train bearing the royal insignia, I explained. Gypsies lived in it now. They'd been living there ever since my mother used to summer here as a girl. The gypsies had hauled the two derailed cars farther inland. Did he want to see them? "Later. Maybe." Polite indifference, as if he'd spotted my misplaced zeal to play up to him and was summarily pushing me away.

But it stung me.

Instead, he said he wanted to open an account in one of the banks in B., then pay a visit to his Italian translator, whom his Italian publisher had engaged for his book.

I decided to take him there by bike.

The conversation was no better on wheels than on foot. Along the way, we stopped for something to drink. The *bartabaccheria* was totally dark and empty. The owner was mopping the floor with a powerful ammonia solution. We stepped outside as soon as we could. A lonely blackbird, sitting in a Mediterranean pine, sang a few notes that were immediately drowned out by the rattle of the cicadas.

I took a long swill from a large bottle of mineral water, passed it to him, then drank from it again. I spilled some on my hand and rubbed my face with it, running my wet fingers through my hair. The water was insufficiently cold, not fizzy enough, leaving behind an unslaked likeness of thirst.

What did one do around here?

Nothing. Wait for summer to end.

What did one do in the winter, then?

I smiled at the answer I was about to give. He got the gist and said, "Don't tell me: wait for summer to come, right?"

I liked having my mind read. He'd pick up on *dinner drudgery* sooner than those before him.

"Actually, in the winter the place gets very gray and dark. We come for Christmas. Otherwise it's a ghost town."

"And what else do you do here at Christmas besides roast chestnuts and drink eggnog?"

He was teasing. I offered the same smile as before. He understood, said nothing, we laughed.

He asked what I did. I played tennis. Swam. Went out at night. Jogged. Transcribed music. Read.

He said he jogged too. Early in the morning. Where did one jog around here? Along the promenade, mostly. I could show him if he wanted.

It hit me in the face just when I was starting to like him again: "Later, maybe."

I had put reading last on my list, thinking that, with the willful, brazen attitude he'd displayed so far, reading would figure last on his. A few hours later, when I remembered that he had just finished writing a book on Heraclitus and that "reading" was probably not an insignificant part of his life, I realized that I needed to perform some clever backpedaling and let him know that my real interests lay right alongside his. What unsettled me, though, was not the fancy footwork needed to redeem myself. It was the unwelcome misgivings with which it finally dawned on me, both then and during our casual conversation by the train tracks, that I had all along, without seeming to, without even admitting it, already been trying—and failing—to win him over.

When I did offer—because all visitors loved the idea—to take him to San Giacomo and walk up to the very top of the belfry we nicknamed To-die-for, I should have known better than to just stand there without a comeback. I thought I'd bring him around simply by taking him up there and letting him take in the view of the town, the sea, eternity. But no. *Later!*

But it might have started way later than I think without my noticing anything at all. You see someone, but you don't really see him, he's in the wings. Or you notice him, but nothing clicks, nothing "catches," and before you're even aware of a presence, or of something troubling you, the six weeks that were offered you have almost passed and he's either already gone or just about to leave, and you're basically scrambling to come to terms with something, which, unbeknownst to you, has been brewing for weeks under your very nose and bears all the symptoms of what you're forced to call *I want*. How couldn't I have known, you ask? I know desire when I see it—and yet, this time, it slipped by completely. I was going for the devious smile that would suddenly light up his face each time he'd read my mind, when all I really wanted was skin, just skin.

At dinner on his third evening, I sensed that he was staring at me as I was explaining Haydn's *Seven Last Words of Christ*, which I'd been transcribing. I was seventeen that year and, being the youngest at the table and the least likely to be listened to, I had developed the habit of smuggling as much information into the fewest possible words. I spoke fast, which gave people the impression that I was always flustered and muffling my words. After I had finished explaining my transcription, I became aware of the keenest glance coming from my left. It thrilled and flattered me; he was obviously interested—he liked me. It hadn't been as difficult as all that, then. But when, after taking my time, I finally turned to face him and take in his glance, I met a cold and icy glare—something at once hostile and vitrified that bordered on cruelty.

It undid me completely. What had I done to deserve this? I wanted him to be kind to me again, to laugh with me as he had done just a few days earlier on the abandoned train tracks, or when I'd explained to him that same afternoon that B. was the only town in Italy where the *corriera*, the regional bus line, carrying Christ, whisked by without ever stopping. He had immediately laughed and recognized the veiled allusion to Carlo Levi's book. I liked how our minds seemed to travel in parallel, how we instantly inferred what words the other was toying with but at the last moment held back.

He was going to be a difficult neighbor. Better stay away from him, I thought. To think that I had almost fallen for the skin of his hands, his chest, his feet that had never touched a rough surface in their existence—and his eyes, which, when their other, kinder gaze fell on you, came like the miracle of the Resurrection. You could never stare long enough but needed to keep staring to find out why you couldn't.

I must have shot him a similarly wicked glance.

For two days our conversations came to a sudden halt.

On the long balcony that both our bedrooms shared, total avoidance: just a makeshift hello, good morning, nice weather, shallow chitchat.

Then, without explanation, things resumed.

Did I want to go jogging this morning? No, not really. Well, let's swim, then.

Today, the pain, the stoking, the thrill of someone new, the promise of so much bliss hovering a fingertip away, the fumbling around people I might misread and don't want to lose and must second-guess at every turn, the desperate cunning I bring to everyone I want and crave to be wanted by, the screens I put up as though between me and the world there were not just one but layers of rice-paper sliding doors, the urge to scramble and un-scramble what was never really coded in the first place—all these started the summer Oliver came into our house. They are em-bossed on every song that was a hit that summer, in every novel I read during and after his stay, on anything from the smell of rosemary on hot days to the frantic rattle of the cicadas in the afternoon—smells and sounds I'd grown up with and known every year of my life until then but that had suddenly turned on me and acquired an inflection forever colored by the events of that summer.

Or perhaps it started after his first week, when I was thrilled to see he still remembered who I was, that he didn't ignore me, and that, therefore, I could allow myself the luxury of passing him on my way to the garden and not having to pretend I was un-aware of him. We jogged early on the first morning—all the way up to B. and back. Early the next morning we swam. Then, the day after, we jogged again. I liked racing by the milk delivery van when it was far from done with its rounds, or by the grocer and the baker as they were just getting ready for business, liked to run along the shore and the promenade when there wasn't a soul about yet and our house seemed a distant mirage. I liked it when our feet were aligned, left with left, and struck the ground at the same time, leaving footprints on the shore that I wished to return to and, in secret, place my foot where his had left its mark.

This alternation of running and swimming was simply his "routine" in graduate school. Did he run on the Sabbath? I joked. He always exercised, even when he was sick; he'd exercise in bed if he had to. Even when he'd slept with someone new the night before, he said, he'd still head out for a jog early in the morning. The only time he didn't exercise was when they operated on him. When I asked him what for, the answer I had promised never to incite in him came at me like the thwack of a jack-in-the-box wearing a baleful smirk. "Later."

Perhaps he was out of breath and didn't want to talk too much or just wanted to concentrate on his swimming or his running. Or perhaps it was his way of spurring me to do the same—totally harmless.

But there was something at once chilling and off-putting in the sudden distance that crept between us in the most unexpected moments. It was almost as though he were doing it on purpose; feeding me slack, and more slack, and then yanking away any semblance of fellowship.

The steely gaze always returned. One day, while I was practicing my guitar at what had become "my table" in the back garden by the pool and he was lying nearby on the grass, I recognized the gaze right away. He had been staring at me while I was focusing on the fingerboard, and when I suddenly raised my face to see if he liked what I was playing, there it was: cutting, cruel, like a glistening blade instantly retracted the moment its victim caught sight of it. He gave me a bland smile, as though to say, *No point hiding it now.*

Stay away from him.

He must have noticed I was shaken and in an effort to make it up to me began asking me questions about the guitar. I was too much on my guard to answer him with candor. Meanwhile, hearing me scramble for answers made him suspect that perhaps more was amiss than I was showing. "Don't bother explaining. Just play it again." But I thought you hated it. Hated it? Whatever gave you that idea? We argued back and forth. "Just play it, will you?" "The same one?" "The same one."

I stood up and walked into the living room, leaving the large French windows open so that he might hear me play it on the piano. He followed me halfway and, leaning on the windows' wooden frame, listened for a while.

"You changed it. It's not the same. What did you do to it?"

"I just played it the way Liszt would have played it had he jimmied around with it."

"Just play it again, *please!*"

I liked the way he feigned exasperation. So I started playing the piece again.

After a while: "I can't believe you changed it again."

"Well, not by much. This is just how Busoni would have played it if he had altered Liszt's version."

"Can't you just play the Bach the way Bach wrote it?"

"But Bach never wrote it for guitar. He may not even have written it for the harpsichord. In fact, we're not even sure it's by Bach at all."

"Forget I asked."

"Okay, okay. No need to get so worked up," I said. It was my turn to feign grudging acquiescence. "This is the Bach as transcribed by me without Busoni and Liszt. It's a very young Bach and it's dedicated to his brother."

I knew exactly what phrase in the piece must have stirred him the first time, and each time I played it, I was sending it to him as a little gift, because it was really dedicated to him, as a token of something very beautiful in me that would take no genius to figure out and that urged me to throw in an extended cadenza. Just for him.

We were—and he must have recognized the signs long before I did—flirting.

Later that evening in my diary, I wrote: *I was exaggerating when I said I thought you hated the piece. What I meant to say was: I thought you hated me. I was hoping you'd persuade me of the opposite—and you did, for a while. Why won't I believe it tomorrow morning?*

So this is who he also is, I said to myself after seeing how he'd flipped from ice to sunshine.

I might as well have asked: Do I flip back and forth in just the same way?

P.S. We are not written for one instrument alone; I am not, neither are you.

I had been perfectly willing to brand him as difficult and unapproachable and have nothing more to do with him. Two words from him, and I had seen my pouting apathy change into I'll play anything for you till you ask me to stop, till it's time for lunch, till the skin on my fingers wears off layer after layer, because I like doing things for you, will do anything for you, just say the word, I liked you from day one, and even when you'll return ice for my renewed offers of friendship, I'll never forget that this conversation occurred between us and that there are easy ways to bring back summer in the snowstorm.

What I forgot to earmark in that promise was that ice and apathy have ways of instantly repealing all truces and resolutions signed in sunnier moments.

Then came that July Sunday afternoon when our house suddenly emptied, and we were the only ones there, and fire tore through my guts—because "fire" was the first and easiest word that came to me later that same evening when I tried to make sense of it in my diary. I'd waited and waited in my room pinioned to my bed in a trancelike state of terror and anticipation. Not a fire of passion, not a ravaging fire, but something paralyzing, like the fire of cluster bombs that suck up the oxygen around them and leave you panting because you've been kicked in the gut and a vacuum has ripped up every living lung tissue and dried your mouth, and you hope nobody speaks, because you can't talk, and you pray no one asks you to move, because your heart is clogged and beats so fast it would sooner spit out shards of glass than let anything else flow through its narrowed chambers. Fire like fear, like panic, like one more minute of this and I'll die if he doesn't knock at my door, but I'd sooner he never knock than knock now. I had learned to leave my French windows ajar, and I'd lie on my bed wearing only my bathing suit, my entire body on fire. Fire like a pleading that says, Please, please, tell me I'm wrong, tell me I've imagined all this, because it can't possibly be true for you as well, and if it's true for you too, then you're the cruelest man alive. This, the afternoon he did finally walk into my room without knocking as if summoned by my prayers and asked how come I wasn't with the others at the beach, and all I could think of saying, though I couldn't bring myself to say it, was, To be with you. To be with you, Oliver. With or without my bathing suit. To be with you on my bed. In your bed. Which is

my bed during the other months of the year. Do with me what
you want. Take me. Just ask if I want to and see the answer you'll
get, just don't let me say no.

And tell me I wasn't dreaming that night when I heard a
noise outside the landing by my door and suddenly knew that
someone was in my room, someone was sitting at the foot of my
bed, thinking, thinking, thinking, and finally started moving up
toward me and was now lying, not next to me, but on top of me,
while I lay on my tummy, and that I liked it so much that, rather
than risk doing anything to show I'd been awakened or to let him
change his mind and go away, I feigned to be fast asleep, thinking, This is not, cannot, had better not be a dream, because the
words that came to me, as I pressed my eyes shut, were, This is
like coming home, like coming home after years away among
Trojans and Lestrygonians, like coming home to a place where
everyone is like you, where people know, they just know—
coming home as when everything falls into place and you suddenly realize that for seventeen years all you'd been doing was
fiddling with the wrong combination. Which was when I decided
to convey without budging, without moving a single muscle in
my body, that I'd be willing to yield if you pushed, that I'd already yielded, was yours, all yours, except that you were suddenly gone and though it seemed too true to be a dream, yet I
was convinced that all I wanted from that day onward was for
you to do the exact same thing you'd done in my sleep.

The next day we were playing doubles, and during a break, as we
were drinking Mafalda's lemonades, he put his free arm around
me and then gently squeezed his thumb and forefingers into my
shoulder in imitation of a friendly hug-massage—the whole thing
very chummy-chummy. But I was so spellbound that I wrenched

myself free from his touch, because a moment longer and I would have slackened like one of those tiny wooden toys whose gimp-legged body collapses as soon as the mainsprings are touched. Taken aback, he apologized and asked if he had pressed a "nerve or something"—he hadn't meant to hurt me. He must have felt thoroughly mortified if he suspected he had either hurt me or touched me the wrong way. The last thing I wanted was to discourage him. Still, I blurted something like, "It didn't hurt," and would have dropped the matter there. But I sensed that if it wasn't pain that had prompted such a reaction, what other explanation could account for my shrugging him off so brusquely in front of my friends? So I mimicked the face of someone trying very hard, but failing, to smother a grimace of pain.

It never occurred to me that what had totally panicked me when he touched me was exactly what startles virgins on being touched for the first time by the person they desire: he stirs nerves in them they never knew existed and that produce far, far more disturbing pleasures than they are used to on their own.

He still seemed surprised by my reaction but gave every sign of believing in, as I of concealing, the pain around my shoulder. It was his way of letting me off the hook and of pretending he wasn't in the least bit aware of any nuance in my reaction. Knowing, as I later came to learn, how thoroughly trenchant was his ability to sort contradictory signals, I have no doubt that he must have already suspected something. "Here, let me make it better." He was testing me and proceeded to massage my shoulder. "Relax," he said in front of the others. "But I am relaxing." "You're as stiff as this bench. Feel this," he said to Marzia, one of the girls closest to us. "It's all knots." I felt her hands on my back. "Here," he ordered, pressing her flattened palm hard against my back. "Feel it? He should relax more," he said. "You should relax more," she repeated.

Perhaps, in this, as with everything else, because I didn't know how to speak in code, I didn't know how to speak at all. I felt like a deaf and dumb person who can't even use sign language. I stammered all manner of things so as not to speak my mind. That was the extent of my code. So long as I had breath to put words in my mouth, I could more or less carry it off. Otherwise, the silence between us would probably give me away— which was why anything, even the most spluttered nonsense, was preferable to silence. Silence would expose me. But what was certain to expose me even more was my struggle to overcome it in front of others.

The despair aimed at myself must have given my features something bordering on impatience and unspoken rage. That he might have mistaken these as aimed at him never crossed my mind.

Maybe it was for similar reasons that I would look away each time he looked at me: to conceal the strain on my timidity. That he might have found my avoidance offensive and retaliated with a hostile glance from time to time never crossed my mind either.

What I hoped he hadn't noticed in my overreaction to his grip was something else. Before shirking off his arm, I knew I had yielded to his hand and had almost leaned into it, as if to say—as I'd heard adults so often say when someone happened to massage their shoulders while passing behind them—Don't stop. Had he noticed I was ready not just to yield but to mold into his body?

This was the feeling I took to my diary that night as well: I called it the "swoon." Why had I swooned? And could it happen so easily—just let him touch me somewhere and I'd totally go limp and will-less? Was this what people meant by butter melting?

And why wouldn't I show him how like butter I was? Because I was afraid of what might happen then? Or was I afraid he would have laughed at me, told everyone, or ignored the whole thing on the pretext I was too young to know what I was doing?

Or was it because if he so much as suspected—and anyone who suspected would of necessity be on the same wavelength—he might be tempted to act on it? Did I want him to act? Or would I prefer a lifetime of longing provided we both kept this little Ping-Pong game going: not knowing, not-not knowing, not-not-not knowing? Just be quiet, say nothing, and if you can't say "yes," don't say "no," say "later." Is this why people say "maybe" when they mean "yes," but hope you'll think it's "no" when all they really mean is, *Please, just ask me once more, and once more after that*?

I look back to that summer and can't believe that despite every one of my efforts to live with the "fire" and the "swoon," life still granted wonderful moments. Italy. Summer. The noise of the cicadas in the early afternoon. My room. His room. Our balcony that shut the whole world out. The soft wind trailing exhalations from our garden up the stairs to my bedroom. The summer I learned to love fishing. Because he did. To love jogging. Because he did. To love octopus, Heraclitus, *Tristan*. The summer I'd hear a bird sing, smell a plant, or feel the mist rise from under my feet on warm sunny days and, because my senses were always on alert, would automatically find them rushing to him.

I could have denied so many things—that I longed to touch his knees and wrists when they glistened in the sun with that viscous sheen I've seen in so very few; that I loved how his white tennis shorts seemed perpetually stained by the color of clay, which, as the weeks wore on, became the color of his skin; that his hair, turning blonder every day, caught the sun before the sun was completely out in the morning; that his billowy blue shirt, becoming ever more billowy when he wore it on gusty days on the patio by the pool, promised to harbor a scent of skin and sweat that made me hard just thinking of it. All this I could have denied. And believed my denials.

But it was the gold necklace and the Star of David with a golden mezuzah on his neck that told me here was something more compelling than anything I wanted from him, for it bound us and reminded me that, while everything else conspired to make us the two most dissimilar beings, this at least transcended all differences. I saw his star almost immediately during his first day with us. And from that moment on I knew that what mystified me and made me want to seek out his friendship, without ever hoping to find ways to dislike him, was larger than anything either of us could ever want from the other, larger and therefore better than his soul, my body, or earth itself. Staring at his neck with its star and telltale amulet was like staring at something timeless, ancestral, immortal in me, in him, in both of us, begging to be rekindled and brought back from its millenary sleep.

What baffled me was that he didn't seem to care or notice that I wore one too. Just as he probably didn't care or notice each time my eyes wandered along his bathing suit and tried to make out the contour of what made us brothers in the desert.

With the exception of my family, he was probably the only other Jew who had ever set foot in B. But unlike us he let you see it from the very start. We were not conspicuous Jews. We wore our Judaism as people do almost everywhere in the world: under the shirt, not hidden, but tucked away. "Jews of discretion," to use my mother's words. To see someone proclaim his Judaism on his neck as Oliver did when he grabbed one of our bikes and headed into town with his shirt wide open shocked us as much as it taught us we could do the same and get away with it. I tried imitating him a few times. But I was too self-conscious, like someone trying to feel natural while walking about naked in a locker room only to end up aroused by his own nakedness. In town, I tried flaunting my Judaism with the silent bluster that comes less from arrogance than from repressed shame. Not him. It's not that he never thought about being Jewish or about the life of Jews in a Catholic country. Sometimes we spoke about just this topic during those long afternoons when both of us would put aside work and enjoy chatting while the entire household and guests had all drifted into every available bedroom to rest for a few hours. He had lived long enough in small towns in New England to know what it felt like to be the odd Jew out. But Judaism never troubled him the way it troubled me, nor was it the subject of an abiding, metaphysical discomfort with himself and the world. It did not even harbor the mystical, unspoken promise of redemptive brotherhood. And perhaps this was why he wasn't ill at ease with being Jewish and didn't constantly have to pick at it, the way children pick at scabs they wish would go away. He was okay with being Jewish. He was okay with himself, the way he was okay with his body, with his looks, with his antic backhand, with his choice of books, music, films, friends. He was okay with losing his prized Mont Blanc pen. "I can buy another one just like it." He was okay with criticism too. He showed my father a few pages he was proud of having written. My father told him his insights into Heraclitus were brilliant but needed firming up, that he needed to accept the paradoxical nature of the philosopher's thinking, not simply explain it away. He was okay with firming things up, he was okay with paradox. Back to the drawing board—he was okay with the drawing board as well. He invited my young aunt for a tête-à-tête midnight *gita*—spin—in our motorboat. She declined. That was okay. He tried again a few days later, was turned down again, and again made light of it. She too was okay with it, and, had she spent another week with us, would probably have been okay with going out to sea for a midnight gita that could easily have lasted till sunrise.

Only once during his very first few days did I get a sense that this willful but accommodating, laid-back, water-over-my-back,

unflappable, unfazed twenty-four-year-old who was so heed-
lessly okay with so many things in life was, in fact, a thoroughly
alert, cold, sagacious judge of character and situations. Nothing
he did or said was unpremeditated. He saw through everybody,
but he saw through them precisely because the first thing he
looked for in people was the very thing he had seen in himself
and may not have wished others to see. He was, as my mother
was scandalized to learn one day, a supreme poker player who'd
escape into town at night twice a week or so to "play a few
hands." This was why, to our complete surprise, he had insisted
on opening a bank account on the very day of his arrival. None
of our residents had ever had a local bank account. Most didn't
have a penny.

It had happened during a lunch when my father had invited
a journalist who had dabbled in philosophy in his youth and
wanted to show that, though he had never written about Heraclitus, he could still spar on any matter under the sun. He and
Oliver didn't hit it off. Afterward, my father had said, "A very
witty man—damn clever too." "Do you really think so, Pro?"
Oliver interrupted, unaware that my father, while very easygoing
himself, did not always like being contradicted, much less being
called Pro, though he went along with both. "Yes, I do," insisted
my father. "Well, I'm not sure I agree at all. I find him arrogant,
dull, flat-footed, and coarse. He uses humor and a lot of
voice"—Oliver mimicked the man's gravitas—"and broad ges-
tures to nudge his audience because he is totally incapable of arguing a case. The voice thing is so over the top, Pro. People laugh
at his humor not because he is funny but because he telegraphs
his desire to be funny. His humor is nothing more than a way of
winning over people he can't persuade.

"If you look at him when you're speaking, he always looks
away, he's not listening, he's just itching to say things he's re-

hearsed while you were speaking and wants to say before he for-
gets them."

How could anyone intuit the manner of someone's thinking
unless he himself was already familiar with this same mode of
thinking? How could he perceive so many devious turns in others unless he had practiced them himself?

What struck me was not just his amazing gift for reading
people, for rummaging inside them and digging out the precise
configuration of their personality, but his ability to intuit things
in exactly the way I myself might have intuited them. This, in the
end, was what drew me to him with a compulsion that overrode
desire or friendship or the allurements of a common religion.
"How about catching a movie?" he blurted out one evening when
we were all sitting together, as if he'd suddenly hit on a solution
to what promised to be a dull night indoors. We had just left the
dinner table where my father, as was his habit these days, had
been urging me to try to go out with friends more often, especially
in the evening. It bordered on a lecture. Oliver was still new with
us and knew no one in town, so I must have seemed as good a
movie partner as any. But he had asked his question in far too
breezy and spontaneous a manner, as though he wanted me and
everyone else in the living room to know that he was hardly invested in going to the movies and could just as readily stay home
and go over his manuscript. The carefee inflection of his offer,
however, was also a wink aimed at my father: he was only pretending to have come up with the idea; in fact, without letting
me suspect it, he was picking up on my father's advice at the dinner table and was offering to go for my benefit alone.

I smiled, not at the offer, but at the double-edged maneuver.
He immediately caught my smile. And having caught it, smiled
back, almost in self-mockery, sensing that if he gave any sign of
guessing I'd seen through his ruse he'd be confirming his guilt,

but that refusing to own up to it, after I'd made clear I'd intercepted it, would indict him even more. So he smiled to confess he'd been caught but also to show he was a good enough sport to own up to it and still enjoy going to the movies together. The whole thing thrilled me.

Or perhaps his smile was his way of countering my reading tit for tat with the unstated suggestion that, much as he'd been caught trying to affect total casualness on the face of his offer, he too had found something to smile about *in me*—namely, the shrewd, devious, guilty pleasure I derived in finding so many imperceptible affinities between us. There may have been nothing there, and I might have invented the whole thing. But both of us knew what the other had seen. That evening, as we biked to the movie theater, I was—and I didn't care to hide it—riding on air.

So, with so much insight, would he *not* have noticed the meaning behind my abrupt shrinking away from his hand? *Not* notice that I'd leaned into his grip? *Not* know that I didn't want him to let go of me? *Not* sense that when he started massaging me, my inability to relax was my last refuge, my last defense, my last pretense, that I had by no means resisted, that mine was fake resistance, that I was incapable of resisting and would never want to resist, no matter what he did or asked me to do? *Not* know, as I sat on my bed that Sunday afternoon when no one was home except for the two of us and watched him enter my room and ask me why I wasn't with the others at the beach, that if I refused to answer and simply shrugged my shoulders under his gaze, it was simply so as not to show that I couldn't gather sufficient breath to speak, that if I so much as let out a sound it might be to utter a desperate confession or a sob—one or the other? Never, since childhood, had anyone brought me to such a pass. Bad allergy, I'd said. Me too, he replied. We probably have the same one. Again I shrugged my shoulders. He picked up my old teddy bear in one hand, turned its face toward him, and whispered something into its ear. Then, turning the teddy's face to me and altering his voice, asked, "What's wrong? You're upset." By then he must have noticed the bathing suit I was wearing. Was I wearing it lower than was decent? "Want to go for a swim?" he asked. "Later, maybe," I said, echoing his word but also trying to say as little as possible before he'd spot I was out of breath. "Let's go now." He extended his hand to help me get up. I grabbed it and, turning on my side facing the wall away from him to prevent him from seeing me, I asked, "Must we?" This was the closest I would ever come to saying, Stay. Just stay with me. Let your hand travel wherever it wishes, take my suit off, take me, I won't make a noise, won't tell a soul, I'm hard and you know it, and if you won't, I'll take that hand of yours and slip it into my suit now and let you put as many fingers as you want inside me.

He *wouldn't* have picked up on any of this?

He said he was going to change and walked out of my room. "I'll meet you downstairs." When I looked at my crotch, to my complete dismay I saw it was damp. Had he seen it? Surely he must have. That's why he wanted us to go to the beach. That's why he walked out of my room. I hit my head with my fist. How could I have been so careless, so thoughtless, so totally stupid? Of course he'd seen.

I should have learned to do what he'd have done. Shrugged my shoulders—and been okay with pre-come. But that wasn't me. It would never have occurred to me to say, So what if he saw? Now he knows.

What never crossed my mind was that someone else who lived under our roof, who played cards with my mother, ate breakfast and supper at our table, recited the Hebrew blessing on

Fridays for the sheer fun of it, slept in one of our beds, used our towels, shared our friends, watched TV with us on rainy days when we sat in the living room with a blanket around us because it got cold and we felt so snug being all together as we listened to the rain patter against the windows—that someone else in my immediate world might like what I liked, want what I wanted, be who I was. It would never have entered my mind because I was still under the illusion that, barring what I'd read in books, in-ferred from rumors, and overheard in bawdy talk all over, no one my age had ever wanted to be both man and woman—with men and women. I had wanted other men my age before and had slept with women. But before he'd stepped out of the cab and walked into our home, it would never have seemed remotely possible that someone so thoroughly okay with himself might want me to share his body as much as I ached to yield up mine.

And yet, about two weeks after his arrival, all I wanted every night was for him to leave his room, not via its front door, but through the French windows on our balcony. I wanted to hear his window open, hear his espadrilles on the balcony, and then the sound of my own window, which was never locked, being pushed open as he'd step into my room after everyone had gone to bed, slip under my covers, undress me without asking, and after mak-ing me want him more than I thought I could ever want another living soul, gently, softly, and, with the kindness one Jew extends to another, work his way into my body, gently and softly, after heeding the words I'd been rehearsing for days now, Please, don't hurt me, which meant, Hurt me all you want.

I seldom stayed in my room during the day. Instead, for the past few summers I had appropriated a round table with an umbrella in the back garden by the pool. Pavel, our previous summer resi-

dent, had liked working in his room, occasionally stepping out
onto the balcony to get a glimpse of the sea or smoke a cigarette.
Maynard, before him, had also worked in his room. Oliver needed
company. He began by sharing my table but eventually grew to
like throwing a large sheet on the grass and lying on it, flanked
by loose pages of his manuscript and what he liked to call his
"things": lemonade, suntan lotion, books, espadrilles, sunglasses,
colored pens, and music, which he listened to with headphones, so
that it was impossible to speak to him unless he was speaking to
you first. Sometimes, when I came downstairs with my scorebook
or other books in the morning, he was already sprawled in the
sun wearing his red or yellow bathing suit and sweating. We'd go
jogging or swimming, and return to find breakfast waiting for us.
Then he got in the habit of leaving his "things" on the grass and
lying right on the tiled edge of the pool—called "heaven," short
for "This is heaven," as he often said after lunch, "I'm going to
heaven now," adding, as an inside joke among Latinists, "to apri-
cate." We would tease him about the countless hours he would
spend soaking in suntan lotion as he lay on the same exact spot
along the pool. "How long were you *in heaven* this morning?" my
mother would ask. "Two straight hours. But I plan to return early
this afternoon for a much longer aprication." Going to the *orle of
paradise* also meant lying on his back along the edge of the pool
with one leg dangling in the water, wearing his headphones and
his straw hat flat on his face.

Here was someone who lacked for nothing. I couldn't understand this feeling. I envied him.

"Oliver, are you sleeping?" I would ask when the air by the
pool had grown oppressively torpid and quiet.

Silence.

Then his reply would come, almost a sigh, without a single
muscle moving in his body. "I was."

"Sorry."

That foot in the water—I could have kissed every toe on it. Then kissed his ankles and his knees. How often had I stared at his bathing suit while his hat was covering his face? He couldn't possibly have known what I was looking at.

Or:

"Oliver, are you sleeping?"

Long silence.

"No. Thinking."

"About what?"

His toes flicking the water.

"About Heidegger's interpretation of a fragment by Heraclitus."

Or, when I wasn't practicing the guitar and he wasn't listening to his headphones, still with his straw hat flat on his face, he would suddenly break the silence:

"Elio."

"Yes?"

"What are you doing?"

"Reading."

"No, you're not."

"Thinking, then."

"About?"

I was dying to tell him.

"Private," I replied.

"So you won't tell me?"

"So I won't tell you."

"So he won't tell me," he repeated, pensively, as if explaining to someone about me.

How I loved the way he repeated what I myself had just repeated. It made me think of a caress, or of a gesture, which happens to be totally accidental the first time but becomes in-

tentional the second time and more so yet the third. It reminded
me of the way Mafalda would make my bed every morning, first
by folding the top sheet over the blanket, then by folding the
sheet back again to cover the pillows on top of the blanket, and
once more yet when she folded the whole thing over the bedspread—back and forth until I knew that tucked in between these
multiple folds were tokens of something at once pious and indulgent, like acquiescence in an instant of passion.

Silence was always light and unobtrusive on those afternoons.

"I'm not telling," I said.

"Then I'm going back to sleep," he'd say.

My heart was racing. He must have known.

Profound silence again. Moments later:

"This is heaven."

And I wouldn't hear him say another word for at least an hour.

There was nothing I loved more in life than to sit at my table
and pore over my transcriptions while he lay on his belly mark-
ing pages he'd pick up every morning from Signora Milani, his
translator in B.

"Listen to this," he'd sometimes say, removing his headphones,
breaking the oppressive silence of those long sweltering summer
mornings. "Just listen to this drivel." And he'd proceed to read
aloud something he couldn't believe he had written months earlier.

"Does it make any sense to you? Not to me."

"Maybe it did when you wrote it," I said.

He thought for a while as though weighing my words.

"That's the kindest thing anyone's said to me in months"—
spoken ever so earnestly, as if he was hit by a sudden revelation
and was taking what I'd said to mean much more than I thought
it did. I felt ill at ease, looked away, and finally muttered the first
thing that came to mind: "Kind?" I asked.

"Yes, kind."

I didn't know what kindness had to do with it. Or perhaps I wasn't seeing clearly enough where all this was headed and preferred to let the matter slide. Silence again. Until the next time he'd speak.

How I loved it when he broke the silence between us to say something—anything—or to ask what I thought about X, or had I ever heard of Y? Nobody in our household ever asked my opinion about anything. If he hadn't already figured out why, he would soon enough—it was only a matter of time before he fell in with everyone's view that I was the baby of the family. And yet here he was in his third week with us, asking me if I'd ever heard of Athanasius Kircher, Giuseppe Belli, and Paul Celan.

"I have."

"I'm almost a decade older than you are and until a few days ago had never heard of any of them. I don't get it."

"What's not to get? Dad's a university professor. I grew up without TV. Get it now?"

"Go back to your plunking, will you!" he said as though crumpling a towel and throwing it at my face.

I even liked the way he told me off.

One day while moving my notebook on the table, I accidentally tipped over my glass. It fell on the grass. It didn't break. Oliver, who was close by, got up, picked it up, and placed it, not just on the table, but right next to my pages.

I didn't know where to find the words to thank him.

"You didn't have to," I finally said.

He let just enough time go by for me to register that his answer might not be casual or carefree.

"I wanted to."

He wanted to, I thought.

I wanted to, I imagined him repeating—kind, complaisant, effusive, as he was when the mood would suddenly strike him.

To me those hours spent at that round wooden table in our garden with the large umbrella imperfectly shading my papers, the chinking of our iced lemonades, the sound of the not-too-distant surf gently lapping the giant rocks below, and in the background, from some neighboring house, the muffled crackle of the hit parade medley on perpetual replay—all these are forever impressed on those mornings when all I prayed for was for time to stop. Let summer never end, let him never go away, let the music on perpetual replay play forever, I'm asking for very little, and I swear I'll ask for nothing more.

What did I want? And why couldn't I know what I wanted, even when I was perfectly ready to be brutal in my admissions?

Perhaps the very least I wanted was for him to tell me that there was nothing wrong with me, that I was no less human than any other young man my age. I would have been satisfied and asked for nothing else than if he'd bent down and picked up the dignity I could so effortlessly have thrown at his feet.

I was Glaucus and he was Diomedes. In the name of some obscure cult among men, I was giving him my golden armor for his bronze. Fair exchange. Neither haggled, just as neither spoke of thrift or extravagance.

The word "friendship" came to mind. But friendship, as defined by everyone, was alien, fallow stuff I cared nothing for. What I may have wanted instead, from the moment he stepped out of the cab to our farewell in Rome, was what all humans ask of one another, what makes life livable. It would have to come from him first. Then possibly from me.

There is a law somewhere that says that when one person is thoroughly smitten with the other, the other must unavoidably be smitten as well. *Amor ch'a null'amato amar perdona.* Love, which exempts no one who's loved from loving, Francesca's words in the *Inferno*. Just wait and be hopeful. I was hopeful, though perhaps this was what I had wanted all along. To wait forever.

As I sat there working on transcriptions at my round table in the morning, what I would have settled for was not his friendship, not anything. Just to look up and find him there, suntan lotion, straw hat, red bathing suit, lemonade. To look up and find you there, Oliver. For the day will come soon enough when I'll look up and you'll no longer be there.

By late morning, friends and neighbors from adjoining houses frequently dropped in. Everyone would gather in our garden and then head out together to the beach below. Our house was the closest to the water, and all you needed was to open the tiny gate by the balustrade, take the narrow stairway down the bluff, and you were on the rocks. Chiara, one of the girls who three years ago was shorter than I and who just last summer couldn't leave me alone, had now blossomed into a woman who had finally mastered the art of not always greeting me whenever we met. Once, she and her younger sister dropped in with the rest, picked up Oliver's shirt on the grass, threw it at him, and said, "Enough. We're going to the beach and you're coming."

He was willing to oblige. "Let me just put away these papers. Otherwise his father"—and with his hands carrying papers he used his chin to point at me—"will skin me alive."

"Talking about skin, come here," she said, and with her fingernails gently and slowly tried to pull a sliver of peeling skin from his tanned shoulders, which had acquired the light golden hue of a wheat field in late June. How I wished I could do that.

"Tell his father that *I* crumpled his papers. See what he says then."

Looking over his manuscript, which Oliver had left on the large dining table on his way upstairs, Chiara shouted from below that she could do a better job translating these pages than the local translator. A child of expats like me, Chiara had an Italian mother and an American father. She spoke English and Italian with both.

"Do you type good too?" came his voice from upstairs as he rummaged for another bathing suit in his bedroom, then in the shower, doors slamming, drawers thudding, shoes kicked.

"I type good," she shouted, looking up into the empty stairwell.

"As good as you speak good?"

"Bettah. And I'd'a gave you a bettah price too."

"I need five pages translated per day, to be ready for pickup every morning."

"Then I won't do nu'in for you," snapped Chiara. "Find yuhsef somebuddy else."

"Well, Signora Milani needs the money," he said, coming downstairs, billowy blue shirt, espadrilles, red trunks, sunglasses, and the red Loeb edition of Lucretius that never left his side. "I'm okay with her," he said as he rubbed some lotion on his shoulders.

"I'm okay with her," Chiara said, tittering. "I'm okay with you, you're okay with me, she's okay with him—"

"Stop clowning and let's go swimming," said Chiara's sister.

He had, it took me a while to realize, four personalities depending on which bathing suit he was wearing. Knowing which to expect gave me the illusion of a slight advantage. Red: bold, set in his ways, very grown-up, almost gruff and ill-tempered—stay away. Yellow: sprightly, buoyant, funny, not without barbs—don't give in too easily; might turn to red in no time. Green, which he seldom wore: acquiescent, eager to learn, eager to speak, sunny—why wasn't he always like this? Blue: the after-

noon he stepped into my room from the balcony, the day he mas-
saged my shoulder, or when he picked up my glass and placed it
right next to me.

Today was red: he was hasty, determined, snappy.

On his way out, he grabbed an apple from a large bowl of
fruit, uttered a cheerful "Later, Mrs. P." to my mother, who was
sitting with two friends in the shade, all three of them in bathing
suits, and, rather than open the gate to the narrow stairway leading to the rocks, jumped over it. None of our summer guests had
ever been as freewheeling. But everyone loved him for it, the way
everyone grew to love *Later!*

"Okay, Oliver, later, okay," said my mother, trying to speak
his lingo, having even grown to accept her new title as Mrs. P.
There was always something abrupt about that word. It wasn't
"See you later" or "Take care, now," or even "Ciao." *Later!* was
a chilling, slam-dunk salutation that shoved aside all our hon-
eyed European niceties. *Later!* always left a sharp aftertaste to
what until then may have been a warm, heart-to-heart moment.
Later! didn't close things neatly or allow them to trail off. It
slammed them shut.

But *Later!* was also a way of avoiding saying goodbye, of
making light of all goodbyes. You said *Later!* not to mean farewell but to say you'd be back in no time. It was the equivalent of
his saying "Just a sec" when my mother once asked him to pass
the bread and he was busy pulling apart the fish bones on his
plate. *"Just a sec."* My mother, who hated what she called his
Americanisms, ended up calling him *Il cauboi*—the cowboy. It
started as a putdown and soon enough became an endearment,
to go along with her other nickname for him, conferred during
his first week, when he came down to the dinner table after show-
ering, his glistening hair combed back. *La star*, she had said,
short for *la muvi star*. My father, always the most indulgent

among us, but also the most observant, had figured the cauboi out. "*É un timido*, he's shy, that's why," he said when asked to explain Oliver's abrasive *Later!*

Oliver *timido*? That was new. Could all of his gruff Americanisms be nothing more than an exaggerated way of covering up the simple fact that he didn't know—or feared he didn't know—how to take his leave gracefully? It reminded me of how for days he had refused to eat soft-boiled eggs in the morning. By the fourth or fifth day, Mafalda insisted he couldn't leave the region without tasting our eggs. He finally consented, only to admit, with a touch of genuine embarrassment that he never bothered to conceal, that he didn't know how to open a soft-boiled egg. "*Lasci fare a me*, Signor Ulliva, leave it to me," she said. From that morning on and well into his stay with us, she would bring Ulliva two eggs and stop serving everyone until she had sliced open the shell of both his eggs.

Did he perhaps want a third? she asked. Some people liked more than two eggs. No, two would do, he replied, and, turning to my parents, added, "I know myself. If I have three, I'll have a fourth, and more." I had never heard someone his age say, *I know myself*. It intimidated me.

But she had been won over well before, on his third morning with us, when she asked him if he liked juice in the morning, and he'd said yes. He was probably expecting orange or grapefruit juice; what he got was a large glass filled to the rim with thick apricot juice. He had never had apricot juice in his life. She stood facing him with her salver flat against her apron, trying to make out his reaction as he quaffed it down. He said nothing at first. Then, probably without thinking, he smacked his lips. She was in heaven. My mother couldn't believe that people who taught at world-famous universities smacked their lips after downing apricot juice. From that day on, a glass of the stuff was waiting for him every morning.

He was baffled to know that apricot trees existed in, of all places, our orchard. On late afternoons, when there was nothing to do in the house, Mafalda would ask him to climb a ladder with a basket and pick those fruits that were almost blushing with shame, she said. He would joke in Italian, pick one out, and ask, Is this one blushing with shame? No, she would say, this one is too young still, youth has no shame, shame comes with age.

I shall never forget watching him from my table as he climbed the small ladder wearing his red bathing trunks, taking forever to pick the ripest apricots. On his way to the kitchen— wicker basket, espadrilles, billowy shirt, suntan lotion, and all— he threw me a very large one, saying, "Yours," in just the same way he'd throw a tennis ball across the court and say, "Your serve." Of course, he had no idea what I'd been thinking minutes earlier, but the firm, rounded cheeks of the apricot with their dimple in the middle reminded me of how his body had stretched across the boughs of the tree with his tight, rounded ass echoing the color and the shape of the fruit. Touching the apricot was like touching him. He would never know, just as the people we buy the newspaper from and then fantasize about all night have no idea that this particular inflection on their face or that tan along their exposed shoulder will give us no end of pleasure when we're alone.

Yours, like *Later!*, had an off-the-cuff, unceremonious, *here, catch* quality that reminded me how twisted and secretive my desires were compared to the expansive spontaneity of everything about him. It would never have occurred to him that in placing the apricot in my palm he was giving me his ass to hold or that, in biting the fruit, I was also biting into that part of his body that must have been fairer than the rest because it never apricated— and near it, if I dared to bite that far, his apricock.

In fact, he knew more about apricots than we did—their

grafts, etymology, origins, fortunes in and around the Mediterranean. At the breakfast table that morning, my father explained
that the name for the fruit came from the Arabic, since the
word—in Italian, *albicocca*, *abricot* in French, *aprikose* in German, like the words "algebra," "alchemy," and "alcohol"—was
derived from an Arabic noun combined with the Arabic article
al- before it. The origin of *albicocca* was *al-birquq*. My father,
who couldn't resist not leaving well enough alone and needed to
top his entire performance with a little fillip of more recent vintage, added that what was truly amazing was that, in Israel and
in many Arab countries nowadays, the fruit is referred to by a totally different name: *mishmish*.

My mother was nonplussed. We all, including my two cousins
who were visiting that week, had an impulse to clap.

On the matter of etymologies, however, Oliver begged to differ. "Ah?!" was my father's startled response.

"The word is actually not an Arabic word," he said.

"How so?"

My father was clearly mimicking Socratic irony, which
would start with an innocent "You don't say," only then to lead
his interlocutor onto turbulent shoals.

"It's a long story, so bear with me, Pro." Suddenly Oliver had
become serious. "Many Latin words are derived from the Greek.
In the case of 'apricot,' however, it's the other way around; the
Greek takes over from Latin. The Latin word was *praecoquum*,
from *pre-coquere*, pre-cook, to ripen early, as in 'precocious,'
meaning premature.

"The Byzantines borrowed *praecox*, and it became *prekokkia*
or *berikokki*, which is finally how the Arabs must have inherited it
as *al-birquq*."

My mother, unable to resist his charm, reached out to him
and tousled his hair and said, "Che muvi star!"

"He is right, there is no denying it," said my father under his breath, as though mimicking the part of a cowered Galileo forced to mutter the truth to himself.

"Courtesy of Philology 101," said Oliver.

All I kept thinking of was *apricock precock, precock apricock.*

One day I saw Oliver sharing the same ladder with the gardener, trying to learn all he could about Anchise's grafts, which explained why our apricots were larger, fleshier, juicier than most apricots in the region. He became fascinated with the grafts, especially when he discovered that the gardener could spend hours sharing everything he knew about them with anyone who cared to ask.

Oliver, it turned out, knew more about all manner of foods, cheeses, and wines than all of us put together. Even Mafalda was wowed and would, on occasion, defer to his opinion—Do you think I should lightly fry the paste with either onions or sage? Doesn't it taste too lemony now? I ruined it, didn't I? I should have added an extra egg—it's not holding! Should I use the new blender or should I stick to the old mortar and pestle? My mother couldn't resist throwing in a barb or two. Like all caubois, she said: they know everything there is to know about food, because they can't hold a knife and fork properly. Gourmet aristocrats with plebian manners. Feed him in the kitchen.

With pleasure, Mafalda would have replied. And indeed, one day when he arrived very late for lunch after spending the morning with his translator, there was Signor Ulliva in the kitchen, eating spaghetti and drinking dark red wine with Mafalda, Manfredi, her husband and our driver, and Anchise, all of them trying to teach him a Neapolitan song. It was not only the national hymn of their southern youth, but it was the best they could offer when they wished to entertain royalty.

Everyone was won over.

Chiara, I could tell, was equally smitten. Her sister as well. Even the crowd of tennis bums who for years had come early every afternoon before heading out to the beach for a late swim would stay much later than usual hoping to catch a quick game with him.

With any of our other summer residents I would have resented it. But seeing everyone take such a liking to him, I found a strange, small oasis of peace. What could possibly be wrong with liking someone everyone else liked? Everyone had fallen for him, including my first and second cousins as well as my other relatives, who stayed with us on weekends and sometimes longer. For someone known to love spotting defects in everyone else, I derived a certain satisfaction from concealing my feelings for him behind my usual indifference, hostility, or spite for anyone in a position to outshine me at home. Because everyone liked him, I had to say I liked him too. I was like men who openly declare other men irresistibly handsome the better to conceal that they're aching to embrace them. To withhold universal approval would simply alert others that I had concealed motives for needing to resist him. Oh, I like him very much, I said during his first ten days when my father asked me what I thought of him. I had used words intentionally compromising because I knew no one would suspect a false bottom in the arcane palette of shadings I applied to everything I said about him. He's the best person I've known in my life, I said on the night when the tiny fishing boat on which he had sailed out with Anchise early that afternoon failed to return and we were scrambling to find his parents' telephone number in the States in case we had to break the terrible news.

On that day I even urged myself to let down my inhibitions and show my grief the way everyone else was showing theirs. But I also did it so none might suspect I nursed sorrows of a far more secret and more desperate kind—until I realized, almost to my shame, that part of me didn't mind his dying, that there was even something almost exciting in the thought of his bloated, eyeless body finally showing up on our shores.

But I wasn't fooling myself. I was convinced that no one in the world wanted him as physically as I did; nor was anyone willing to go the distance I was prepared to travel for him. No one had studied every bone in his body, ankles, knees, wrists, fingers, and toes, no one lusted after every ripple of muscle, no one took him to bed every night and on spotting him in the morning lying in his *heaven* by the pool, smiled at him, watched a smile come to his lips, and thought, Did you know I came in your mouth last night?

Perhaps even the others nursed an extra something for him, which each concealed and displayed in his or her own way. Unlike the others, though, I was the first to spot him when he came into the garden from the beach or when the flimsy silhouette of his bicycle, blurred in the midafternoon mist, would appear out of the alley of pines leading to our house. I was the first to recognize his steps when he arrived late at the movie theater one night and stood there looking for the rest of us, not uttering a sound until I turned around knowing he'd be overjoyed I'd spotted him. I recognized him by the inflection of his footfalls up the stairway to our balcony or on the landing outside my bedroom door. I knew when he stopped outside my French windows, as if debating whether to knock and then thinking twice, and continued walking. I knew it was he riding a bicycle by the way the bike skidded ever so mischievously on the deep gravel path and still kept going when it was obvious there couldn't be any traction left, only to come to a sudden, bold, determined stop, with something of a declarative *voilà* in the way he jumped off.

I always tried to keep him within my field of vision. I never let him drift away from me except when he wasn't with me. And

when he wasn't with me, I didn't much care what he did so long
as he remained the exact same person with others as he was with
me. Don't let him be someone else when he's away. Don't let him
be someone I've never seen before. Don't let him have a life other
than the life I know he has with us, with me.

Don't let me lose him.

I knew I had no hold on him, nothing to offer, nothing to
lure him by.

I was nothing.

Just a kid.

He simply doled out his attention when the occasion suited
him. When he came to my assistance to help me understand a
fragment by Heraclitus, because I was determined to read "his"
author, the words that sprang to me were not "gentleness" or
"generosity" but "patience" and "forbearance," which ranked
higher. Moments later, when he asked if I liked a book I was
reading, his question was prompted less by curiosity than by an
opportunity for casual chitchat. Everything was casual.

He was okay with casual.

How come you're not at the beach with the others?

Go back to your plunking.

Later!

Yours!

Just making conversation.

Casual chitchat.

Nothing.

Oliver was receiving many invitations to other houses. This had
become something of a tradition with our other summer residents as well. My father always wanted them to feel free to
"talk" their books and expertise around town. He also believed

that scholars should learn how to speak to the layman, which
was why he always had lawyers, doctors, businessmen over for
meals. Everyone in Italy has read Dante, Homer, and Virgil, he'd
say. Doesn't matter whom you're talking to, so long as you
Dante-and-Homer them first. Virgil is a must, Leopardi comes
next, and then feel free to dazzle them with everything you've
got, Celan, celery, salami, who cares. This also had the advantage of allowing all of our summer residents to perfect their Italian, one of the requirements of the residency. Having them on
the dinner circuit around B. also had another benefit: it relieved
us from having them at our table every single night of the week.

But Oliver's invitations had become vertiginous. Chiara and
her sister wanted him at least twice a week. A cartoonist from
Brussels, who rented a villa all summer long, wanted him for his
exclusive Sunday *soupers* to which writers and scholars from the
environs were always invited. Then the Moreschis, from three villas down, the Malaspinas from N., and the occasional acquain-
tance struck up at one of the bars on the *piazzetta*, or at Le
Danzing. All this to say nothing of his poker and bridge playing
at night, which flourished by means totally unknown to us.

His life, like his papers, even when it gave every impression
of being chaotic, was always meticulously compartmentalized.
Sometimes he skipped dinner altogether and would simply tell
Mafalda, "*Esco*, I'm going out."

His *Esco*, I realized soon enough, was just another version of
Later! A summary and unconditional goodbye, spoken not as
you were leaving, but after you were out the door. You said it
with your back to those you were leaving behind. I felt sorry for
those on the receiving end who wished to appeal, to plead.

Not knowing whether he'd show up at the dinner table was
torture. But bearable. Not daring to ask whether he'd be there
was the real ordeal. Having my heart jump when I suddenly heard

his voice or saw him seated at his seat when I'd almost given up hoping he'd be among us tonight eventually blossomed like a poisoned flower. Seeing him and thinking he'd join us for dinner tonight only to hear his peremptory *Esco* taught me there are certain wishes that must be clipped like wings off a thriving butterfly.

I wanted him gone from our home so as to be done with him.

I wanted him dead too, so that if I couldn't stop thinking about him and worrying about when would be the next time I'd see him, at least his death would put an end to it. I wanted to kill him myself, even, so as to let him know how much his mere existence had come to bother me, how unbearable his ease with everything and everyone, taking all things in stride, his tireless I'm-okay-with-this-and-that, his springing across the gate to the beach when everyone else opened the latch first, to say nothing of his bathing suits, his spot in *paradise*, his cheeky *Later!*, his lip-smacking love for apricot juice. If I didn't kill him, then I'd cripple him for life, so that he'd be with us in a wheelchair and never go back to the States. If he were in a wheelchair, I would always know where he was, and he'd be easy to find. I would feel superior to him and become his master, now that he was crippled.

Then it hit me that I could have killed myself instead, or hurt myself badly enough and let him know why I'd done it. If I hurt my face, I'd want him to look at me and wonder why, why might anyone do this to himself, until, years and years later—yes, *Later!*—he'd finally piece the puzzle together and beat his head against the wall.

Sometimes it was Chiara who had to be eliminated. I knew what she was up to. At my age, her body was more than ready for him. More than mine? I wondered. She was after him, that much was clear, while all I really wanted was one night with him, just one night—one hour, even—if only to determine whether I

wanted him for another night after that. What I didn't realize
was that wanting to test desire is nothing more than a ruse to get
what we want without admitting that we want it. I dreaded to
think how experienced he himself was. If he could make friends
so easily within weeks of arriving here, you had only to think of
what life at home was like. Just imagine letting him loose on an
urban campus like Columbia's, where he taught.

The thing with Chiara happened so easily it was past reck-
oning. With Chiara he loved heading out into the deep on our
twin-hulled rowboat for a gita, with him rowing while she
lounged in the sun on one of the hulls, eventually removing her
bra once they had stopped and were far from shore.

I was watching. I dreaded losing him to her. Dreaded losing
her to him too. Yet thinking of them together did not dismay me.
It made me hard, even though I didn't know if what aroused me
was her naked body lying in the sun, his next to hers, or both of
theirs together. From where I stood against the balustrade along
the garden overlooking the bluff, I would strain my eyes and finally catch sight of them lying in the sun next to one another,
probably necking, she occasionally dropping a thigh on top of
his, until minutes later he did the same. They hadn't removed
their suits. I took comfort in that, but when later one night I saw
them dancing, something told me that these were not the moves
of people who'd stopped at heavy petting.

Actually, I liked watching them dance together. Perhaps seeing him dance this way with someone made me realize that he
was taken now, that there was no reason to hope. And this was a
good thing. It would help my recovery. Perhaps thinking this way
was already a sign that recovery was well under way. I had grazed
the forbidden zone and been let off easily enough.

But when my heart jolted the next morning when I saw him

at our usual spot in the garden, I knew that wishing them my
best and longing for recovery had nothing to do with what I still
wanted from him.

Did his heart jolt when he saw me walk into a room?

I doubted it.

Did he ignore me the way I ignored him that morning: on
purpose, to draw me out, to protect himself, to show I was nothing to him? Or was he oblivious, the way sometimes the most per-
ceptive individuals fail to pick up the most obvious cues because
they're simply not paying attention, not tempted, not interested?

When he and Chiara danced I saw her slip her thigh between
his legs. And I'd seen them mock-wrestle on the sand. When had
it started? And how was it that I hadn't been there when it
started? And why wasn't I told? Why wasn't I able to reconstruct
the moment when they progressed from x to y? Surely the signs
were all around me. Why didn't I see them?

I began thinking of nothing but what they might do together.
I would have done anything to ruin every opportunity they had
to be alone. I would have slandered one to the other, then used
the reaction of one to report it back to the other. But I also
wanted to see them do it, I wanted to be in on it, have them owe
me and make me their necessary accomplice, their go-between,
the pawn that has become so vital to king and queen that it is
now master of the board.

I began to say nice things about each, pretending I had no
inkling where things stood between them. He thought I was being coy. She said she could take care of herself.

"Are you trying to fix us up?" she asked, derision crackling in
her voice.

"What's it to you anyway?" he asked.

I described her naked body, which I'd seen two years before. I
wanted him aroused. It didn't matter what he desired so long as he

was aroused. I described him to her too, because I wanted to see if her arousal took the same turns as mine, so that I might trace mine on hers and see which of the two was the genuine article.

"Are you trying to make me like her?"

"What would the harm be in that?"

"No harm. Except I like to go it alone, if you don't mind."

It took me a while to understand what I was really after. Not just to get him aroused in my presence, or to make him need me, but in urging him to speak about her behind her back, I'd turn Chiara into the object of man-to-man gossip. It would allow us to warm up to one another through her, to bridge the gap between us by admitting we were drawn to the same woman.

Perhaps I just wanted him to know I liked girls.

"Look, it's very nice of you—and I appreciate it. But don't."

His rebuke told me he wasn't going to play my game. It put me in my place.

No, he's the noble sort, I thought. Not like me, insidious, sinister, and base. Which pushed my agony and shame up a few notches. Now, over and above the shame of desiring him as Chiara did, I respected and feared him and hated him for making me hate myself.

The morning after seeing them dance I made no motions to go jogging with him. Neither did he. When I eventually brought up jogging, because the silence on the matter had become unbearable, he said he'd already gone. "You're a late riser these days."

Clever, I thought.

Indeed, for the past few mornings, I had become so used to finding him waiting for me that I'd grown bold and didn't worry too much about when I got up. That would teach me.

The next morning, though I wanted to swim with him, coming downstairs would have looked like a chastened response to a casual chiding. So I stayed in my room. Just to prove a point. I heard him step lightly across the balcony, on tiptoes almost. He was avoiding me.

I came downstairs much later. By then he had already left to deliver his corrections and retrieve the latest pages from Signora Milani.

We stopped talking.

Even when we shared the same spot in the morning, talk was at best idle and stopgap. You couldn't even call it chitchat.

It didn't upset him. He probably hadn't given it another thought.

How is it that some people go through hell trying to get close to you, while you haven't the haziest notion and don't even give them a thought when two weeks go by and you haven't so much as exchanged a single word between you? Did he have any idea? Should I let him know?

The romance with Chiara started on the beach. Then he neglected tennis and took up bike rides with her and her friends in the late afternoons in the hill towns farther west along the coast. One day, when there was one too many of them to go biking, Oliver turned to me and asked if I minded letting Mario borrow my bike since I wasn't using it.

It threw me back to age six.

I shrugged my shoulders, meaning, Go ahead, I couldn't care less. But no sooner had they left than I scrambled upstairs and began sobbing into my pillow.

At night sometimes we'd meet at Le Danzing. There was never any telling when Oliver would show up. He just bounded onto the scene, and just as suddenly disappeared, sometimes alone, sometimes with others. When Chiara came to our home as she'd been in the habit of doing ever since childhood, she would sit in the garden and stare out, basically waiting for him to show up. Then, when the minutes wore on and there was nothing much to say between us, she'd finally ask, "C'è Oliver?" He went to see the translator. Or: He's in the library with my dad. Or: He's down somewhere at the beach. "Well, I'm leaving, then. Tell him I came by."

It's over, I thought.

Mafalda shook her head with a look of compassionate re-buke. "She's a baby, he's a university professor. Couldn't she have found someone her own age?"

"Nobody asked you anything," snapped Chiara, who had overheard and was not about to be criticized by a cook.

"Don't you talk to me that way or I'll split your face in two," said our Neapolitan cook, raising the palm of her hand in the air. "She's not seventeen yet and she goes about having bare-breasted crushes. Thinks I haven't seen anything?"

I could just see Mafalda inspecting Oliver's sheets every morn-ing. Or comparing notes with Chiara's housemaid. No secret could escape this network of informed *perpetue*, housekeepers.

I looked at Chiara. I knew she was in pain.

Everyone suspected something was going on between them. In the afternoon he'd sometimes say he was going to the shed by the garage to pick up one of the bikes and head to town. An hour and a half later he would be back. The translator, he'd explain.

"The translator," my father's voice would resound as he nursed an after-dinner cognac.

"*Traduttrice*, my eye," Mafalda would intone.

Sometimes we'd run into each other in town.

Sitting at the *caffè* where several of us would gather at night after the movies or before heading to the disco, I saw Chiara and Oliver walking out of a side alley together, talking. He was eat-ing an ice cream, while she was hanging on his free arm with both of hers. When had they found the time to become so inti-mate? Their conversation seemed serious.

"What are you doing here?" he said when he spotted me.

Banter was both how he took cover and tried to conceal we'd altogether stopped talking. A cheap ploy, I thought.

"Hanging out."

"Isn't it past your bedtime?"

"My father doesn't believe in bedtimes," I parried.

Chiara was still deep in thought. She was avoiding my eyes. Had he told her the nice things I'd been saying about her? She seemed upset. Did she mind my sudden intrusion into their little world? I remembered her tone of voice on the morning when she'd lost it with Mafalda. A smirk hovered on her face; she was about to say something cruel.

"Never a bedtime in their house, no rules, no supervision, nothing. That's why he's such a well-behaved boy. Don't you see? Nothing to rebel against."

"Is that true?"

"I suppose," I answered, trying to make light of it before they went any further. "We all have our ways of rebelling."

"We do?" he asked.

"Name one," chimed in Chiara.

"You wouldn't understand."

"He reads Paul Celan," Oliver broke in, trying to change the subject but also perhaps to come to my rescue and show, without quite seeming to, that he had not forgotten our previous conversation. Was he trying to rehabilitate me after that little jab about my late hours, or was this the beginnings of yet another joke at my expense? A steely, neutral glance sat on his face.

"E chi è?" She'd never heard of Paul Celan.

I shot him a complicit glance. He intercepted it, but there was no hint of mischief in his eyes when he finally returned my glance. Whose side was he on?

"A poet," he whispered as they started ambling out into the heart of the piazzetta, and he threw me a casual *Later!*

I watched them look for an empty table at one of the adjoining caffès.

My friends asked me if he was hitting on her.

I don't know, I replied.

Are they doing it, then?

Didn't know that either.

I'd love to be in his shoes.

Who wouldn't?

But I was in heaven. That he hadn't forgotten our conversation about Celan gave me a shot of tonic I hadn't experienced in many, many days. It spilled over everything I touched. Just a word, a gaze, and I was in heaven. To be happy like this maybe wasn't so difficult after all. All I had to do was find the source of happiness in me and not rely on others to supply it the next time.

I remembered the scene in the Bible when Jacob asks Rachel for water and on hearing her speak the words that were prophesied for him, throws up his hands to heaven and kisses the ground by the well. Me Jewish, Celan Jewish, Oliver Jewish—we were in a half ghetto, half oasis, in an otherwise cruel and unflinching world where fuddling around strangers suddenly stops, where we misread no one and no one misjudges us, where one person simply knows the other and knows him so thoroughly that to be taken away from such intimacy is *galut*, the Hebrew word for exile and dispersal. Was he my home, then, my homecoming? You are my homecoming. When I'm with you and we're well together, there is nothing more I want. You make me like who I am, who I become when you're with me, Oliver. If there is any truth in the world, it lies when I'm with you, and if I find the courage to speak my truth to you one day, remind me to light a candle in thanksgiving at every altar in Rome.

It never occurred to me that if one word from him could make me so happy, another could just as easily crush me, that if

I didn't want to be unhappy, I should learn to beware of such small joys as well.

But on that same night I used the heady elation of the moment to speak to Marzia. We danced past midnight, then I walked her back by way of the shore. Then we stopped. I said I was tempted to take a quick swim, expecting she would hold me back. But she said she too loved swimming at night. Our clothes were off in a second. "You're not with me because you're angry with Chiara?"

"Why am I angry with Chiara?"

"Because of him."

I shook my head, feigning a puzzled look meant to show that I couldn't begin to guess where she'd fished such a notion from.

She asked me to turn around and not stare while she used her sweater to towel her body dry. I pretended to sneak a clandestine glance, but was too obedient not to do as I was told. I didn't dare ask her not to look when I put my clothes on but was glad she looked the other way. When we were no longer naked, I took her hand and kissed her on the palm, then kissed the space between her fingers, then her mouth. She was slow to kiss me back, but then she didn't want to stop.

We were to meet at the same spot on the beach the following evening. I'd be there before her, I said.

"Just don't tell anyone," she said.

I motioned that my mouth was zipped shut.

"We almost did it," I told both my father and Oliver the next morning as we were having breakfast.

"And why didn't you?" asked my father.

"Dunno."

"Better to have tried and failed . . ." Oliver was half mocking and half comforting me with that oft-rehashed saw. "All I had to do was find the courage to reach out and touch, she would have said yes," I said, partly to parry further criticism from either of them but also to show that when it came to self-mockery, I could administer my own dose, thank you very much. I was showing off.

"Try again later," said Oliver. This was what people who were okay with themselves did. But I could also sense he was onto something and wasn't coming out with it, perhaps because there was something mildly disquieting behind his fatuous though well-intentioned *try again later*. He was criticizing me. Or making fun of me. Or seeing through me.

It stung me when he finally came out with it. Only someone who had completely figured me out would have said it. "If not later, when?"

My father liked it. "If not later, when?" It echoed Rabbi Hillel's famous injunction, "If not now, when?"

Oliver instantly tried to take back his stinging remark. "I'd definitely try again. And again after that," came the watered-down version. But *try again later* was the veil he'd drawn over *If not later, when?*

I repeated his phrase as if it were a prophetic mantra meant to reflect how he lived his life and how I was attempting to live mine. By repeating this mantra that had come straight from his mouth, I might trip on a secret passageway to some nether truth that had hitherto eluded me, about me, about life, about others, about me with others.

Try again later were the last words I'd spoken to myself every night when I'd sworn to do something to bring Oliver closer to me. *Try again later* meant, I haven't the courage now. Things weren't ready *just yet*. Where I'd find the will and the courage to *try again later* I didn't know. But resolving to do something rather than sit passively made me feel that I was already doing something, like reaping a profit on money I hadn't invested, much less earned yet.

But I also knew that I was circling wagons around my life with *try again later*s, and that months, seasons, entire years, a lifetime could go by with nothing but Saint Try-again-later stamped on every day. *Try again later* worked for people like Oliver. *If not later, when?* was my shibboleth.

If not later, when? What if he had found me out and uncovered each and every one of my secrets with those four cutting words?

I had to let him know I was totally indifferent to him.

What sent me into a total tailspin was talking to him a few mornings later in the garden and finding, not only that he was turning a deaf ear to all of my blandishments on behalf of Chiara, but that I was on the totally wrong track.

"What do you mean, wrong track?"

"I'm not interested."

I didn't know if he meant not interested in discussing it, or not interested in Chiara.

"Everyone is interested."

"Well, maybe. But not me."

Still unclear.

There was something at once dry, irked, and fussy in his voice.

"But I saw you two."

"What you saw was not your business to see. Anyway, I'm not playing this game with either her or you."

He sucked on his cigarette and looking back at me gave me his usual menacing, chilly gaze that could cut and bore into your guts with arthroscopic accuracy.

I shrugged my shoulders. "Look, I'm sorry"—and went back to my books. I had overstepped my bounds again and there was no getting out of it gracefully except by owning that I'd been terribly indiscreet.

"Maybe *you* should try," he threw in.

I'd never heard him speak in that lambent tone before. Usually, it was I who teetered on the fringes of propriety.

"She wouldn't want to have anything to do with me."

"Would you want her to?"

Where was this going, and why did I feel that a trap lay a few steps ahead?

"No?" I replied gingerly, not realizing that my diffidence had made my "no" sound almost like a question.

"Are you sure?"

Had I, by any chance, convinced him that I'd wanted her all along?

I looked up at him as though to return challenge for challenge.

"What would you know?"

"I know you like her."

"You have no idea what I like," I snapped. "No idea."

I was trying to sound arch and mysterious, as though referring to a realm of human experience about which someone like him wouldn't have the slightest clue. But I had only managed to sound peevish and hysterical.

A less canny reader of the human soul would have seen in my persistent denials the terrified signs of a flustered admission about Chiara scrambling for cover.

A more canny observer, however, would have considered it a lead-in to an entirely different truth: push open the door at your own peril—believe me, you don't want to hear this. Maybe you should go away now, while there's still time.

But I also knew that if he so much as showed signs of suspecting the truth, I'd make every effort to cast him adrift right away. If, however, he suspected nothing, then my flustered words would have left him marooned just the same. In the end, I was happier if he thought I wanted Chiara than if he pushed the issue further and had me tripping all over myself. Speechless, I would have admitted things I hadn't mapped out for myself or didn't know I had it in me to admit. Speechless, I would have gotten to where my body longed to go far sooner than with any bon mot prepared hours ahead of time. I would have blushed, and blushed because I had blushed, fuddled with words and ultimately broken down—and then where would I be? What would he say?

Better break down now, I thought, than live another day juggling all of my implausible resolutions to *try again later.*

No, better he should never know. I could live with that. I could always, always live with that. It didn't even surprise me to see how easy it was to accept.

And yet, out of the blue, a tender moment would erupt so suddenly between us that the words I longed to tell him would almost slip out of my mouth. Green bathing suit moments, I called them—even after my color theory was entirely disproved and gave me no confidence to expect kindness on "blue" days or to watch out for "red" days.

Music was an easy subject for us to discuss, especially when I was at the piano. Or when he'd want me to play something in the manner of so-and-so. He liked my combinations of two, three, even four composers chiming in on the same piece, and then transcribed by me. One day Chiara started to hum a hit-parade tune and suddenly, because it was a windy day and no one was heading for the beach or even staying outdoors, our friends gathered around the piano in the living room as I improvised a Brahms variation on a Mozart rendition of that very same song. "How do you do this?" he asked me one morning while he lay in *heaven.*

"Sometimes the only way to understand an artist is to wear his shoes, to get inside him. Then everything else flows naturally."

We talked about books again. I had seldom spoken to anyone about books except my father.

Or we talked about music, about the pre-Socratic philosophers, about college in the U.S.

Or there was Vimini.

The first time she intruded on our mornings was precisely when I'd been playing a variation on Brahms's last variations on Handel.

Her voice broke up the intense midmorning heat.

"What are you doing?"

"Working," I replied.

Oliver, who was lying flat on his stomach on the edge of the pool, looked up with the sweat pouring down between his shoulder blades.

"Me too," he said when she turned and asked him the same question.

"You were talking, not working."

"Same thing."

"I wish I could work. But no one gives me any work."

Oliver, who had never seen Vimini before, looked up to me, totally helpless, as though he didn't know the rules of this conversation.

"Oliver, meet Vimini, literally our next-door neighbor."

She offered him her hand and he shook it.

"Vimini and I have the same birthday, but she is ten years old. Vimini is also a genius. Isn't it true you're a genius, Vimini?"

"So they say. But it seems to me that I may not be."

"Why is that?" Oliver inquired, trying not to sound too patronizing.

"It would be in rather bad taste for nature to have made me a genius."

Oliver looked more startled than ever: "Come again?"

"He doesn't know, does he?" she was asking me in front of him.

I shook my head.

"They say I may not live long."

"Why do you say that?" He looked totally stunned. "How do you know?"

"Everyone knows. Because I have leukemia."

"But you're so beautiful, so healthy-looking, and so smart," he protested.

"As I said, a bad joke."

Oliver, who was now kneeling on the grass, had literally dropped his book on the ground.

"Maybe you can come over one day and read to me," she said. "I'm really very nice—and you look very nice too. Well, goodbye."

She climbed over the wall. "And sorry if I spooked you—well—"

You could almost watch her trying to withdraw the ill-chosen metaphor.

If the music hadn't already brought us closer together at least for a few hours that day, Vimini's apparition did.

We spoke about her all afternoon. I didn't have to look for anything to say. He did most of the talking and the asking. Oliver was mesmerized. For once, I wasn't speaking about myself.

Soon they became friends. She was always up in the morning after he returned from his morning jog or swim, and together they would walk over to our gate, and clamber down the stairs ever so cautiously, and head to one of the huge rocks, where they sat and talked until it was time for breakfast. Never had I seen a friendship so beautiful or more intense. I was never jealous of it, and no one, certainly not I, dared come between them or eavesdrop on them. I shall never forget how she would give him her hand once they'd opened the gate to the stairway leading to the rocks. She seldom ever ventured that far unless accompanied by someone older.

When I think back to that summer, I can never sort the sequence of events. There are a few key scenes. Otherwise, all I remember are the "repeat" moments. The morning ritual before and after breakfast: Oliver lying on the grass, or by the pool, I sitting at my table. Then the swim or the jog. Then his grabbing a bicycle and riding to see the translator in town. Lunch at the large, shaded dining table in the other garden, or lunch indoors, always a guest or two for *lunch drudgery*. The afternoon hours, splendid and lush with abundant sun and silence.

Then there are the leftover scenes: my father always wondering what I did with my time, why I was always alone; my mother urging me to make new friends if the old ones didn't interest me, but above all to stop hanging around the house all the time— books, books, books, always books, and all these scorebooks, both of them begging me to play more tennis, go dancing more often, get to know people, find out for myself why others are so necessary in life and not just foreign bodies to be sidled up to. Do crazy things if you must, they told me all the while, forever prying to unearth the mysterious, telltale signs of heartbreak which, in their clumsy, intrusive, devoted way, both would instantly wish to heal, as if I were a soldier who had strayed into their garden and needed his wound immediately stanched or else he'd die.

You can always talk to me. I was your age once, my father used
to say. The things you feel and think only you have felt, believe
me, I've lived and suffered through all of them, and more than
once—some I've never gotten over and others I'm as ignorant
about as you are today, yet I know almost every bend, every toll-
booth, every chamber in the human heart.

There are other scenes: the postprandial silence—some of us
napping, some working, others reading, the whole world basking
away in hushed semitones. Heavenly hours when voices from the
world beyond our house would filter in so softly that I was sure I
had drifted off. Then afternoon tennis. Shower and cocktails.
Waiting for dinner. Guests again. Dinner. His second trip to the
translator. Strolling into town and back late at night, sometimes
alone, sometimes with friends.

Then there are the exceptions: the stormy afternoon when
we sat in the living room, listening to the music and to the hail
pelting every window in the house. The lights would go out, the
music would die, and all we had was each other's faces. An aunt
twittering away about her dreadful years in St. Louis, Missouri,
which she pronounced *San Lui*, Mother trailing the scent of Earl
Grey tea, and in the background, all the way from the kitchen
downstairs, the voices of Manfredi and Mafalda—spare whispers
of a couple bickering in loud hisses. In the rain, the lean, cloaked,
hooded figure of the gardener doing battle with the elements, always pulling up weeds even in the rain, my father signaling with
his arms from the living room window, *Go back, Anchise, go
back.*

"That man gives me the creeps," my aunt would say.

"That creep has a heart of gold," my father would say.

But all of these hours were strained by fear, as if fear were
a brooding specter, or a strange, lost bird trapped in our little
town, whose sooty wing flecked every living thing with a shadow

that would never wash. I didn't know what I was afraid of, nor why I worried so much, nor why this thing that could so easily cause panic felt like hope sometimes and, like hope in the darkest moments, brought such joy, unreal joy, joy with a noose tied around it. The thud my heart gave when I saw him unannounced both terrified and thrilled me. I was afraid when he showed up, afraid when he failed to, afraid when he looked at me, more frightened yet when he didn't. The agony wore me out in the end, and, on scalding afternoons, I'd simply give out and fall asleep on the living room sofa and, though still dreaming, know exactly who was in the room, who had tiptoed in and out, who was standing there, who was looking at me and for how long, who was trying to pick out today's paper while making the least rustling sound, only to give up and look for tonight's film listings whether they woke me or not.

The fear never went away. I woke up to it, watched it turn to joy when I heard him shower in the morning and knew he'd be downstairs with us for breakfast, only to watch it curdle when, rather than have coffee, he would dash through the house and right away set to work in the garden. By noon, the agony of waiting to hear him say anything to me was more than I could bear. I knew that the sofa awaited me in an hour or so. It made me hate myself for feeling so hapless, so thoroughly invisible, so smitten, so callow. Just say something, just touch me, Oliver. Look at me long enough and watch the tears well in my eyes. Knock at my door at night and see if I haven't already left it ajar for you. Walk inside. There's always room in my bed.

What I feared most were the days when I didn't see him for stretches at a time—entire afternoons and evenings sometimes without knowing where he'd been. I'd sometimes spot him crossing the piazzetta or talking to people I'd never seen there. But that didn't count, because in the small piazzetta where people gathered around closing time, he seldom gave me a second look, just a nod which might have been intended less for me than for my father, whose son I happened to be.

My parents, my father especially, couldn't have been happier with him. Oliver was working out better than most of our summer residents. He helped my father organize his papers, managed a good deal of his foreign correspondence, and was clearly coming along with his own book. What he did in his private life and his time was his business—*If youth must canter, then who'll do the galloping?* was my father's clumsy adage. In our household, Oliver could do no wrong.

Since my parents never paid any attention to his absences, I thought it was safer never to show that they caused me any anxiety. I mentioned his absence only when one of them wondered where he'd been; I would pretend to look as startled as they were. Oh, that's right, he's been gone so long. No, no idea. And I had to worry not to look too startled either, for that might ring false and alert them to what was eating at me. They'd know bad faith as soon as they spotted it. I was surprised they hadn't already. They had always said I got *too easily attached* to people. This summer, though, I finally realized what they meant by being *too easily attached*. Obviously, it had happened before, and they must have already picked up on it when I was probably too young to notice anything myself. It had sent alarming ripples through their lives. They worried for me. I knew they were right to worry. I just hoped they'd never know how far things stood beyond their ordinary worries now. I knew they didn't suspect a thing, and it bothered me—though I wouldn't have wanted it otherwise. It told me that if I were no longer transparent and could disguise so much of my life, then I was finally safe from them, and from him—but at what price, and did I want to be so safe from anyone?

There was no one to speak to. Whom could I tell? Mafalda? She'd leave the house. My aunt? She'd probably tell everyone. Marzia, Chiara, my friends? They'd desert me in a second. My cousins when they came? Never. My father held the most liberal views—but on this? Who else? Write to one of my teachers? See a doctor? Say I needed a shrink? Tell Oliver?

Tell Oliver. There is no one else to tell, Oliver, so I'm afraid it's going to have to be you . . .

One afternoon, when I knew that the house was totally empty, I went up to his room. I opened his closet and, as this was my room when there were no residents, pretended to be looking for something I'd left behind in one of the bottom drawers. I'd planned to rifle through his papers, but as soon as I opened his closet, I saw it. Hanging on a hook was this morning's red bathing suit which he hadn't swum in, which was why it was hanging there and not drying on the balcony. I picked it up, never in my life having pried into anyone's personal belongings before. I brought the bathing suit to my face, then rubbed my face inside of it, as if I were trying to snuggle into it and lose myself inside its folds—So this is what he smells like when his body isn't covered in suntan lotion, this is what he smells like, this is what he smells like, I kept repeating to myself, looking inside the suit for something more personal yet than his smell and then kissing every corner of it, almost wishing to find hair, anything, to lick it, to put the whole bathing suit into my mouth, and, if I could only steal it, keep it with me forever, never ever let Mafalda wash it, turn to it in the winter months at home and, on sniffing it, bring him back to life, as naked as he was with me at this very moment. On impulse, I removed my bathing suit and began to put his on. I knew what I wanted, and I wanted it with the kind of intoxicated rapture that makes people take risks they would never take even with plenty of alcohol in their system. I wanted to come in his suit, and leave the evidence for him to find there. Which was when a crazier notion possessed me. I undid his bed, took off his suit, and cuddled it between his sheets, naked. Let him find me—I'll deal with it, one way or another. I recognized the feel of the bed. My bed. But the smell of him was all around me, wholesome and forgiving, like the strange scent which had suddenly come over my entire body when an elderly man who happened to be standing right next to me in a temple on Yom Kippur placed his tallis over my head till I had all but disappeared and was now united with a nation that is forever dispersed but which, from time to time, comes together again when one being and another wrap themselves under the same piece of cloth. I put his pillow over my face, kissed it savagely, and, wrapping my legs around it, told it what I lacked the courage to tell everyone else in the world. Then I told him what I wanted. It took less than a minute.

The secret was out of my body. So what if he saw. So what if he caught me. So what, so what, so what.

On my way from his room to mine I wondered if I'd ever be mad enough to try the same thing again.

That evening I caught myself keeping careful tabs on where everyone was in the house. The shameful urge was upon me sooner than I'd ever imagined. It would have taken nothing to sneak back upstairs.

While reading in my father's library one evening, I came upon the story of a handsome young knight who is madly in love with a princess. She too is in love with him, though she seems not to be entirely aware of it, and despite the friendship that blossoms between them, or perhaps because of that very friendship, he finds himself so humbled and speechless owing to her forbidding candor that he is totally unable to bring up the subject of his love. One day he asks her point-blank: "Is it better to speak or die?"

I'd never even have the courage to ask such a question.

But what I'd spoken into his pillow revealed to me that, at least for a moment, I'd rehearsed the truth, gotten it out into the open, that I had in fact enjoyed speaking it, and if he happened to pass by at the very moment I was muttering things I wouldn't have dared speak to my own face in the mirror, I wouldn't have cared, wouldn't have minded—let him know, let him see, let him pass judgment too if he wants—just don't tell the world—even if you're the world for me right now, even if in your eyes stands a horrified, scornful world. That steely look of yours, Oliver, I'd rather die than face it once I've told you.

PART 2

Monet's Berm

Toward the end of July things finally came to a head. It seemed clear that after Chiara there had been a succession of *cotte*, crushes, mini-crushes, one-night crushes, flings, who knows. To me all of it boiled down to one thing only: his cock had been everywhere in B. Every girl had touched it, that cock of his. It had been in who knows how many vaginas, how many mouths. The image amused me. It never bothered me to think of him between a girl's legs as she lay facing him, his broad, tanned, glistening shoulders moving up and down as I'd imagined him that afternoon when I too had wrapped my legs around his pillow.

Just looking at his shoulders when he happened to be going over his manuscript in his *heaven* made me wonder where they'd been last night. How effortless and free the movement of his shoulder blades each time he shifted, how thoughtlessly they caught the sun. Did they taste of the sea to the woman who had lain under him last night and bitten into him? Or of his suntan lotion? Or of the smell that had risen from his sheets when I went into them?

How I wished I had shoulders like his. Maybe I wouldn't long for them if I had them?

Muvi star.

Did I want to be like him? Did I want to be him? Or did I just want to have him? Or are "being" and "having" thoroughly in-accurate verbs in the twisted skein of desire, where having some-one's body to touch and being that someone we're longing to touch are one and the same, just opposite banks on a river that passes from us to them, back to us and over to them again in this perpetual circuit where the chambers of the heart, like the trapdoors of desire, and the wormholes of time, and the false-bottomed drawer we call identity share a beguiling logic accord-ing to which the shortest distance between real life and the life unlived, between who we are and what we want, is a twisted stair-case designed with the impish cruelty of M. C. Escher. When had they separated us, you and me, Oliver? And why did I know it, and why didn't you? Is it your body that I want when I think of lying next to it every night or do I want to slip into it and own it as if it were my own, as I did when I put on your bathing suit and took it off again, all the while craving, as I craved nothing more in my life that afternoon, to feel you slip inside me as if my entire body were your bathing suit, your home? You in me, me in you . . .

Then came the day. We were in the garden, I told him of the novella I had just finished reading.

"About the knight who doesn't know whether to speak or die. You told me already."

Obviously I had mentioned it and forgotten.

"Yes."

"Well, does he or doesn't he?"

"Better to speak, she said. But she's on her guard. She senses a trap somewhere."

"So does he speak?"

"No, he fudges."

"Figures."

It was just after breakfast. Neither of us felt like working that day.

"Listen, I need to pick up something in town."

Something was always the latest pages from the translator.

"I'll go, if you want me to."

He sat silently a moment.

"No, let's go together."

"Now?" What I might have meant was, Really?

"Why, have you got anything better to do?"

"No."

"So let's go." He put some pages in his frayed green back-pack and slung it over his shoulders.

Since our last bike ride to B., he had never asked me to go anywhere with him.

I put down my fountain pen, closed my scorebook, placed a half-full glass of lemonade on top of my pages, and was ready to go.

On our way to the shed, we passed the garage.

As usual, Manfredi, Mafalda's husband, was arguing with Anchise. This time he was accusing him of dousing the tomatoes with too much water, and that it was all wrong, because they were growing too fast. "They'll be mealy," he complained.

"Listen. I do the tomatoes, you do the driving, and we're all happy."

"You don't understand. In my day you moved the tomatoes at some point, from one place to another, from one place to the other"—he insisted—"and you planted basil nearby. But of course you people who've been in the army know everything."

"That's right." Anchise was ignoring him.

"Of course I'm right. No wonder they didn't keep you in the army."

"That's right. They didn't keep me in the army."

Both of them greeted us. The gardener handed Oliver his bicycle. "I straightened the wheel last night, it took some doing. I also put some air in the tires."

Manfredi couldn't have been more peeved.

"From now on, I fix the wheels, you grow the tomatoes," said the piqued driver.

Anchise gave a wry smile. Oliver smiled back.

Once we had reached the cypress lane that led onto the main road to town, I asked Oliver, "Doesn't he give you the creeps?"

"Who?"

"Anchise."

"No, why? I fell the other day on my way back and scraped myself pretty badly. Anchise insisted on applying some sort of witch's brew. He also fixed the bike for me."

With one hand on the handlebar he lifted his shirt and exposed a huge scrape and bruise on his left hip.

"Still gives me the creeps," I said, repeating my aunt's verdict.

"Just a lost soul, really."

I would have touched, caressed, worshipped that scrape.

On our way, I noticed that Oliver was taking his time. He wasn't in his usual rush, no speeding, no scaling the hill with his usual athletic zeal. Nor did he seem in a rush to go back to his paperwork, or join his friends on the beach, or, as was usually the case, ditch me. Perhaps he had nothing better to do. This was my moment in *heaven* and, young as I was, I knew it wouldn't last and that I should at least enjoy it for what it was rather than ruin it with my oft-cranked resolution to firm up our friendship or take it to another plane. There'll never be a friendship, I thought, this is nothing, just a minute of grace. *Zwischen Immer und Nie. Zwischen Immer und Nie.* Between always and never. Celan.

When we arrived at the piazzetta overlooking the sea, Oliver stopped to buy cigarettes. He had started smoking Gauloises. I had never tried Gauloises and asked if I could. He took out a *cerino* from the box, cupped his hands very near my face, and lit my cigarette. "Not bad, right?" "Not bad at all." They'd remind me of him, of this day, I thought, realizing that in less than a month he'd be totally gone, without a trace.

This was probably the first time I allowed myself to count down his remaining days in B.

"Just take a look at this," he said as we ambled with our bikes in the midmorning sun toward the edge of the piazzetta overlooking the rolling hills below.

Farther out and way below was a magnificent view of the sea with scarcely a few stripes of foam streaking the bay like giant dolphins breaking the surf. A tiny bus was working its way up-hill, while three uniformed bikers straggled behind it, obviously complaining of the fumes. "You do know who is said to have drowned near here," he said.

"Shelley."

"And do you know what his wife Mary and friends did when they found his body?"

"*Cor cordium*, heart of hearts," I replied, referring to the moment when a friend had seized Shelley's heart before the flames had totally engulfed his swollen body as it was being cremated on the shore. Why was he quizzing me?

"Is there anything you don't know?"

I looked at him. This was my moment. I could seize it or I could lose it, but either way I knew I would never live it down. Or I could gloat over his compliment—but live to regret everything else. This was probably the first time in my life that I spoke to an adult without planning some of what I was going to say. I was too nervous to plan anything.

"I know nothing, Oliver. Nothing, just nothing."

"You know more than anyone around here."

Why was he returning my near-tragic tone with bland ego-boosting?

"If you only knew how little I know about the things that really matter."

I was treading water, trying neither to drown nor to swim to safety, just staying in place, because here was the truth—even if I couldn't speak the truth, or even hint at it, yet I could swear it lay around us, the way we say of a necklace we've just lost while swimming: I know it's down there somewhere. If he knew, if he only knew that I was giving him every chance to put two and two together and come up with a number bigger than infinity.

But if he understood, then he must have suspected, and if he suspected he would have been there himself, watching me from across a parallel lane with his steely, hostile, glass-eyed, trenchant, all-knowing gaze.

He must have hit on something, though God knows what. Perhaps he was trying not to seem taken aback.

"What things that matter?"

Was he being disingenuous?

"You know what things. By now *you* of all people should know."

Silence.

"Why are you telling me all this?"

"Because I thought you should know."

"Because you thought I should know." He repeated my words slowly, trying to take in their full meaning, all the while sorting them out, playing for time by repeating the words. The iron, I knew, was burning hot.

"Because I want *you* to know," I blurted out. "Because there is no one else I can say it to but you."

There, I had said it.

Was I making any sense?

I was about to interrupt and sidetrack the conversation by saying something about the sea and the weather tomorrow and whether it might be a good idea to sail out to E. as my father kept promising this time every year.

But to his credit he didn't let me loose.

"Do you know what you're saying?"

This time I looked out to the sea and, with a vague and weary tone that was my last diversion, my last cover, my last getaway, said, "Yes, I know what I'm saying and you're not mistaking *any* of it. I'm just not very good at speaking. But you're welcome never to speak to me again."

"Wait. Are you saying what I think you're saying?"

"Ye-es." Now that I had spilled the beans I could take on the laid-back, mildly exasperated air with which a felon, who's surrendered to the police, confesses yet once more to yet one more police officer how he robbed the store.

"Wait for me here, I have to run upstairs and get some papers. Don't go away."

I looked at him with a confiding smile.

"You know very well I'm not going anywhere."

If that's not another admission, then what is? I thought.

As I waited, I took both our bikes and walked them toward the war memorial dedicated to the youth of the town who'd perished in the Battle of the Piave during the First World War. Every small town in Italy has a similar memorial. Two small buses had just stopped nearby and were unloading passengers—older women arriving from the adjoining villages to shop in town. Around the small piazza, the old folk, men mostly, sat on small, rickety, straw-backed chairs or on park benches wearing drab, old, dun-colored suits. I wondered how many people here still remembered the young men they'd lost on the Piave River. You'd have to be at least eighty years old today to have known them. And at least one hundred, if not more, to have been older than they were then. At one hundred, surely you learn to overcome loss and grief—or do they hound you till the bitter end? At one hundred, siblings forget, sons forget, loved ones forget, no one remembers anything, even the most devastated forget to remember. Mothers and fathers have long since died. Does anyone remember?

A thought raced through my mind: Would my descendants know what was spoken on this very piazzetta today? Would anyone? Or would it dissolve into thin air, as I found part of me wishing it would? Would they know how close to the brink their fate stood on this day on this piazzetta? The thought amused me and gave me the necessary distance to face the remainder of this day.

In thirty, forty years, I'll come back here and think back on a conversation I knew I'd never forget, much as I might want to someday. I'd come here with my wife, my children, show them the sights, point to the bay, the local caffès, Le Danzing, the Grand Hotel. Then I'd stand here and ask the statue and the straw-backed chairs and shaky wooden tables to remind me of someone called Oliver.

When he returned, the first thing he blurted out was, "That idiot Milani mixed the pages and has to retype the whole thing. So I have nothing to work on this afternoon, which sets me back a whole day."

It was his turn to look for excuses to dodge the subject. I could easily let him off the hook if he wanted. We could talk about the sea, the Piave, or fragments of Heraclitus, such as "Nature loves to hide" or "I went in search of myself." And if not these, there was the trip to E. we'd been discussing for days now. There was also the chamber music ensemble due to arrive any day.

On our way we passed a shop where my mother always ordered flowers. As a child I liked to watch the large storefront window awash in a perpetual curtain of water which came sliding
down ever so gently, giving the shop an enchanted, mysterious
aura that reminded me of how in many films the screen would
blur to announce that a flashback was about to occur.

"I wish I hadn't spoken," I finally said.

I knew as soon as I'd said it that I'd broken the exiguous spell
between us.

"I'm going to pretend you never did."

Well, that was an approach I'd never expected from a man
who was so okay with the world. I'd never heard such a sentence
used in our house.

"Does this mean we're on speaking terms—but not really?"

He thought about it.

"Look, we can't talk about such things. We really can't."

He slung his bag around him and we were off downhill.

Fifteen minutes ago, I was in total agony, every nerve ending,
every emotion bruised, trampled, crushed as in Mafalda's mortar, all of it pulverized till you couldn't tell fear from anger from
the merest trickle of desire. But at that time there was something
to look forward to. Now that we had laid our cards on the table,
the secrecy, the shame were gone, but with them so was that dash
of unspoken hope that had kept everything alive these weeks.

Only the scenery and the weather could buoy my spirits now.
As would the ride together on the empty country road, which was
entirely ours at this time of day and where the sun started pounding exposed patches along the route. I told him to follow me, I'd
show him a spot most tourists and strangers had never seen.

"If you have time," I added, not wishing to be pushy this
time.

"I have time." It was spoken with a noncommittal lilt in his voice, as though he had found the overplayed tact in my words slightly comical. But perhaps this was a small concession to make up for not discussing the matter at hand.

We veered off the main road and headed toward the edge of the cliff.

"This," I said by way of a preface meant to keep his interest alive, "is the spot where Monet came to paint."

Tiny, stunted palm trees and gnarled olive trees studded the copse. Then through the trees, on an incline leading toward the very edge of the cliff, was a knoll partly shaded by tall marine pines. I leaned my bike against one of the trees, he did the same, and I showed him the way up to the berm. "Now take a look," I said, extremely pleased, as if revealing something more eloquent than anything I might say in my favor.

A soundless, quiet cove stood straight below us. Not a sign of civilization anywhere, no home, no jetty, no fishing boats. Farther out, as always, was the belfry of San Giacomo, and, if you strained your eyes, the outline of N., and farther still was something that looked like our house and the adjoining villas, the one where Vimini lived, and the Moreschi family's, with their two daughters whom Oliver had probably slept with, alone or together, who knew, who cared at this point.

"This is my spot. All mine. I come here to read. I can't tell you the number of books I've read here."

"Do you like being alone?" he asked.

"No. No one likes being alone. But I've learned how to live with it."

"Are you always so very wise?" he asked. Was he about to adopt a condescending, pre-lecture tone before joining everyone else on my needing to get out more, make more friends, and, having made friends, not to be so selfish with them? Or was this a preamble to his role as shrink/part-time-friend-of-the-family? Or was I yet again misreading him completely?

"I'm not wise at all. I told you, I know nothing. I know books, and I know how to string words together—it doesn't mean I know how to speak about the things that matter most to me."

"But you're doing it now—in a way."

"Yes, in a way—that's how I always say things: in a way."

Staring out at the offing so as not to look at him, I sat down on the grass and noticed he was crouching a few yards away from me on the tips of his toes, as though he would any moment now spring to his feet and go back to where we'd left our bicycles.

It never occurred to me that I had brought him here not just to show him my little world, but to ask my little world to let him in, so that the place where I came to be alone on summer afternoons would get to know him, judge him, see if he fitted in, take him in, so that I might come back here and remember. Here I would come to escape the known world and seek another of my own invention; I was basically introducing him to my launchpad. All I had to do was list the works I'd read here and he'd know all the places I'd traveled to.

"I like the way you say things. Why are you always putting yourself down?"

I shrugged my shoulders. Was he criticizing me for criticizing myself?

"I don't know. So you won't, I suppose."

"Are you so scared of what others think?"

I shook my head. But I didn't know the answer. Or perhaps the answer was so obvious that I didn't have to answer. It was moments such as these that left me feeling so vulnerable, so naked. Push me, make me nervous, and, unless I push you back, you've already found me out. No, I had nothing to say in reply.

But I wasn't moving either. My impulse was to let him ride home by himself. I'd be home in time for lunch.

He was waiting for me to say something. He was staring at me.

This, I think, is the first time I dared myself to stare back at him. Usually, I'd cast a glance and then look away—look away because I didn't want to swim in the lovely, clear pool of his eyes unless I'd been invited to—and I never waited long enough to know whether I was even wanted there; look away because I was too scared to stare anyone back; look away because I didn't want to give anything away; look away because I couldn't acknowledge how much he mattered. Look away because that steely gaze of his always reminded me of how tall he stood and how far below him I ranked. Now, in the silence of the moment, I stared back, not to defy him, or to show I wasn't shy any longer, but to surrender, to tell him this is who I am, this is who you are, this is what I want, there is nothing but truth between us now, and where there's truth there are no barriers, no shifty glances, and if nothing comes of this, let it never be said that either of us was unaware of what might happen. I hadn't a hope left. And maybe I stared back because there wasn't a thing to lose now. I stared back with the all-knowing, I-dare-you-to-kiss-me gaze of someone who both challenges and flees with one and the same gesture.

"You're making things very difficult for me."

Was he by any chance referring to our staring?

I didn't back down. Neither did he. Yes, he was referring to our staring.

"Why am I making things difficult?"

My heart was beating too fast for me to speak coherently. I wasn't even ashamed of showing how flushed I was. So let him know, let him.

"Because it would be very wrong."

"*Would?*" I asked.

Was there a ray of hope, then?

He sat down on the grass, then lay down on his back, his arms under his head, as he stared at the sky.

"Yes, *would*. I'm not going to pretend this hasn't crossed my mind."

"I'd be the last to know."

"Well, it has. There! What did you think was going on?"

"Going on?" I fumbled by way of a question. "Nothing." I thought about it some more. "Nothing," I repeated, as if what I was vaguely beginning to get a hint of was so amorphous that it could just as easily be shoved away by my repeated "nothing" and thereby fill the unbearable gaps of silence. "Nothing."

"I see," he finally said. "You've got it wrong, my friend"— chiding condescension in his voice. "If it makes you feel any better, I have to hold back. It's time you learned too."

"The best I can do is pretend I don't care."

"That much we've known for a while already," he snapped right away.

I was crushed. All these times when I thought I was slighting him by showing how easy it was to ignore him in the garden, on the balcony, at the beach, he had been seeing right through me and taken my move for the peevish, textbook gambit it was.

His admission, which seemed to open up all the sluiceways between us, was precisely what drowned my budding hopes. Where would we go from here? What was there to add? And what would happen the next time we pretended not to speak but were no longer sure the frost between us was still sham?

We spoke awhile longer, then the conversation petered out. Now that we had put our cards on the table, it felt like small talk.

"So this is where Monet came to paint."

"I'll show you at home. We have a book with wonderful re-productions of the area around here."

"Yes, you'll have to show me."

He was playing the role of the patronizing understudy. I hated it.

Each leaning on one arm, we both stared out at the view.

"You're the luckiest kid in the world," he said.

"You don't know the half of it."

I let him ponder my statement. Then, perhaps to fill the silence that was becoming unbearable, I blurted out, "So much of it is wrong, though."

"What? Your family?"

"That too."

"Living here all summer long, reading by yourself, meeting all those dinner drudges your father dredges up at every meal?" He was making fun of me again.

I smirked. No, that wasn't it either.

He paused a moment.

"Us, you mean."

I did not reply.

"Let's see, then—" And before I knew it, he sidled up to me. We were too close, I thought, I'd never been so close to him except in a dream or when he cupped his hand to light my cigarette. If he brought his ear any closer he'd hear my heart. I'd seen it written in novels but never believed it until now. He stared me right in the face, as though he liked my face and wished to study it and to linger on it, then he touched my nether lip with his finger and let it travel left and right and right and left again and again as I lay there, watching him smile in a way that made me fear anything might happen now and there'd be no turning back, that this was his way of asking, and here was my chance to say no or to say something and play for time, so that I might still debate the matter with myself, now that it had reached this point—except that I didn't have any time left, because he brought his lips to my mouth, a warm, conciliatory, I'll-meet-you-halfway-but-no-further kiss till he realized how famished mine was. I wished I knew how to calibrate my kiss the way he did. But passion allows us to hide more, and at that moment on Monet's berm, if I wished to hide everything about me in this kiss, I was also desperate to forget the kiss by losing myself in it.

"Better now?" he asked afterward.

I did not answer but lifted my face to his and kissed him again, almost savagely, not because I was filled with passion or even because his kiss still lacked the zeal I was looking for, but because I was not so sure our kiss had convinced me of anything about myself. I was not even sure I had enjoyed it as much as I'd expected and needed to test it again, so that even in the act itself, I needed to test the test. My mind was drifting to the most mundane things. *So much denial?* a two-bit disciple of Freud would have observed. I squelched my doubts with a yet more violent kiss. I did not want passion, I did not want pleasure. Perhaps I didn't even want proof. And I did not want words, small talk, big talk, bike talk, book talk, any of it. Just the sun, the grass, the occasional sea breeze, and the smell of his body fresh from his chest, from his neck and his armpits. Just take me and molt me and turn me inside out, till, like a character in Ovid, I become one with your lust, that's what I wanted. Give me a blindfold, hold my hand, and don't ask me to think—will you do that for me?

I did not know where all this was leading, but I was surrendering to him, inch by inch, and he must have known it, for I sensed he was still keeping a distance between us. Even with our faces touching, our bodies were angles apart. I knew that anything I did now, any movement I'd make, might disturb the harmony of the moment. So, sensing there was probably not going to be a sequel to our kiss, I began to test the eventual separation of our mouths, only to realize, now that I was making mere motions of ending the kiss, how much I'd wanted it not to stop, wanted his tongue in my mouth and mine in his—because all we had become, after all these weeks and all the strife and all the fits and starts that ushered a chill draft each time, was just two wet tongues flailing away in each other's mouths. Just two tongues, all the rest was nothing. When, finally, I lifted one knee and moved it toward him to face him, I knew I had broken the spell.

"I think we should go."

"Not yet."

"We can't do this—I know myself. So far we've behaved. We've been good. Neither of us has done anything to feel ashamed of. Let's keep it that way. I want to be good."

"Don't be. I don't care. Who is to know?"

In a desperate move which I knew I'd never live down if he did not relent, I reached for him and let my hand rest on his crotch. He did not move. I should have slipped my hand straight into his shorts. He must have read my intention and, with total composure, bordering on a gesture that was very gentle but also quite glacial, brought his hand there and let it rest on mine for a second, then, twining his fingers into mine, lifted my hand.

A moment of unbearable silence settled between us.

"Did I offend you?"

"Just don't."

It sounded a bit like *Later!* when I'd first heard it weeks earlier—biting and blunted, and altogether mirthless, without any inflection of either the joy or the passion we'd just shared. He gave me his hand and helped me stand up again.

He suddenly winced.

I remembered the scrape on his side.

"I should make sure it doesn't get infected," he said.

"We'll stop by the pharmacist on the way back."

He didn't reply. But it was about the most sobering thing we could have said. It let the intrusive real world gust into our lives—Anchise, the mended bike, the bickering over tomatoes, the music score hastily left under a glass of lemonade, how *long ago* they all seemed.

Indeed, as we rode away from my spot we saw two tourist vans heading south to N. It must have been nearing noon.

"We'll never speak again," I said as we glided down the never-ending slope, the wind in our hair.

"Don't say that."

"I just know it. We'll chitchat. Chitchat, chitchat. That's all. And the funny thing is, I can live with that."

"You just rhymed," he said.

I loved the way he'd flip on me.

Two hours later, at lunch, I gave myself all the proof I needed that I would never be able to live with that.

Before dessert, while Mafalda was clearing away the plates and while everyone's attention was focused on a conversation about Jacopone da Todi, I felt a warm, bare foot casually brush mine.

I remembered that, on the berm, I should have seized my chance to feel if the skin of his foot was as smooth as I'd imagined it. Now this was all the chance I'd get.

Perhaps it was my foot that had strayed and touched his. It withdrew, not immediately, but soon enough, as though it had consciously waited an appropriate interval of time so as not to give the impression of having recoiled in panic. I too waited a few seconds more and, without actually planning my move, allowed my foot to begin seeking the other out. I had just begun searching for it when my toe suddenly bumped into his foot; his had hardly budged at all, like a pirate ship that gave every indication of having fled miles away but was really hiding in a fog no more than fifty yards away, waiting to pounce as soon as the chance presented itself. I had barely enough time to do anything with my foot when, without warning, without giving me time to work my way to his or to let mine rest at a safe distance again, softly, gently, suddenly his foot moved over to mine and began caressing it, rubbing it, never holding still, the smooth round ball of his heel holding my foot in place, occasionally bringing its weight to bear but lightening it right away with another caress of the toes, indicating, all the while, that this was being done in the spirit of fun and games, because it was his way of pulling the rug out from under the lunch drudges sitting right across from us, but also telling me that this had nothing to do with others and would remain strictly between us, because it was about us, but that I shouldn't read into it more than there was. The stealth and stubbornness of his caresses sent chills down my spine. A sudden giddiness overtook me. No, I wasn't going to cry, this wasn't a panic attack, it wasn't a "swoon," and I wasn't going to come in my shorts either, though I liked this very, very much, especially when the arch of his foot lay on top of my foot. When I looked at my dessert plate and saw the chocolate cake speckled with raspberry juice, it seemed to me that someone was pouring more and more red sauce than usual, and that the sauce seemed to be coming from the ceiling above my head until it suddenly hit me that it was streaming from my nose. I gasped, and quickly crumpled my napkin and brought it to my nose, holding my head as far back as I could. "*Ghiaccio*, ice, Mafalda, *per favore, presto,*" I said, softly, to show that I was in perfect control of the situation. "I was up at the hill this morning. Happens all the time," I said, apologizing to the guests.

There was a scuffle of quick sounds as people rushed in and out of the dining room. I had shut my eyes. Get a grip, I kept saying to myself, get a grip. Don't let your body give the whole thing away.

"Was it my fault?" he asked when he stepped into my bedroom after lunch.

I did not reply. "I'm a mess, aren't I?"

He smiled and said nothing.

"Sit for a second."

He sat at the far corner of my bed. He was visiting a hospitalized friend who was injured in a hunting accident.

"Are you going to be okay?"

"I thought I was. I'll get over it." I'd heard too many characters say the same thing in too many novels. It let the runaway lover off the hook. It allowed everyone to save face. It restored dignity and courage to the one whose cover had been completely blown.

"I'll let you sleep now." Spoken like an attentive nurse.

On his way out he said, "I'll stick around," the way people might say, I'll leave the light on for you. "Be good."

As I tried to doze, the incident on the piazzetta, lost somewhere amid the Piave war memorial and our ride up the hill with fear and shame and who knows what else pressing on me, seemed to come back to me from summers and ages ago, as though I'd biked up to the piazzetta as a little boy before World War I and had returned a crippled ninety-year-old soldier confined to this bedroom that was not even my own, because mine had been given over to a young man who was the light of my eyes.

The light of my eyes, I said, light of my eyes, light of the world, that's what you are, light of my life. I didn't know what light of my eyes meant, and part of me wondered where on earth had I fished out such claptrap, but it was nonsense like this that brought tears now, tears I wished to drown in his pillow, soak in his bathing suit, tears I wanted him to touch with the tip of his tongue and make sorrow go away.

I didn't understand why he had brought his foot on mine. Was it a pass, or a well-meaning gesture of solidarity and comradeship, like his chummy hug-massage, a lighthearted nudge between lovers who are no longer sleeping together but have decided to remain friends and occasionally go to the movies? Did it mean, *I haven't forgotten, it'll always remain between us, even though nothing will come of it*?

I wanted to flee the house. I wanted it to be next fall already and be as far away as I could. Leave our town with its silly Le Danzing and its silly youth no one in his right mind would wish to befriend. Leave my parents and my cousins, who always competed with me, and those horrible summer guests with their arcane scholarly projects who always ended up hogging all the bathrooms on my side of the house.

What would happen if I saw him again? Would I bleed again, cry, come in my shorts? And what if I saw him with someone else, ambling as he so often did at night around Le Danzing? What if instead of a woman, it was a man?

I should learn to avoid him, sever each tie, one by one, as neurosurgeons do when they split one neuron from another, one thought-tormented wish from the next, stop going to the back garden, stop spying, stop heading to town at night, wean myself a bit at a time each day, like an addict, one day, one hour, one minute, one slop-infested second after the other. It could be done. I knew there was no future in this. Supposing he did come into my bedroom tonight. Better yet, supposing I had a few drinks and went into his and told him the plain honest truth square in your face, Oliver: Oliver, I want you to take me. Someone has to, and it might as well be you. Correction: I want it to be you. I'll try not to be the worst lay of your life. Just do with me as you would with anyone you hope never to run into again. I know this doesn't sound remotely romantic but I'm tied up in so many knots that I need the Gordian treatment. So get on with it.

We'd do it. Then I'd go back to my bedroom and clean up. After that, I'd be the one to occasionally place my foot on his, and see how he liked that.

This was my plan. This was going to be my way of getting him out of my system. I'd wait for everyone to go to bed. Watch for his light. I'd enter his room from the balcony.

Knock knock. No, no knocking. I was sure he slept naked. What if he wasn't alone? I'd listen outside the balcony before stepping in. If there was someone else with him and it was too late to beat a hasty retreat, I'd say, "Oops, wrong address." Yes: Oops, wrong address. A touch of levity to save face. And if he was alone? I'd walk in. Pajamas. No, just pajama bottoms. It's me, I'd say. Why are you here? I can't sleep. Want me to get you something to drink? It's not a drink I need. I've already had enough to find the courage to walk from my room to your room. It's you I've come for. I see. Don't make it difficult, don't talk, don't give me reasons, and don't act as if you're any moment going to shout for help. I'm way younger than you and you'd only make a fool of yourself by ringing the house alarm or threatening to tell my mommy. And right away I'd take off my pajama bottoms and slip into his bed. If he didn't touch me, then I'd be the one to touch him, and if he didn't respond, I'd let my mouth boldly go to places it'd never been before. The humor of the words themselves amused me. Intergalactic slop. My Star of David, his Star of David, our two necks like one, two cut Jewish men joined together from time immemorial. If none of this worked I'd go for *him*, he'd fight me back, and we'd wrestle, and I'd make sure to turn him on as he pinned me down while I wrapped my legs around him like a woman, even hurt him on the hip he'd scraped in his bicycle fall, and if all this didn't work then I'd commit the ultimate indignity, and with this indignity show him that the shame was all his, not mine, that I had come with truth and human kindness in my heart and that I was leaving it on his sheets now to remind him how he'd said no to a young man's plea for fellowship. Say no to that and they should have you in hell feet first.

What if he didn't like me? In the dark they say all cats . . . What if he doesn't like it at all? He'll just have to try, then. What if he gets really upset and offended? "Get out, you sick, wretched, twisted piece of shit." The kiss was proof enough he could be pushed that way. To say nothing of the foot? *Amor ch'a null'amato amar perdona.*

The foot. The last time he'd brought out such a reaction in me was not when he'd kissed me but when he'd pressed his thumb into my shoulders.

No, there'd been another time yet. In my sleep, when he came into my bedroom and lay on top of me, and I pretended to be asleep. Correction there again: in my sleep I'd heaved ever so slightly, just enough to tell him, Don't leave, you're welcome to go on, just don't say I knew.

When I awoke later that afternoon, I had an intense desire for yogurt. Childhood memories. I went to the kitchen and found Mafalda lazily stowing away the china, which had been washed hours earlier. She must have napped too, and just awakened. I found a large peach in the fruit bowl and began to pare it.

"Faccio io," she said, trying to grab the knife from my hand.

"No, no, faccio da me," I replied, trying not to offend her.

I wanted to slice it and then cut the pieces into smaller pieces, and the smaller pieces into yet smaller ones. Till they became atoms. Therapy. Then I picked a banana, peeled it ever so slowly, and then proceeded to slice it into the thinnest slices, which I then diced. Then an apricot. A pear. Dates. Then I took the large container of yogurt from the refrigerator and poured its contents and the minced fruit into the blender. Finally, for coloring, a few fresh strawberries picked from the garden. I loved the purr of the blender.

This was not a dessert she was familiar with. But she was going to let me have my way in her kitchen without interfering, as if humoring someone who'd been hurt enough already. The bitch knew. She must have seen the foot. Her eyes followed me every step of the way as if ready to pounce on my knife before I slit my veins with it.

After blending my concoction, I poured it into a large glass, aimed a straw into it as if it were a dart, and proceeded toward the patio. On my way there, I stepped into the living room and took out the large picture book of Monet reproductions. I placed it on a tiny stool by the ladder. I wouldn't show him the book. I'd just leave it there. He'd know.

On the patio, I saw my mother having tea with two sisters who had come all the way from S. to play bridge. The fourth player was due to arrive any minute.

In the back, from the garage area, I could hear their driver discussing soccer players with Manfredi.

I brought my drink to the far end of the patio, took out a chaise longue, and, facing the long balustrade, tried to enjoy the last half hour of full sun. I liked to sit and watch the waning day spread itself out into pre-dusk light. This was when one went for a late afternoon swim, but it was good to read then as well.

I liked feeling so rested. Maybe the ancients were right: it never hurt to be bled from time to time. If I continued to feel this way, later I might try to play one or two preludes and fugues, maybe a fantasy by Brahms. I swallowed more of the yogurt and put my leg on the chair next to mine.

It took me a while to realize that I was striking a pose.

I wanted him to come back and catch me ever so relaxed. Little did he know what I was planning for tonight.

"Is Oliver around?" I said, turning to my mother.

"Didn't he go out?"

I didn't say anything. So much for "I'll stick around," then.

In a while, Mafalda came to remove the empty glass. *Vuoi un altro di questi*, did I want another of *these*? she seemed to say as though referring to a strange brew whose foreign, un-Italian name, if it had one, was of no interest to her.

"No, maybe I'll go out."

"But where will you go at this time?" she asked, implying dinner. "Especially in the state you were in at lunch. *Mi preoccupo*, I worry."

"I'll be okay."

"I'd advise against it."

"Don't worry."

"Signora," she shouted, trying to enlist my mother's support. My mother agreed it was a bad idea.

"Then I'll go for a swim."

Anything but count the hours until tonight.

On my way down the stairway to the beach, I encountered a group of friends. They were playing volleyball on the sand. Did I want to play? No, thank you, I've been sick. I left them alone and ambled toward the large rock, stared at it for a while, and then looked out to the sea, which seemed to aim a rippling shaft of sunlight on the water directly toward me, as in a Monet painting. I stepped into the warm water. I was not unhappy. I wanted to be with someone. But it didn't trouble me that I was alone.

Vimini, who must have been brought there by one of the others, said she heard I'd been unwell. "We sick ones—," she began.

"Do you know where Oliver is?" I asked.

"I don't know. I thought he went fishing with Anchise."

"With Anchise? He's crazy! He almost got killed the last time."

No response. She was looking away from the setting sun.

"You like him, don't you?"

"Yes," I said.

"He likes you too—more than you do, I think."

Was this her impression?

No, it was Oliver's.

When had he told her?

A while ago.

It corresponded to the time when we had almost stopped speaking to each other. Even my mother had taken me aside that week and suggested I be more polite with our cauboi—all that walking in and out of rooms without even a perfunctory hello, not nice.

"I think he is right," said Vimini.

I shrugged my shoulders. But I had never been visited by such powerful contradictions before. This was agony, for something like rage was brimming over inside me. I tried to still my mind and think of the sunset before us, the way people about to be given a polygraph like to visualize serene and placid settings to disguise their agitation. But I was also forcing myself to think of other things because I did not want to touch or use up any thoughts bearing on tonight. He might say no, he might even decide to leave our house and, if pressed, explain why. This was as far as I would let myself think.

A horrible thought gripped me. What if, right now, among some of the townsfolk he had befriended, or among all those people who clamored to invite him for dinner, he were to let out, or just hint at, what had happened during our bike ride into town? In his place, would *I* have been able to keep a lid on such a secret? No.

And yet, he had shown me that what I wanted could be given and taken so naturally that one wonders why it needed such hand-wringing torment and shame, seeing it was no more complicated a gesture than, say, buying a pack of cigarettes, or passing a reefer, or stopping by one of the girls behind the piazzetta late at night and, having settled on a price, going upstairs for a few minutes.

When I returned after swimming, there was still no sign of him. I asked. No, he wasn't back. His bike was in the same place where we'd left it just before noon. And Anchise had returned hours ago. I went up to my room and from my balcony tried to make my way through the French windows of his room. They were shut. All I saw through the glass was the shorts he had been wearing at lunch.

I tried to remember. He was wearing a bathing suit when he came into my bedroom that afternoon and promised to stick around. I looked out of the balcony hoping to spot the boat, in case he had decided to take it out again. It was moored to our wharf.

When I came downstairs, Father was having cocktails with a reporter from France. Why don't you play something? he asked. *"Non mi va,"* I said, "don't feel like it." "E perché non ti va?" he asked, as though taking issue with the tone of my words. "Perché non mi va!" I shot back.

Having finally crossed a major barrier this morning, it seemed I could openly express the petty stuff that was on my mind right now.

Perhaps I too should have a drop of wine, said my father.

Mafalda announced dinner.

"Isn't it too early for dinner?" I asked.

"It's past eight."

My mother was escorting one of her friends who had come by car and had to leave.

I was grateful that the Frenchman was sitting on the edge of his armchair, as though on the verge of standing up to be shown to the dining room, yet still sitting down, not budging. He was holding an empty glass in both hands, forcing my father, who had just asked him what he thought of the upcoming opera season, to remain seated while he finished answering him.

Dinner was pushed back by another five to ten minutes. If he was late for dinner, he wouldn't eat with us. But if he was late that meant he was having dinner elsewhere. I didn't want him to have dinner anywhere but with us tonight.

"*Noi ci mettiamo a tavola*, we'll sit down," said my mother. She asked me to sit next to her.

Oliver's seat was empty. My mother complained that he should at least have let us know he wasn't coming for dinner.

Father said it might be the boat's fault again. That boat should be totally dismantled.

But the boat was downstairs, I said.

"Then it must be the translator. Who was it who told me he needed to see the translator this evening?" asked my mother.

Must not show anxiety. Or that I cared. Stay calm. I didn't want to bleed again. But that moment of what seemed like bliss now when we'd walked our bikes on the piazzetta both before and after our talk belonged to another time segment, as though it had happened to another me in some other life that was not too different from my own, but removed enough to make the few seconds that kept us apart seem like light-years away. If I put my foot on the floor and pretend that his is just behind the leg of the table, will that foot, like a starship that has turned on its cloaking

device, like a ghost summoned by the living, suddenly materialize
from its dimple in space and say, *I know you've beckoned. Reach
and you'll find me?*

Before long, my mother's friend, who, at the last minute, decided to stay for dinner, was asked to sit where I'd sat at lunch.
Oliver's place setting was instantly removed.

The removal was performed summarily, without a hint of regret or compunction, the way you'd remove a bulb that was no
longer working, or scrape out the entrails of a butchered sheep
that had once been a pet, or take off the sheets and blankets from
a bed where someone had died. Here, take these, and remove
them from sight. I watched his silverware, his place mat, his napkin, his entire being disappear. It presaged exactly what would
happen less than a month from now. I did not look at Mafalda.
She hated these last-minute changes at the dinner table. She was
shaking her head at Oliver, at my mother, at our world. At me
too, I suppose. Without looking at her I knew her eyes were scanning my face to pounce on mine and make eye contact, which
was why I avoided lifting my eyes from my *semifreddo*, which I
loved, and which she knew I loved and had placed there for me
because, despite the chiding look on her face that was stalking
my every glance, she knew I knew she felt sorry for me.

Later that night, while I was playing something on the piano,
my heart leapt when I thought I'd heard a scooter stop by our
gate. Someone had given him a ride. But I could have been mistaken. I strained for his footsteps, from the sound of gravel un-
derfoot to the muted flap of his espadrilles when he climbed the
stairway leading to our balcony. But no one came into the house.

Much, much later, in bed, I made out the sound of music
coming from a car that had stopped by the main road, beyond
the alley of pines. Door opens. Door slams shut. Car pulls away.
Music begins to fade. Just the sound of the surf and of gravel

gently raked by the idle steps of someone who's deep in thought or just slightly drunk.

What if on the way to his room he were to step into my bedroom, as in: *Thought I'd stick my head in before turning in and see how you're feeling. You okay?*

No answer.

Pissed?

No answer.

You are pissed?

No, not at all. It's just that you said you'd stick around.

So you are pissed.

So why didn't you stick around?

He looks at me, and like one adult to another, *You know exactly why.*

Because you don't like me.

No.

Because you never liked me.

No. Because I'm not good for you.

Silence.

Believe me, just believe me.

I lift the corner of my sheets.

He shakes his head.

Just for a second?

Shakes it again. *I know myself*, he says.

I'd heard him use these very same words before. They meant *I'm dying to, but may not be able to hold back once I start, so I'd rather not start.* What aplomb to tell someone you can't touch him because you know yourself.

Well, since you're not going to do anything with me—can you at least read me a story?

I'd settle for that. I wanted him to read me a story. Something by Chekhov or Gogol or Katherine Mansfield. Take your clothes

off, Oliver, and come into my bed, let me feel your skin, your
hair against my flesh, your foot on mine, even if we won't do a
thing, let us cuddle up, you and I, when the night is spread out
against the sky, and read stories of restless people who always
end up alone and hate being alone because it's always themselves
they can't stand being alone with . . .

Traitor, I thought as I waited to hear his bedroom door
squeak open and squeak shut. Traitor. How easily we forget. *I'll
stick around.* Sure. Liar.

It never crossed my mind that I too was a traitor, that somewhere on a beach near her home a girl had waited for me tonight,
as she waited every night now, and that I, like Oliver, hadn't given
her a second thought.

I heard him step onto the landing. I had left my bedroom
door intentionally ajar, hoping that the light from the foyer
would stream in just enough to reveal my body. My face was
turned toward the wall. It was up to him. He walked past my
room, didn't stop. Didn't even hesitate. Nothing.

I heard his door shut.

Barely a few minutes later, he opened it. My heart jumped.
By now I was sweating and could feel the dampness on my pillow. I heard a few more footsteps. Then I heard the bathroom
door click shut. If he ran the shower it meant he'd had sex. I
heard the bathtub and then the shower run. Traitor. Traitor.

I waited for him to come out of the shower. But he was taking forever.

When I finally turned to take a peek at the corridor, I noticed
that my room was completely dark. The door was shut—was
someone in my room? I could make out the scent of his Roger &
Gallet shampoo, so near me that if I so much as lifted my arm I
knew I'd touch his face. He was in my room, standing in the
dark, motionless, as though trying to make up his mind whether

to rouse me or just find my bed in the dark. Oh, bless this night, I thought, bless this night. Without saying a word, I strained to make out the outline of the bathrobe I had worn so many times after he'd used it, its long terrycloth belt hanging so close to me now, rubbing my cheek ever so lightly as he stood there ready to let the robe drop to the floor. Had he come barefoot? And had he locked my door? Was he as hard as I was, and was his cock already pushing out of the bathrobe, which was why the belt was just about caressing my face, was he doing it on purpose, tickling me in the face, don't stop, don't stop, don't ever stop. Without warning the door began to open. Why open the door now?

It was only a draft. A draft had pushed it shut. And a draft was pulling it open. The belt that had so impishly tickled my face was none other than the mosquito net rubbing by my face each time I breathed. Outside, I could hear the water running in the bathroom, hours and hours seemed to have gone by since he'd gone to take a bath. No, not the shower, but the flushing of the toilet. It didn't always work and would periodically empty itself when it was just about to overflow, only to refill and be emptied, again and again, all through the night. When I stepped out onto the balcony and made out the delicate light blue outline of the sea, I knew it was already dawn.

I woke up again an hour later.

At breakfast, as was our habit, I pretended not even to be aware of him. It was my mother who, on looking at him, first exclaimed, *Ma guardi un po' quant'è pallido*, just look how gaunt you look! Despite her bluff remarks she continued using the formal address when speaking to Oliver. My father looked up and continued reading the paper. "I pray to God you made a killing last night, otherwise I'll have to answer to your father." Oliver cracked open the top of his soft-boiled egg by tapping it with the flat of his teaspoon. He still hadn't learned. "I never lose, Pro."

He was speaking to his egg the way my father had spoken into his newspaper. "Does your father approve?" "I pay my own way. I've paid my way since prep school. My father couldn't possibly disapprove." I envied him. "Did you have a lot to drink last night?"

"That—and other things." This time he was buttering his bread.

"I don't think I want to know," said my father.

"Neither does my father. And to be perfectly frank, I don't think I care to remember myself."

Was this for my benefit? *Look, there's never going to be anything between us, and the sooner you get it through your head, the better off we'll all be.*

Or was it all diabolical posturing?

How I admired people who talked about their vices as though they were distant relatives they'd learned to put up with because they couldn't quite disown them. *That and other things. I don't care to remember*—like *I know myself*—hinted at a realm of human experience only others had access to, not I. How I wished I could say such a thing one day—that I didn't care to remember what I'd done at night in full morning glory. I wondered what were the other things that necessitated taking a shower. Did you take a shower to perk yourself up because your system wouldn't hold up otherwise? Or did you shower to forget, to wash away all traces of last night's smut and degradation? Ah, to proclaim your vices by shaking your head at them and wash the whole thing down with apricot juice freshly prepared by Mafalda's arthritic fingers and smack your lips afterward!

"Do you save your winnings?"

"Save and invest, Pro."

"I wish I'd had your head at your age; I would have spared myself many mistaken turns," said my father.

"You, mistaken turns, Pro? Frankly, I can't picture you even imagining a mistaken turn."

"That's because you see me as a figure, not a human being. Worse yet: as an old figure. But there were. Mistaken turns, that is. Everyone goes through a period of *traviamento*—when we take, say, a different turn in life, the other *via*. Dante himself did. Some recover, some pretend to recover, some never come back, some chicken out before even starting, and some, for fear of taking any turns, find themselves leading the wrong life all life long."

My mother sighed melodiously, her way of warning present company that this could easily turn into an improvised lecture from the great man himself.

Oliver proceeded to crack another egg.

He had big bags under his eyes. And he did look gaunt.

"Sometimes the traviamento turns out to be the right way, Pro. Or as good a way as any."

My father, who was already smoking at this point, nodded pensively, his way of signifying that he was not an expert on such matters and was more than willing to yield to those who were. "At your age I knew nothing. But today everyone knows everything, and everyone talks, talks, talks."

"Perhaps what Oliver needs is sleep, sleep, sleep."

"Tonight, I promise, Signora P., no poker, no drinking. I'll put on clean clothes, go over my manuscript, and after dinner we'll all watch TV and play canasta, like old folks in Little Italy.

"But first," he added, with something of a smirk on his face, "I need to see Milani for a short while. But tonight, I promise, I'll be the best-behaved boy on the whole Riviera."

Which was what happened. After a brief escape to B., he was the "green" Oliver all day, a child no older than Vimini, with all her candor and none of her barbs. He also had an enormous selection of flowers sent from the local flower shop. "You've lost your mind," my mother said. After lunch, he said he would take a nap—the first, and last, during his entire stay with us. And indeed he did nap, because when he woke up at around five, he looked as flush as someone who had lost ten years of his life: ruddy cheeks, eyes all rested, the gauntness gone. He could have passed for my age. As promised, that night we all sat down—there were no guests—and watched television romances. The best part was how everyone, including Vimini, who wandered in, and Mafalda, who had her "seat" near the door of the living room, talked back to every scene, predicted its end, by turns outraged by and derisive of the stupidity of the story, the actors, the characters. Why, what would you have done in her place? I would have left him, that's what. And you, Mafalda? Well, in my opinion, I think she should have accepted him the first time he asked and not shilly-shallied so long. My point exactly! She got what was coming to her. That she did.

We were interrupted only once. It was a phone call from the States. Oliver liked to keep his telephone conversations extremely short, curt almost. We heard him utter his unavoidable *Later!*, hang up, and, before we knew it, he was back asking what he'd missed. He never commented after hanging up. We never asked. Everyone volunteered to fill him in on the plot at the same time, including my father, whose version of what Oliver had missed was less accurate than Mafalda's. There was a lot of noise, with the result that we missed more of the film than Oliver had during his brief call. Much laughter. At some point, while we were intently focused on the high drama, Anchise walked into the living room and, unrolling a soaking old T-shirt, produced the evening's catch: a gigantic sea bass, instantly destined for tomorrow's lunch and dinner, with plenty for everyone who cared to join in. Father decided to pour some grappa for everyone, including a few drops for Vimini.

That night we all went to bed early. Exhaustion was the order of the day. I must have slept very soundly, because when I awoke they were already removing breakfast from the table.

I found him lying on the grass with a dictionary to his left and a yellow pad directly under his chest. I was hoping he'd look gaunt or be in the mood he'd been in all day yesterday. But he was already hard at work. I felt awkward breaking the silence. I was tempted to fall back on my habit of pretending not to notice him, but that seemed hard to do now, especially when he'd told me two days earlier that he'd seen through my little act.

Would knowing we were shamming change anything between us once we were back to not speaking again?

Probably not. It might dig the ditch even deeper, because it would be difficult for either of us to believe we were stupid enough to pretend the very thing we'd already confessed was a sham. But I couldn't hold back.

"I waited for you the other night." I sounded like my mother reproaching my father when he came home inexplicably late. I never knew I could sound so peevish.

"Why didn't you come into town?" came his answer.

"Dunno."

"We had a nice time. You would have too. Did you rest at least?"

"In a way. Restless. But okay."

He was back to staring at the page he had just been reading and was mouthing the syllables, perhaps to show his mind was very focused on the page.

"Are you headed into town this morning?"

I knew I was interrupting and hated myself.

"Later, maybe."

I should have taken the hint, and I did. But part of me refused to believe anyone could change so soon.

"I was going to head into town myself."

"I see."

"A book I ordered has finally arrived. I'm to pick it up at the bookstore this morning."

"What book?"

"*Armance*."

"I'll pick it up for you if you want."

I looked at him. I felt like a child who, despite all manner of indirect pleas and hints, finds himself unable to remind his parents they'd promised to take him to the toy store. No need beating around the bush.

"It was just that I was hoping we'd go together."

"You mean like the other day?" he added, as though to help me say what I couldn't bring myself to say, but making things no easier by pretending to have forgotten the exact day.

"I don't think we'll ever do anything like that again." I was trying to sound noble and grave in my defeat. "But, yes, like that." I could be vague too.

That I, an extremely shy boy, found the courage to say such things could come from one place only: from a dream I'd had two, perhaps three nights running. In my dream he had pleaded with me, saying, "You'll kill me if you stop." I thought I remembered the context, but it embarrassed me so much that I was reluctant, even vis-à-vis myself, to own up to it. I had put a cloak around it and could only take furtive, hasty peeks.

"That day belongs to a different time warp. We should learn to leave sleeping dogs—"

Oliver listened.

"This voice of wisdom is your most winning trait." He had

lifted his eyes from his pad and was staring me straight in the face, which made me feel terribly uneasy. "Do you like me that much, Elio?"

"Do I like you?" I wanted to sound incredulous, as though to question how he could ever have doubted such a thing. But then I thought better of it and was on the point of softening the tone of my answer with a meaningfully evasive *Perhaps* that was supposed to mean *Absolutely*, when I let my tongue loose: "Do I like you, Oliver? I worship you." There, I'd said it. I wanted the word to startle him and to come like a slap in the face so that it might be instantly followed with the most languorous caresses. What's *liking* when we're talking about *worshipping*? But I also wanted my verb to carry the persuasive knockout punch with which, not the person who has a crush on us, but their closest friend, takes us aside and says, *Look, I think you ought to know, so-and-so worships you.* "To worship" seemed to say more than anyone might dare say under the circumstances; but it was the safest, and ultimately murkiest, thing I could come up with. I gave myself credit for getting the truth off my chest, all the while finding a loophole for immediate retreat in case I'd ventured too far.

"I'll go with you to B.," he said. "But—no speeches."

"No speeches, nothing, not a word."

"What do you say we grab our bikes in half an hour?"

Oh, Oliver, I said to myself on my way to the kitchen for a quick bite to eat, I'll do anything for you. I'll ride up the hill with you, and I'll race you up the road to town, and won't point out the sea when we reach the berm, and I'll wait at the bar in the piazzetta while you meet with your translator, and I'll touch the memorial to the unknown soldier who died on the Piave, and I won't utter a word, I'll show you the way to the bookstore, and we'll park our bikes outside the shop and go in together and leave together, and I promise, I promise, I promise, there'll be no hint of Shelley, or Monet, nor will I ever stoop to tell you that two nights ago you added an annual ring to my soul.

I am going to enjoy this for its own sake, I kept telling myself. We are two young men traveling by bike, and we're going to go to town and come back, and we'll swim, play tennis, eat, drink, and late at night run into each other on the very same piazzetta where two mornings ago so much but really nothing was said between us. He'll be with a girl, I'll be with a girl, and we're even going to be happy. Every day, if I don't mess things up, we can ride into town and be back, and even if this is all he is willing to give, I'll take it—I'll settle for less, even, if only to live with these thread-bare scraps.

We rode our bicycles to town that morning and were done with his translator before long, but even after a hasty coffee at the bar, the bookstore wasn't open yet. So we lingered on the piazzetta, I staring at the war memorial, he looking out at the view of the speckling bay, neither of us saying a word about Shelley's ghost, which shadowed our every step through town and beckoned louder than Hamlet's father. Without thinking, he asked how anyone could drown in such a sea. I smiled right away, because I caught his attempt to backpedal, which instantly brought complicit smiles to our faces, like a passionate wet kiss in the midst of a conversation between two individuals who, without thinking, had reached for each other's lips through the scorching red desert both had intentionally placed between them so as not to grope for each other's nakedness.

"I thought we weren't going to mention—," I began.

"No speeches. I know."

When we returned to the bookshop, we left our bikes outside and went in.

This felt special. Like showing someone your private chapel, your secret haunt, the place where, as with the berm, one comes to be alone, to dream of others. This is where I dreamed of you before you came into my life.

I liked his bookstore manner. He was curious but not entirely focused, interested yet nonchalant, veering between a *Look what I've found* and *Of course, how could any bookstore not carry so-and-so!*

The bookseller had ordered two copies of Stendhal's *Armance*, one a paperback edition and the other an expensive hardbound. An impulse made me say I'd take both and to put them on my father's bill. I then asked his assistant for a pen, opened up the hardbound edition, and wrote, *Zwischen Immer und Nie, for you in silence, somewhere in Italy in the mid-eighties.*

In years to come, if the book was still in his possession, I wanted him to ache. Better yet, I wanted someone to look through his books one day, open up this tiny volume of *Armance*, and ask, *Tell me who was in silence, somewhere in Italy in the mid-eighties?* And then I'd want him to feel something as darting as sorrow and fiercer than regret, maybe even pity for me, because in the bookstore that morning I'd have taken pity too, if pity was all he had to give, if pity could have made him put an arm around me, and underneath this surge of pity and regret, hovering like a vague, erotic undercurrent that was years in the making, I wanted him to remember the morning on Monet's berm when I'd kissed him not the first but the second time and given him my spit in his mouth because I so desperately wanted his in mine.

He said something about the gift being the best thing he'd received all year. I shrugged my shoulders to make light of perfunctory gratitude. Perhaps I just wanted him to repeat it.

"I am glad, then. I just want to thank you for this morning." And before he even thought of interrupting, I added, "I know. No speeches. Ever."

On our way downhill, we passed my spot, and it was I this

time who looked the other way, as though it had all but slipped my mind. I'm sure that if I had looked at him then, we would have exchanged the same infectious smile we'd immediately wiped off our faces on bringing up Shelley's death. It might have brought us closer, if only to remind us how far apart we needed to be now. Perhaps in looking the other way, and knowing we had looked the other way to avoid "speeches," we might have found a reason to smile at each other, for I'm sure he knew I knew he knew I was avoiding all mention of Monet's berm, and that this avoidance, which gave every indication of drawing us apart, was, instead, a perfectly synchronized moment of intimacy which neither of us wished to dispel. This too is in the picture book, I might have said, but bit my tongue instead. No speeches.

But, if on our rides together the following mornings he were to ask, then I'd spill everything.

I'd tell him that though we rode our bicycles every day and took them up to our favorite piazzetta where I was determined never to speak out of turn, yet, each night, when I knew he was in bed, I'd still open my shutters and would step out onto the balcony, hoping he'd have heard the shaking glass of my French windows, followed by the telltale squeak of its old hinges. I'd wait for him there, wearing only my pajama bottoms, ready to claim, if he asked what I was doing there, that the night was too hot, and the smell of the citronella intolerable, and that I preferred to stay up, not sleep, not read, just stare, because I couldn't bring myself to sleep, and if he asked why I couldn't sleep, I'd simply say, You don't want to know, or, in a roundabout way, just say that I had promised never to cross over to his side of the balcony, partly because I was terrified of offending him now, but also because I didn't want to test the invisible trip wire between us— *What trip wire are you talking about?*—The trip wire which one night, if my dream is too powerful or if I've had more wine than usual, I could easily cross, then push open your glass door and say, Oliver, it's me, I can't sleep, let me stay with you. *That* trip wire!

The trip wire loomed at all hours of the night. An owl, the sound of Oliver's own window shutters squeaking against the wind, the music from a distant, all-night discotheque in an adjoining hill town, the scuffling of cats very late at night, or the creak of the wooden lintel of my bedroom door, anything could wake me. But I'd known these since childhood and, like a sleeping fawn flicking his tail at an intrusive insect, knew how to brush them away and fall instantly back to sleep. Sometimes, though, a mere nothing, like a sense of dread or shame, would slip its way out of my sleep and hover undefined about me and watch me sleep and, bending down to my ear, finally whisper, *I'm not trying to wake you, I'm really not, go back to sleep, Elio, keep sleeping*—while I made every effort to recover the dream I was about to reenter any moment now and could almost rescript if only I tried a bit harder.

But sleep would not come, and sure enough not one but two troubling thoughts, like paired specters materializing out of the fog of sleep, stood watch over me: desire and shame, the longing to throw open my window and, without thinking, run into his room stark-naked, and, on the other hand, my repeated inability to take the slightest risk to bring any of this about. There they were, the legacy of youth, the two mascots of my life, hunger and fear, watching over me, saying, *So many before you have taken the chance and been rewarded, why can't you?* No answer. *So many have balked, so why must you?* No answer. And then it came, as ever deriding me: *If not later, Elio, when?*

That night, yet again, an answer did come, though it came in a dream that was itself a dream within a dream. I awoke with an image that told me more than I wanted to know, as though, de-

spite all of my frank admissions to myself about what I wanted
from him, and how I'd want it, there were still a few corners I'd
avoided. In this dream I finally learned what my body must have
known from the very first day. We were in his room, and, contrary to all my fantasies, it was not I who had my back on the
bed, but Oliver; I was on top of him, watching, on his face, an
expression at once so flushed, so readily acquiescent, that even in
my sleep it tore every emotion out of me and told me one thing I
could never have known or guessed so far: that not to give what I
was dying to give him at whatever price was perhaps the greatest
crime I might ever commit in my life. I desperately wanted to give
him something. By contrast, taking seemed so bland, so facile,
so mechanical. And then I heard it, as I knew by now I would.
"You'll kill me if you stop," he was gasping, conscious that he'd
already spoken these selfsame words to me a few nights before
in another dream but that, having said them once, he was also
free to repeat them whenever he came into my dreams, even
though neither of us seemed to know whether it was his voice
that was breaking from inside me or whether my memory of
these very words was exploding in him. His face, which seemed
both to endure my passion and by doing so to abet it, gave me an
image of kindness and fire I had never seen and could never have
imagined on anyone's face before. This very image of him would
become like a night-light in my life, keeping vigil on those days
when I'd all but given up, rekindling my desire for him when I
wanted it dead, stoking the embers of courage when I feared a
snub might dispel every semblance of pride. The look on his face
became like the tiny snapshot of a beloved that soldiers take with
them to the battlefield, not only to remember there are good
things in life and that happiness awaits them, but to remind themselves that this face might never forgive them for coming back in
a body bag.

These words made me long for things and try things I would never have thought myself capable of.

Regardless of how much he wished to have nothing to do with me, regardless of those he'd befriended and was surely sleeping with each night, anyone who'd revealed his entire humanity to me while lying naked under me, even in my dream, could not be any different in real life. This was who he truly was; the rest was incidental.

No: he was also the other man, the one in the red bathing suit.

It was just that I couldn't allow myself to hope I'd ever see him wearing no bathing suit at all.

If on our second morning after the piazzetta I found the courage to insist on going to town with him though it was obvious he didn't even want to speak with me, it was only because as I looked at him and saw him mouthing the words he had just written on his yellow pad, I kept remembering his other, pleading words: "You'll kill me if you stop." When I offered him the book in the bookstore, and later even insisted on being the one to pay for our ice cream because buying an ice cream also meant walking our bikes through the narrow, shaded lanes of B. and therefore being together awhile longer, it was also to thank him for giving me "You'll kill me if you stop." Even when I ribbed him and promised to make no speeches, it was because I was secretly cradling "You'll kill me if you stop"—far more precious now than any other admission from him. That morning, I'd written it down in my diary but omitted to say I had dreamt it. I wanted to come back years later and believe, if only for a moment, that he had truly spoken these pleading words to me. What I wanted to preserve was the turbulent gasp in his voice which lingered with me for days afterward and told me that, if I could have him like this in my dreams every night of my life, I'd stake my entire life on dreams and be done with the rest.

As we sped downhill past my spot, past the olive groves and the sunflowers that turned their startled faces to us as we glided past the marine pines, past the two old train cars that had lost their wheels generations ago but still bore the royal insignia of the House of Savoy, past the string of gypsy vendors screaming murder at us for almost grazing their daughters with our bikes, I turned to him and yelled, "Kill me if I stop."

I had said it to put his words in my mouth, to savor them awhile longer before squirreling them back in my hideaway, the way shepherds take their sheep out uphill when it's warm but rush them back indoors when the weather cools. By shouting his words I was fleshing them out and giving them longer life, as though they had a life of their own now, a longer and louder life that no one could govern, like the life of echoes once they've bounced off the cliffs of B. and gone to dive by the distant shoals where Shelley's boat slammed into the squall. I was returning to Oliver what was his, giving him back his words with the implicit wish that he repeat them back to me again, as in my dream, because now it was his turn to say them.

At lunch, not a word. After lunch he sat in the shade in the garden doing, as he announced before coffee, two days' work. No, he wasn't going to town tonight. Maybe tomorrow. No poker either. Then he went upstairs.

A few days ago his foot was on mine. Now, not even a glance.

Around dinner, he came back down for a drink. "I'll miss all this, Mrs. P.," he said, his hair glistening after his late-afternoon shower, the "star" look beaming all over his features. My mother smiled; *la muvi star* was welcome *ennnnni taim*. Then he took the usual short walk with Vimini to help her look for her pet chameleon. I never quite understood what the two of them saw in each other, but it felt far more natural and spontaneous than anything he and I shared. Half an hour later, they were back. Vimini had scaled a fig tree and was told by her mother to go wash before dinner.

At dinner not a word. After dinner he disappeared upstairs.

I could have sworn that sometime around ten or so he'd make a quiet getaway and head to town. But I could see the light drifting from his end of the balcony. It cast a faint, oblique orange band toward the landing by my door. From time to time, I heard him moving.

I decided to call a friend to ask if he was headed to town. His mother replied that he'd already left, and yes, had probably gone to the same place as well. I called another. He too had already left. My father said, "Why don't you call Marzia? Are you avoiding her?" Not avoiding—but she seemed full of complications. "As if you aren't!" he added. When I called she said she wasn't going anywhere tonight. There was a dusky chill in her voice. I was calling to apologize. "I heard you were sick." It was nothing, I replied. I could come and pick her up by bike, and together we'd ride to B. She said she'd join me.

My parents were watching TV when I walked out of the house. I could hear my steps on the gravel. I didn't mind the noise. It kept me company. He'd hear it too, I thought.

Marzia met me in her garden. She was seated on an old, wrought-iron chair, her legs extended in front of her, with just her heels touching the ground. Her bike was leaning against another chair, its handlebar almost touching the ground. She was wearing a sweater. You made me wait a lot, she said. We left her house via a shortcut that was steeper but that brought us to town in no time. The light and the sound of bustling nightlife from the piazzetta were brimming over into the side alleys. One of the restaurants was in the habit of taking out tiny wooden tables and putting them on the sidewalk whenever its clientele overflowed the allotted space on the square. When we entered the piazza the bustle and commotion filled me with the usual sense of anxiety and inadequacy. Marzia would run into friends, others were bound to tease. Even being with her would challenge me in one way or another. I didn't want to be challenged.

Rather than join some of the people we knew at a table in the caffès, we stood in line to buy two ice creams. She asked me to buy her cigarettes as well.

Then, with our ice-cream cones, we began to walk casually through the crowded piazzetta, threading our way along one street, then another, and still another. I liked it when cobblestones glistened in the dark, liked the way she and I ambled about lazily as we walked our bikes through town, listening to the muffled chatter of TV stations coming from behind open windows. The bookstore was still open, and I asked her if she minded. No, she didn't mind, she'd come in with me. We leaned our bikes against the wall. The beaded fly curtain gave way to a smoky, musty room littered with overbrimming ashtrays. The owner was thinking of closing soon, but the Schubert quartet was still playing and a couple in their mid-twenties, tourists, were thumbing through books in the English-language section, probably looking for a novel with local color. How different from that morning when there hadn't been a soul about and blinding sunlight and the smell of fresh coffee had filled the shop. Marzia looked over my shoulder while I picked up a book of poetry on the table and began to read one of the poems. I was about to turn the page when she said she hadn't finished reading yet. I liked this. Seeing the couple next to us about to purchase an Italian novel in translation, I interrupted their conversation and advised against it. "This is much, much better. It's set in Sicily, not here, but it's probably the best Italian novel written this century." "We've seen the movie," said the girl. "Is it as good as Calvino, though?" I shrugged my shoulders. Marzia was still interested in the same poem and was actually rereading it. "Calvino is nothing in comparison—lint and tinsel. But I'm just a kid, and what do I know?"

Two other young adults, wearing stylish summer sports jackets, without ties, were discussing literature with the owner, all three of them smoking. On the table next to the cashier stood a clutter of mostly emptied wine glasses, and next to them one large bottle of port. The tourists, I noticed, were holding emptied glasses. Obviously, they'd been offered wine during the book party. The owner looked over to us and with a silent glance that wished to apologize for interrupting asked if we wanted some port as well. I looked at Marzia and shrugged back, meaning, She doesn't seem to want to. The owner, still silent, pointed to the bottle and shook his head in mock disapproval, to suggest it was a pity to throw away such good port tonight, so why not help him finish it before closing the shop. I finally accepted, as did Marzia. Out of politeness, I asked what was the book being celebrated tonight. Another man, whom I hadn't noticed because he'd been reading something in the tiny alcove, named the book: *Se l'amore. If Love.* "Is it good?" I asked. "Pure junk," he replied. "I should know. I wrote it."

I envied him. I envied him the book reading, the party, the friends and aficionados who had come in from the surrounding areas to congratulate him in the little bookstore off our little piazzetta in this little town. They had left more than fifty emptied glasses behind. I envied him the privilege of putting himself down.

"Would you inscribe a copy for me?"

"Con piacere," he replied, and before the owner had handed him a felt-tip pen, the author had already taken out his Pelikan. "I'm not sure this book is for you, but . . ." He let the sentence trail into silence with a mix of utter humility tinted with the faintest suggestion of affected swagger, which translated into, *You asked me to sign and I'm only too happy to play the part of the famous poet which we both know I'm not.*

I decided to buy Marzia a copy as well, and begged him to inscribe it for her, which he did, adding an endless doodle next to his name. "I don't think it's for you either, signorina, but . . ."

Then, once again, I asked the bookseller to put both books on my father's bill.

As we stood by the cashier, watching the bookseller take forever to wrap each copy in glossy yellow paper, to which he added a ribbon and, on the ribbon, the store's silver seal-sticker, I sidled up to her and, maybe because she simply stood there so close to me, kissed her behind the ear.

She seemed to shudder, but did not move. I kissed her again. Then, catching myself, I whispered, "Did it bother you?" "Of course not," she whispered back.

Outside, she couldn't help herself. "Why did you buy me this book?"

For a moment I thought she was going to ask me why I'd kissed her.

"*Perché mi andava*, because I felt like it."

"Yes, but why did you buy it for me—why buy *me* a book?"

"I don't understand why you're asking."

"Any idiot would understand why I'm asking. But you don't. Figures!"

"I still don't follow."

"You're hopeless."

I gazed at her, looking totally startled by the flutters of anger and vexation in her voice.

"If you don't tell me, I'll imagine all sorts of things—and I'll just feel terrible."

"You're an ass. Give me a cigarette."

It's not that I didn't suspect where she was headed, but that I couldn't believe that she had seen through me so clearly. Perhaps I didn't want to believe what she was implying for fear of having to answer for my behavior. Had I been purposely disingenuous? Could I continue to misconstrue what she was saying without feeling entirely dishonest?

Then I had a brilliant insight. Perhaps I'd been ignoring every one of her signals on purpose: to draw her out. This the shy and ineffectual call strategy.

Only then, by a ricochet mechanism that totally surprised me, did it hit me. Had Oliver been doing the same with me? Intentionally ignoring me all the time, the better to draw me in?

Wasn't this what he'd implied when he said he'd seen through my own attempts to ignore him?

We left the bookstore and lit two cigarettes. A minute later we heard a loud metallic rattle. The owner was lowering the steel shutter. "Do you really like to read that much?" she asked as we ambled our way casually in the dark toward the piazzetta.

I looked at her as if she had asked me if I loved music, or bread and salted butter, or ripe fruit in the summertime. "Don't get me wrong," she said. "I like to read too. But I don't tell anyone." At last, I thought, someone who speaks the truth. I asked her why she didn't tell anyone. "I don't know . . ." This was more her way of asking for time to think or to hedge before answering, "People who read are hiders. They hide who they are. People who hide don't always like who they are."

"Do you hide who you are?"

"Sometimes. Don't you?"

"Do I? I suppose." And then, contrary to my every impulse, I found myself stumbling into a question I might otherwise never have dared ask. "Do you hide from me?"

"No, not from you. Or maybe, yes, a bit."

"Like what?"

"You know exactly *like what*."

"Why do you say that?"

"Why? Because I think you can hurt me and I don't want to be hurt." Then she thought for a moment. "Not that you mean to hurt anyone, but because you're always changing your mind, always slipping, so no one knows where to find you. You scare me."

We were both walking so slowly that when we stopped our bicycles, neither took note. I leaned over and kissed her lightly on the lips. She took her bike, placed it against the door of a closed shop, and, leaning against a wall, said, "Kiss me again?" Using my kickstand, I stood the bike in the middle of the alley and, once we were close, I held her face with both hands, then leaned into her as we began to kiss, my hands under her shirt, hers in my hair. I loved her simplicity, her candor. It was in every word she'd spoken to me that night—untrammeled, frank, human—and in the way her hips responded to mine now, without inhibition, without exaggeration, as though the connection between lips and hips in her body was fluid and instantaneous. A kiss on the mouth was not a prelude to a more comprehensive contact, it was already contact in its totality. There was nothing between our bodies but our clothes, which was why I was not caught by surprise when she slipped a hand between us and down into my trousers, and said, "*Sei duro, duro*, you're so hard." And it was her frankness, unfettered and unstrained, that made me harder yet now.

I wanted to look at her, stare in her eyes as she held me in her hand, tell her how long I'd wanted to kiss her, say something to show that the person who'd called her tonight and picked her up at her house was no longer the same cold, lifeless boy—but she cut me short: "*Baciami ancora*, kiss me again."

I kissed her again, but my mind was racing ahead to the berm. Should I propose it? We would have to ride our bikes for five minutes, especially if we took her shortcut and made our way directly through the olive groves. I knew we'd run into other lovers around there. Otherwise there was the beach. I'd used the spot before. Everyone did. I might propose my room, no one at home would have known or for that matter cared.

An image flitted through my mind: she and I sitting in the garden every morning after breakfast, she wearing her bikini, always urging me to walk downstairs and join her for a swim.

"*Ma tu mi vuoi veramente bene*, do you really care for me?" she asked. Did it come from nowhere—or was this the same wounded look in need of soothing which had been shadowing our steps ever since we'd left the bookstore?

I couldn't understand how boldness and sorrow, how *you're so hard* and *do you really care for me?* could be so thoroughly bound together. Nor could I begin to fathom how someone so seemingly vulnerable, hesitant, and eager to confide so many uncertainties about herself could, with one and the same gesture, reach into my pants with unabashed recklessness and hold on to my cock and squeeze it.

While kissing her more passionately now, and with our hands straying all over each other's bodies, I found myself composing the note I resolved to slip under his door that night: *Can't stand the silence. I need to speak to you.*

By the time I was ready to slip the note under his door it was already dawn. Marzia and I had made love in a deserted spot on the beach, a place nicknamed the Aquarium, where the night's condoms would unavoidably gather and be seen floating among the rocks like returning salmon in trapped water. We planned to meet later in the day.

Now, as I made my way home, I loved her smell on my body, on my hands. I would do nothing to wash it away. I'd keep it on me till we met in the evening. Part of me still enjoyed luxuriating in this newfound, beneficent wave of indifference, verging on distaste, for Oliver that both pleased me and told me how fickle I ultimately was. Perhaps he sensed that all I'd wanted from him was to sleep with him to be done with him and had instinctively resolved to have nothing to do with me. To think that a few nights ago I had felt so strong an urge to host his body in mine that I'd nearly jumped out of bed to seek him out in his room. Now the idea couldn't possibly arouse me. Perhaps this whole thing with Oliver had been canicular rut, and I was well rid of it. By contrast, all I had to do was smell Marzia on my hand and I loved the all-woman in every woman.

I knew the feeling wouldn't last long and that, as with all addicts, it was easy to forswear an addiction immediately after a fix.

Scarcely an hour later, and Oliver came back to me *au galop*. To sit in bed with him and offer him my palm and say, Here, smell this, and then to watch him sniff at my hand, holding it ever so gently in both of his, finally placing my middle finger to his lips and then suddenly all the way into his mouth.

I tore out a sheet of paper from a school notebook.

Please don't avoid me.

Then I rewrote it:

Please don't avoid me. It kills me.

Which I rewrote:

Your silence is killing me.

Way over the top.

Can't stand thinking you hate me.

Too plangent. No, make it less lachrymose, but keep the trite death speech.

I'd sooner die than know you hate me.

At the last minute I came back to the original.

Can't stand the silence. I need to speak to you.

I folded the piece of lined paper and slipped it under his door with the resigned apprehension of Caesar crossing the Rubicon. There was no turning back now. *Iacta alea est*, Caesar had said, the die is cast. It amused me to think that the verb "to throw," *iacere* in Latin, has the same root as the verb "to ejaculate." No sooner had I thought this than I realized that what I wanted was to bring him not just her scent on my fingers but, dried on my hand, the imprint of my semen.

Fifteen minutes later I was prey to two countervailing emotions: regret that I had sent the message, and regret that there wasn't a drop of irony in it.

At breakfast, when he finally showed up after his jog, all he asked without raising his head was whether I had enjoyed myself last night, the implication being I had gone to bed very late. "*Insomma*, so-so," I replied, trying to keep my answer as vague as possible, which was also my way of suggesting I was minimizing a report that would have been too long otherwise. "Must be tired, then," was my father's ironic contribution to the conversation. "Or was it poker that you were playing too?" "I don't play poker." My father and Oliver exchanged significant glances. Then they began discussing the day's workload. And I lost him. Another day of torture.

When I went back upstairs to fetch my books, I saw the same folded piece of lined notebook paper on my desk. He must have stepped into my room using the balcony door and placed it where I'd spot it. If I read it now it would ruin my day. But if I put

off reading it, the whole day would become meaningless, and I
wouldn't be able to think of anything else. In all likelihood, he
was tossing it back to me without adding anything on it, as
though to mean: *I found this on the floor. It's probably yours.
Later!* Or it might mean something far more blunted: *No reply.
Grow up. I'll see you at midnight.*

That's what he had added under my words.

He had delivered it before breakfast.

This realization came with a few minutes' delay but it filled
me with instant yearning and dismay. Did I want this, now that
something was being offered? And was it in fact being offered?
And if I wanted or didn't want it, how would I live out the day till
midnight? It was barely ten in the morning: fourteen hours to
go . . . The last time I had waited so long for something was for
my report card. Or on the Saturday two years ago when a girl
had promised we'd meet at the movies and I wasn't sure she
hadn't forgotten. Half a day watching my entire life being put on
hold. How I hated waiting and depending on the whim of others.

Should I answer his note?

You can't answer an answer!

As for the note: was its tone intentionally light, or was it
meant to look like an afterthought scribbled away minutes after
jogging and seconds before breakfast? I didn't miss the little jab
at my operatic sentimentalism, followed by the self-confident,
let's-get-down-to-basics *see you at midnight.* Did either bode
well, and which would win the day, the swat of irony, or the
jaunty *Let's get together tonight and see what comes of it?* Were
we going to talk—just talk? Was this an order or a consent to see
me at the hour specified in every novel and every play? And where
were we going to meet at midnight? Would he find a moment
during the day to tell me where? Or, being aware that I had fret-
ted all night long the other night and that the trip wire dividing

our respective ends of the balcony was entirely artificial, did he assume that one of us would eventually cross the unspoken Maginot Line that had never stopped anyone?

And what did this do to our near-ritual morning bike rides? Would "midnight" supersede the morning ride? Or would we go on as before, as though nothing had changed, except that now we had a "midnight" to look forward to? When I run into him now, do I flash him a significant smile, or do I go on as before, and offer, instead, a cold, glazed, discreet *American* gaze?

And yet, among the many things I wished to show him the next time I crossed paths with him was gratitude. One could show gratitude and still not be considered intrusive and heavy-handed. Or does gratitude, however restrained, always bear that extra dollop of treacle that gives every Mediterranean passion its unavoidably mawkish, histrionic character? Can't let things well enough alone, can't play down, must exclaim, proclaim, declaim . . .

Say nothing and he'll think you regret having written.

Say anything and it will be out of place.

Do what, then?

Wait.

I knew this from the very start. Just wait. I'd work all morning. Swim. Maybe play tennis in the afternoon. Meet Marzia. Be back by midnight. No, eleven-thirty. Wash? No wash? Ah, to go from one body to the other.

Wasn't this what he might be doing as well? Going from one to the other.

And then a terrible panic seized me: was midnight going to be a talk, a clearing of the air between us—as in, buck up, lighten up, grow up!

But why wait for midnight, then? Who ever picks midnight to have such a conversation?

Or was midnight going to be *midnight*?

What to wear at midnight?

The day went as I feared. Oliver found a way to leave without telling me immediately after breakfast and did not come back until lunch. He sat in his usual place next to me. I tried to make light conversation a few times but realized that this was going to be another one of our let's-not-speak-to-each-other days when we both tried to make it very clear that we were no longer just pretending to be quiet.

After lunch, I went to take a nap. I heard him follow me upstairs and shut his door.

Later I called Marzia. We met on the tennis court. Luckily, no one was there, so it was quiet and we played for hours under the scorching sun, which both of us loved. Sometimes, we would sit on the old bench in the shade and listen to the crickets. Mafalda brought us refreshments and then warned us that she was too old for this, that the next time we'd have to fetch whatever we wanted ourselves. "But we never asked you for anything," I protested. "You shouldn't have drunk, then." And she shuffled away, having scored her point.

Vimini, who liked to watch people play, did not come that day. She must have been with Oliver at their favorite spot.

I loved August weather. The town was quieter than usual in the late summer weeks. By then, everyone had left for *le vacanze*, and the occasional tourists were usually gone before seven in the evening. I loved the afternoons best: the scent of rosemary, the heat, the birds, the cicadas, the sway of palm fronds, the silence that fell like a light linen shawl on an appallingly sunny day, all of these highlighted by the walk down to the shore and the walk back upstairs to shower. I liked looking up to our house from the tennis court and seeing the empty balconies bask in the sun, knowing that from any one of them you could spot the limitless sea. This was my balcony, my world. From where I sat now, I could look around me and say, Here is our tennis court, there our garden, our orchard, our shed, our house, and below is our wharf—everyone and everything I care for is here. My family, my instruments, my books, Mafalda, Marzia, Oliver.

That afternoon, as I sat with Marzia with my hand resting on her thighs and knees, it did occur to me that I was, in Oliver's words, one of the luckiest persons on earth. There was no saying how long all this would last, just as there was no sense in second-guessing how the day might turn out, or the night. Every minute felt as though stretched on tenterhooks. Everything could snap in a flash.

But sitting here I knew I was experiencing the mitigated bliss of those who are too superstitious to claim they may get all they've ever dreamed of but are far too grateful not to know it could easily be taken away.

After tennis, and just before heading to the beach, I took her upstairs by way of the balcony into my bedroom. No one passed there in the afternoon. I closed the shutters but left the windows open, so that the subdued afternoon light drew slatted patterns on the bed, on the wall, on Marzia. We made love in utter silence, neither of us closing our eyes.

Part of me hoped we'd bang against the wall, or that she'd be unable to smother a cry, and that all this might alert Oliver to what was happening on the other side of his wall. I imagined him napping and hearing my bedsprings and being upset.

On our way to the cove below I was once again pleased to feel I didn't care if he found out about us, just as I didn't care if he never showed up tonight. I didn't even care for him or his shoulders or the white of his arms. The bottom of his feet, the flat of his palms, the underside of his body—didn't care. I would much rather spend the night with her than wait up for him and hear him declaim bland pieties at the stroke of midnight. What had I been thinking this morning when I'd slipped him my note?

And yet another part of me knew that if he showed up tonight and I disliked the start of whatever was in store for me, I'd still go through with it, go with it all the way, because better to find out once and for all than to spend the rest of the summer, or my life perhaps, arguing with my body.

I'd make a decision in cold blood. And if he asked, I'd tell him. I'm not sure I want to go ahead with this, but I need to know, and better with you than anyone else. I want to know your body, I want to know how you feel, I want to know you, and through you, me.

Marzia left just before dinnertime. She had promised to go to the movies. There'd be friends, she said. Why didn't I come? I made a face when I heard their names. I'd stay home and practice, I said. I thought you practiced every morning. This morning I started late, remember? She intercepted my meaning and smiled.

Three hours to go.

There'd been a mournful silence between us all afternoon. If I hadn't had his word that we were going to talk later, I don't know how I'd have survived another day like this.

At dinner, our guests were a semi-employed adjunct professor of music and a gay couple from Chicago who insisted on speaking terrible Italian. The two men sat next to each other, facing my mother and me. One of them decided to recite some verses by Pascoli, to which Mafalda, catching my look, made her usual *smorfia* meant to elicit a giggle from me. My father had warned me not to misbehave in the presence of the scholars from Chicago. I said I would wear the purple shirt given me by a distant cousin from Uruguay. My father laughed it off, saying I was too old not to accept people as they were. But there was a glint in his eyes when both showed up wearing purple shirts. They had both stepped out from either side of the cab at the same time and each carried a bunch of white flowers in his hand. They looked, as my father must have realized, like a flowery, gussied-up version of Tintin's Thomson and Thompson twins.

I wondered what their life together was like.

It seemed strange to be counting the minutes during supper, shadowed by the thought that tonight I had more in common with Tintin's twins than with my parents or anyone else in my world.

I looked at them, wondering who was top and who was bottom, Tweedle-Dee or Tweedle-Dum.

It was almost eleven when I said I was going to sleep and said goodnight to my parents and the guests. "What about Marzia?" asked my father, that unmistakable lambent look in his eyes. Tomorrow, I replied.

I wanted to be alone. Shower. A book. A diary entry, perhaps. Stay focused on midnight yet keep my mind off every aspect of it.

On my way up the staircase, I tried to imagine myself coming down this very same staircase tomorrow morning. By then I might be someone else. Did I even like this someone else whom I didn't yet know and who might not want to say good morning then or have anything to do with me for having brought him to this pass? Or would I remain the exact same person walking up this staircase, with nothing about me changed, and not one of my doubts resolved?

Or nothing at all might happen. He could refuse, and, even if no one found out I had asked him, I'd still be humiliated, and for nothing. He'd know; I'd know.

But I was past humiliation. After weeks of wanting and waiting and—let's face it—begging and being made to hope and fight
every access of hope, I'd be devastated. How do you go back to
sleep after that? Slink back into your room and pretend to open
a book and read yourself to sleep?

Or: how do you go back to sleep no longer a virgin? There
was no coming back from that! What had been in my head for so
long would now be out in the real world, no longer afloat in my
foreverland of ambiguities. I felt like someone entering a tattoo
parlor and taking a last, long look at his bare left shoulder.

Should I be punctual?

Be punctual and say: Whooo-hooo, the witching hour.

Soon I could hear the voices of the two guests rising from the
courtyard. They were standing outside, probably waiting for the
adjunct professor to drive them back to their pension. The adjunct was taking his time and the couple were simply chatting
outside, one of them giggling.

At midnight there wasn't a sound coming from his room.
Could he have stood me up again? That would be too much. I
hadn't heard him come back. He'd just have to come to my
room, then. Or should I still go to his? Waiting would be torture.

I'll go to him.

I stepped out onto the balcony for a second and peered in the
direction of his bedroom. No light. I'd still knock anyway.

Or I could wait. Or not go at all.

Not going suddenly burst on me like the one thing I wanted
most in life. It kept tugging at me, straining toward me ever so
gently now, like someone who'd already whispered once or twice
in my sleep but, seeing I wasn't waking, had finally tapped me on
the shoulder and was now encouraging me to look for every in-
ducement to put off knocking on his window tonight. The

thought washed over me like water on a flower shop window, like a soothing, cool lotion after you've showered and spent the whole day in the sun, loving the sun but loving the balsam more. Like numbness, the thought works on your extremities first and then penetrates to the rest of your body, giving all manner of arguments, starting with the silly ones—it's way too late for anything tonight—rising to the major ones—how will you face the others, how will you face yourself?

Why hadn't I thought of this before? Because I wanted to savor and save it for last? Because I wanted the counterarguments to spring on their own, without my having any part in summoning them at all, so that I wouldn't be blamed for them? *Don't try, don't try this, Elio.* It was my grandfather's voice. I was his namesake, and he was speaking to me from the very bed where he'd crossed a far more menacing divide than the one between my room and Oliver's. *Turn back. Who knows what you'll find once you're in that room. Not the tonic of discovery but the pall of despair when disenchantment has all but shamed every ill-stretched nerve in your body. The years are watching you now, every star you see tonight already knows your torment, your ancestors are gathered here and have nothing to give or say,* Non c'andà, *don't go there.*

But I loved the fear—if fear it really was—and this they didn't know, my ancestors. It was the underside of fear I loved, like the smoothest wool found on the underbelly of the coarsest sheep. I loved the boldness that was pushing me forward; it aroused me, because it was born of arousal itself. "You'll kill me if you stop"—or was it: "I'll die if you stop." Each time I heard these words, I couldn't resist.

I knock on the glass panel, softly. My heart is beating like crazy. I am afraid of nothing, so why be so frightened? Why? Because everything scares me, because both fear and desire are busy equivocating with each other, with me, I can't even tell the difference between wanting him to open the door and hoping he's stood me up.

Instead, no sooner have I knocked on the glass panel than I hear something stir inside, like someone looking for his slippers. Then I make out a weak light going on. I remembered buying this night-light at Oxford with my father one evening early last spring when our hotel room was too dark and he had gone downstairs and come back up saying he'd been told there was a twenty-four-hour store that sold night-lights just around the corner. *Wait here, and I'll be back in no time.* Instead, I said I'd go with him. I threw on my raincoat on top of the very same pajamas I was wearing tonight.

"I'm so glad you came," he said. "I could hear you moving in your room and for a while I thought you were getting ready to go to bed and had changed your mind."

"Me, change my mind? Of course I was coming."

It was strange seeing him fussing awkwardly this way. I had expected a hailstorm of mini-ironies, which was why I was nervous. Instead, I was greeted with excuses, like someone apologizing for not having had time to buy better biscuits for afternoon tea.

I stepped into my old bedroom and was instantly taken aback by the smell which I couldn't quite place, because it could have been a combination of so many things, until I noticed the rolled-up towel tucked under the bedroom door. He had been sitting in bed, a half-full ashtray sitting on his right pillow.

"Come in," he said, and then shut the French window behind us. I must have been standing there, lifeless and frozen.

Both of us were whispering. A good sign.

"I didn't know you smoked."

"Sometimes." He went to the bed and sat squarely in the middle of it.

Not knowing what else to do or say, I muttered, "I'm nervous."

"Me too."

"Me more than you."

He tried to smile away the awkwardness between us and passed me the reefer.

It gave me something to do.

I remembered how I'd almost hugged him on the balcony but had caught myself in time, thinking that an embrace after such chilly moments between us all day was unsuitable. Just because someone says he'll see you at midnight doesn't mean you're automatically bound to hug him when you've barely shaken hands all week. I remembered thinking before knocking: To hug. Not to hug. To hug.

Now I was inside the room.

He was sitting on the bed, with his legs crossed. He looked smaller, younger. I was standing awkwardly at the foot of the bed, not knowing what to do with my hands. He must have seen me struggling to keep them on my hips and then put them in my pockets and then back to my hips again.

I look ridiculous, I thought. This and the would-be hug I'd suppressed and which I kept hoping he hadn't noticed.

I felt like a child left alone for the first time with his homeroom teacher. "Come, sit."

Did he mean on a chair or on the bed itself?

Hesitantly, I crawled onto the bed and sat facing him, crosslegged like him, as though this were the accepted protocol among men who meet at midnight. I was making sure our knees didn't touch. Because he'd mind if our knees touched, just as he'd mind the hug, just as he minded when, for want of a better way to show I wanted to stay awhile longer on the berm, I'd placed my hand on his crotch.

But before I had a chance to exaggerate the distance between us, I felt as though washed by the sliding water on the flower shop's storefront window, which took all my shyness and inhibitions away. Nervous or not nervous, I no longer cared to cross-examine every one of my impulses. If I'm stupid, let me be stupid. If I touch his knee, so I'll touch his knee. If I want to hug, I'll hug. I needed to lean against something, so I sidled up to the top of the bed and leaned my back against the headboard next to him.

I looked at the bed. I could see it clearly now. This was where I'd spent so many nights dreaming of just such a moment. Now here I was. In a few weeks, I'd be back here on this very same bed. I'd turn on my Oxford night-light and remember standing outside on the balcony, having caught the rustle of his feet scrambling to find his slippers. I wondered whether I would look back on this with sorrow. Or shame. Or indifference, I hoped.

"You okay?" he asked.

"Me okay."

There was absolutely nothing to say. With my toes, I reached over to his toes and touched them. Then, without thinking, I slipped my big toe in between his big toe and his second toe. He did not recoil, he did not respond. I wanted to touch each toe with my own. Since I was sitting to his left, these were probably not the toes that had touched me at lunch the other day. It was his right foot that was guilty. I tried to reach it with my right foot, all the while avoiding touching both his knees, as if something told me knees were off bounds. "What are you doing?" he finally asked. "Nothing." I didn't know myself, but his body gradually began to reciprocate the movement, somewhat absentmindedly, without conviction, no less awkward than mine, as if to say, *What else is there to do but to respond in kind when someone touches your toes with his toes?* After that, I moved closer to him and then hugged him. A child's hug which I hoped he'd read as an embrace. He did not respond. "That's a start," he finally said, perhaps with a tad more humor in his voice than I'd wish. Instead of speaking, I shrugged my shoulders, hoping he'd feel my shrug and not ask any more questions. I did not want us to speak. The less we spoke, the more unrestrained our movements. I liked hugging him.

"Does this make you happy?" he asked.

I nodded, hoping, once again, that he'd feel my head nodding without the need for words.

Finally, as if my position urged him to do likewise, he brought his arm around me. The arm didn't stroke me, nor did it hold me tight. The last thing I wanted at this point was comradeship. Which was why, without interrupting my embrace, I loosened my hold for a moment, time enough to bring both my arms under his loose shirt and resume my embrace. I wanted his skin.

"You sure you want this?" he asked, as if this doubt was why he'd been hesitant all along.

I nodded again. I was lying. By then I wasn't sure at all. I wondered when my hug would run its course, when I, or he, would grow tired of this. Soon? Later? Now?

"We haven't talked," he said.

I shrugged my shoulders, meaning, No need to.

He lifted my face with both hands and stared at me as we had done that day on the berm, this time even more intensely because both of us knew we'd already crossed the bar. "Can I kiss you?" What a question, coming after our kiss on the berm! Or had we wiped the slate clean and were starting all over again?

I did not give him an answer. Without nodding, I had already brought my mouth to his, just as I'd kissed Marzia the night before. Something unexpected seemed to clear away between us, and, for a second, it seemed there was absolutely no difference in age between us, just two men kissing, and even this seemed to dissolve, as I began to feel we were not even two men, just two beings. I loved the egalitarianism of the moment. I loved feeling younger and older, human to human, man to man, Jew to Jew. I loved the night-light. It made me feel snug and safe. As I'd felt that night in the hotel bedroom in Oxford. I even loved the stale, wan feel of my old bedroom, which was littered with his things but which somehow became more livable under his stewardship than mine: a picture here, a chair turned into an end table, books, cards, music.

I decided to get under the covers. I loved the smell. I wanted to love the smell. I even liked the fact that there were things on the bed that hadn't been removed and which I kept kneeing into and didn't mind encountering when I slipped a foot under them, because they were part of his bed, his life, his world.

He got under the covers too and, before I knew it, started to undress me. I had worried about how I'd go about undressing, how, if he wasn't going to help, I'd do what so many girls did in the movies, take off my shirt, drop my pants, and just stand there, stark-naked, arms hanging down, meaning: This is who I am, this is how I'm made, here, take me, I'm yours. But his move had solved the problem. He was whispering, "Off, and off, and off, and off," which made me laugh, and suddenly I was totally naked, feeling the weight of the sheet on my cock, not a secret left in the world, because wanting to be in bed with him was my only secret and here I was sharing it with him. How wonderful to feel his hands all over me under the sheets, as if part of us, like an advance scouting party, had already arrived at intimacy, while the rest of us, exposed outside the sheets, was still struggling with niceties, like latecomers stamping their feet in the cold while everyone else is warming hands inside a crowded nightclub. He was still dressed and I wasn't. I loved being naked before him. Then he kissed me, and kissed me again, deeply this second time, as if he too was finally letting go. At some point I realized he'd been naked for a long while, though I hadn't noticed him undress, but there he was, not a part of him wasn't touching me. Where had I been? I'd been meaning to ask the tactful health question, but that too seemed to have been answered a while ago, because when I finally did find the courage to ask him, he replied, "I already told you, I'm okay." "Did I tell you I was okay too?" "Yes." He smiled. I looked away, because he was staring at me, and I knew I was flushed, and I knew I'd made a face, though I still wanted him to stare at me even if it embarrassed me, and I wanted to keep staring at him too as we settled in our mock wrestling position, his shoulders rubbing my knees. How far we had come from the afternoon when I'd taken off my underwear and put on his bathing suit and thought this was the closest his body would ever come to mine. Now this. I was on the cusp of something, but I also wanted it to last forever, because I knew there'd be no coming back from this. When it happened, it happened not as I'd dreamed it would, but with a degree of discomfort that forced me to reveal more of myself than I cared to reveal. I had an impulse to stop him, and when he noticed, he did ask, but I did not answer, or didn't know what to answer, and an eternity seemed to pass between my reluctance to make up my mind and his instinct to make it up for me. From this moment on, I thought, from this moment on—I had, as I'd never before in my life, the distinct feeling of arriving somewhere very dear, of wanting this forever, of being me, me, me, me, and no one else, just me, of finding in each shiver that ran down my arms something totally alien and yet by no means unfamiliar, as if all this had been part of me all of my life and I'd misplaced it and he had helped me find it. The dream had been right—this was like coming home, like asking, Where have I been all my life? which was another way of asking, Where were you in my childhood, Oliver?

which was yet another way of asking, What is life without this? which was why, in the end, it was I, and not he, who blurted out, not once, but many, many times, You'll kill me if you stop, you'll kill me if you stop, because it was also my way of bringing full circle the dream and the fantasy, me and him, the longed-for words from his mouth to my mouth back into his mouth, swapping words from mouth to mouth, which was when I must have begun using obscenities that he repeated after me, softly at first, till he said, "Call me by your name and I'll call you by mine," which I'd never done in my life before and which, as soon as I said my own name as though it were his, took me to a realm I never shared with anyone in my life before, or since.

Had we made noise?

He smiled. Nothing to worry about.

I think I might have sobbed even, but I wasn't sure. He took his shirt and cleaned me with it. Mafalda always looks for signs. She won't find any, he said. I call this shirt "Billowy," you wore it on your first day here, it has more of you than me. I doubt it, he said. He wouldn't let go of me yet, but as our bodies separated I seemed to remember, though ever so distantly, that a while back I had absentmindedly shoved away a book which had ended up under my back while he was still inside me. Now it was on the floor. When had I realized it was a copy of *Se l'amore*? Where had I found time in the heat of passion even to wonder whether he'd been to the book party on the same night I'd gone there with Marzia? Strange thoughts that seemed to drift in from long, long ago, no more than half an hour later.

It must have come to me a while later when I was still in his arms. It woke me up before I even realized I had dozed off, filling me with a sense of dread and anxiety I couldn't begin to fathom. I felt queasy, as if I had been sick and needed not just many showers to wash everything off but a bath in mouthwash. I needed to be far away—from him, from this room, from what we'd done together. It was as though I were slowly landing from an awful nightmare but wasn't quite touching the ground yet and wasn't sure I wanted to, because what awaited was not going to be much better, though I knew I couldn't go on hanging on to that giant, amorphous blob of a nightmare that felt like the biggest cloud of self-loathing and remorse that had ever wafted into my life. I would never be the same. How had I let him do these things to me, and how eagerly had I participated in them, and spurred them on, and then waited for him, begging him, Please don't stop. Now his goo was matted on my chest as proof that I had crossed a terrible line, not vis-à-vis those I held dearest, not even vis-à-vis myself, or anything sacred, or the race itself that had brought us this close, not even vis-à-vis Marzia, who stood now like a far-flung siren on a sinking reef, distant and irrelevant, cleansed by lapping summer waves while I struggled to swim out to her, clamoring from a whirlpool of anxiety in the hope that she'd be part of the collection of images to help me rebuild myself by daybreak. It was not these I had offended, but those who were yet unborn or unmet and whom I'd never be able to love without remembering this mass of shame and revulsion rising between my life and theirs. It would haunt and sully my love for them, and between us, there would be this secret that could tarnish everything good in me.

Or had I offended something even deeper? What was it?

Had the loathing I felt always been there, though camouflaged, and all I'd needed was a night like this to let it out?

Something bordering on nausea, something like remorse—

was that it, then?—began to grip me and seemed to define itself ever more clearly the more I became aware of incipient daylight through our windows.

Like the light, though, remorse, if remorse indeed it was, seemed to fade for a little while. But when I lay in bed and felt uncomfortable, it came back on the double as if to score a point each time I thought I'd felt the last of it. I had known it would hurt. What I hadn't expected was that the hurt would find itself coiled and twisted into sudden pangs of guilt. No one had told me about this either.

Outside it was clearly dawn now.

Why was he staring at me? Had he guessed what I was feeling?

"You're not happy," he said.

I shrugged my shoulders.

It was not him I hated—but the thing we'd done. I didn't want him looking into my heart just yet. Instead, I wanted to remove myself from this bog of self-loathing and didn't know how to do it.

"You're feeling sick about it, aren't you?"

Again I shrugged the comment away.

"I knew we shouldn't have. I knew it," he repeated. For the first time in my life I watched him balk, prey to self-doubt. "We should have talked . . ."

"Maybe," I said.

Of all the things I could have uttered that morning, this insignificant "maybe" was the cruelest.

"Did you hate it?"

No, I didn't hate it at all. But what I felt was worse than hate. I didn't want to remember, didn't want to think about it. Just put it away. It had never happened. I had tried it and it didn't work for me, now I wanted my money back, roll back the film, take me back to that moment when I'm almost stepping out onto the balcony barefoot, I'll go no farther, I'll sit and stew and never know—better to argue with my body than feel what I was feeling now. *Elio, Elio, we warned you, didn't we?*

Here I was in his bed, staying put out of an exaggerated sense of courtesy. "You can go to sleep, if you want," he said, perhaps the kindest words he'd ever spoken to me, a hand on my shoulder, while I, Judas-like, kept saying to myself, If only he knew. If only he knew I want to be leagues and a lifetime away from him. I hugged him. I closed my eyes. "You're staring at me," I said, with my eyes still shut. I liked being stared at with my eyes shut.

I needed him as far away as possible if I was to feel better and forget—but I needed him close by in case this thing took a turn for the worse and there was no one to turn to.

Meanwhile, another part of me was actually happy the whole thing was behind me. He was out of my system. I would pay the price. The questions were: Would he understand? And would he forgive?

Or was this another trick to stave off another access of loathing and shame?

Early in the morning, we went for a swim together. It felt to me that this was the last time we'd ever be together like this. I would go back into my room, fall asleep, wake up, have breakfast, take out my scorebook, and spend those marvelous morning hours immersed in transcribing the Haydn, occasionally feeling a sting of anxiety in anticipating his renewed snub at the breakfast ta- ble, only to remember that we were past that stage now, that I'd had him inside me barely a few hours ago and that later he had come all over my chest, because he said he wanted to, and I let him, perhaps because I hadn't come yet and it thrilled me to watch him make faces and peak before my very eyes.

Now he walked almost knee-deep into the water with his shirt on. I knew what he was doing. If Mafalda asked, he'd claim it got wet by accident.

Together, we swam to the big rock. We spoke. I wanted him to think that I was happy being with him. I had wanted the sea to wash away the gunk on my chest, yet here was his semen, clinging to my body. In a short while, after soap and shower, all my doubts about myself, which had started three years before when an anonymous young man riding a bike had stopped, gotten off, put a hand around my shoulder, and with that gesture either stirred or hastened something that might have taken much, much longer to work itself to consciousness—all these could now finally be washed away as well, dispelled as an evil rumor about me, or a false belief, released like a genie who'd served his sentence and was now being cleansed with the soft, radiant scent of chamomile soap found in every one of our bathrooms.

We sat on one of the rocks and talked. Why hadn't we talked like this before? I'd have been less desperate for him had we been able to have this kind of friendship weeks earlier. Perhaps we might have avoided sleeping together. I wanted to tell him that I had made love to Marzia the other night not two hundred yards away from where we stood right now. But I kept quiet. Instead we spoke of Haydn's "It Is Finished," which I'd just finished transcribing. I could speak about this and not feel I was doing it to impress him or to draw his attention or to put up a wobbly footbridge between us. I could speak about the Haydn for hours—what a lovely friendship this might have been.

It never occurred to me, as I was going through the heady motions of feeling over and done with him and even a tad disappointed that I had so easily recovered after a spell of so many weeks, that this desire to sit and discuss Haydn in so unusually relaxed a manner as we were doing right now was my most vulnerable spot, that if desire had to resurface, it could just as easily sneak in through this very gate, which I'd always assumed the safest, as through the sight of his near-naked body by the swimming pool.

At some point he interrupted me.

"You okay?"

"Fine. Fine," I replied.

Then, with an awkward smile, as if correcting his initial question: "Are you okay everywhere?"

I smiled back faintly, knowing I was already clamming up, shutting the doors and windows between us, blowing out the candles because the sun was finally up again and shame cast long shadows.

"I meant—"

"I know what you meant. Sore."

"But did you mind when I—?"

I turned my face the other way, as though a chill draft had touched my ear and I wished to avoid having it hit my face. "Do we need to speak about it?" I asked.

I had used the same words that Marzia had uttered when I wished to know if she liked what I'd done to her.

"Not if you don't want to."

I knew exactly what he wanted to talk about. He wanted to go over the moment when I'd almost asked him to stop.

Now all I thought of, as we spoke, was that today I'd be walking with Marzia and each time we'd try to sit somewhere I would hurt. The indignity of it. Sitting on the town's ramparts—which was where everyone our age congregated at night when we weren't sitting in the caffès—and be forced to squirm and be reminded each time of what I'd just done that night. The standing joke among schoolboys. Watch Oliver watch me squirm and think, *I did that to you, didn't I?*

I wished we hadn't slept together. Even his body left me in-

different. On the rock where we sat now I looked at his body as
one looks at old shirts and trousers being boxed for pick up by
the Salvation Army.

Shoulder: check.

Area between inner and outer elbow that I'd worshipped
once: check.

Crotch: check.

Neck: check.

Curves of the apricot: check.

Foot—oh, that foot: but, yes, check.

Smile, when he'd said, *Are you okay everywhere*: yes, check
that too. Leave nothing to chance.

I had worshipped them all once. I had touched them the way
a civet rubs itself on the objects it covets. They'd been mine for a
night. I didn't want them now. What I couldn't remember, much
less understand, was how I could have brought myself to desire
them, to do all I'd done to be near them, touch them, sleep
with them. After our swim I'd take that much-awaited shower.
Forget, forget.

As we were swimming back, he asked as though it were an
afterthought, "Are you going to hold last night against me?"

"No," I answered. But I had answered too swiftly for someone who meant what he was saying. To soften the ambiguity of
my no, I said I'd probably want to sleep all day. "I don't think I'll
be able to ride my bike today."

"Because . . ." He was not asking me a question, he was sup-
plying the answer.

"Yes, because."

It occurred to me that one of the reasons I'd decided not to
distance him too quickly was not just to avoid hurting his feelings or alarming him or stirring up an awkward and unwieldy

situation at home, but because I was not sure that within a few hours I wouldn't be desperate for him again.

When we reached our balcony, he hesitated at the door and then stepped into my room. It took me by surprise. "Take your trunks off." This was strange, but I didn't have it in me to disobey. So I lowered them and got out of them. It was the first time I'd been naked with him in broad daylight. I felt awkward and was starting to grow nervous. "Sit down." I had barely done as I was told when he brought his mouth to my cock and took it all in. I was hard in no time. "We'll save it for later," he said with a wry smile on his face and was instantly gone.

Was this his revenge on me for presuming to be done with him?

But there they went—my self-confidence and my checklist and my craving to be done with him. Great work. I dried myself, put on the pajama bottoms I had worn last night, threw myself on my bed, and didn't awake till Mafalda knocked at my door asking whether I wanted eggs for breakfast.

The same mouth that was going to eat eggs had been everywhere last night.

As with a hangover, I kept wondering when the sickness would wear off.

Every once in a while, sudden soreness triggered a twinge of discomfort and shame. Whoever said the soul and the body met in the pineal gland was a fool. It's the asshole, stupid.

When he came down for breakfast he was wearing my bathing suit. No one would have given it another thought since everyone was always swapping suits in our house, but this was the first time he had done so and it was the same suit I had worn that very dawn when we'd gone out for a swim. Watching him wearing my clothes was an unbearable turn-on. And he knew it. It was turning both of us on. The thought of his cock rubbing the netted fabric where mine had rested reminded me how, before my very eyes, and after so much exertion, he had finally shot his load on my chest. But what turned me on wasn't this. It was the porousness, the fungibility, of our bodies—what was mine was suddenly his, just as what belonged to him could be all mine now. Was I being lured back again? At the table, he decided to sit at my side and, when no one was looking, slipped his foot not on top of but under mine. I knew my foot was rough from always walking barefoot; his was smooth; last night I had kissed his foot and sucked his toes; now they were snuggled under my callused foot and I needed to protect my protector.

He was not allowing me to forget him. I was reminded of a married chatelaine who, after sleeping with a young vassal one night, had him seized by the palace guards the next morning and summarily executed in a dungeon on trumped-up charges, not only to eliminate all evidence of their adulterous night together and to prevent her young lover from becoming a nuisance now that he thought he was entitled to her favors, but to stem the temptation to seek him out on the following evening. Was he becoming a nuisance going after me? And what was I to do—tell my mother?

That morning he went into town alone. Post office, Signora Milani, the usual rounds. I saw him pedal down the cypress lane, still wearing my trunks. No one had ever worn my clothes. Perhaps the physical and the metaphorical meanings are clumsy ways of understanding what happens when two beings need, not just to be close together, but to become so totally ductile that each becomes the other. To be who I am because of you. To be who he was because of me. To be in his mouth while he was in mine and no longer know whose it was, his cock or mine, that was in my mouth. He was my secret conduit to myself—like a catalyst that allows us to become who we are, the foreign body, the pacer, the graft, the patch that sends all the right impulses, the steel pin that keeps a soldier's bone together, the other man's heart that makes us more us than we were before the transplant.

The very thought of this suddenly made me want to drop everything I would do today and run to him. I waited about ten minutes, then took out my bike and, despite my promise not to go biking that day, headed out by way of Marzia's home and scaled the steep hillside road as fast as I could. When I reached the piazzetta I realized I had arrived minutes after him. He was parking his bike, had already purchased the *Herald Tribune*, and was heading for the post office—his first errand. "I had to see you," I said as I rushed to him. "Why, something wrong?" "I just had to see you." "Aren't you sick of me?" I thought I was—I was about to say—and I wanted to be—"I just wanted to be with you," I said. Then it hit me: "If you want, I'll go back now," I said. He stood still, dropped his hand with the bundle of unsent letters still in it, and simply stood there staring at me, shaking his head. "Do you have any idea how glad I am we slept together?"

I shrugged my shoulders as though to put away another compliment. I was unworthy of compliments, most of all coming from him. "I don't know."

"It would be just like you not to know. I just don't want to regret any of it—including what you wouldn't let me talk about this morning. I just dread the thought of having messed you up. I don't want either of us to have to pay one way or another."

I knew exactly what he was referring to but pretended otherwise. "I'm not telling anyone. There won't be any trouble."

"I didn't mean *that*. I'm sure I'll pay for it somehow, though." And for the first time in daylight I caught a glimpse of a different Oliver. "For you, however you think of it, it's still fun and games, which it should be. For me it's something else which I haven't figured out, and the fact that I can't scares me."

"Are you sorry I came?" Was I being intentionally fatuous?

"I'd hold you and kiss you if I could."

"Me too."

I came up to his ear as he was just about to enter the post office and whispered, "Fuck me, Elio."

He remembered and instantly moaned his own name three times, as we'd done during that night. I could feel myself already getting hard. Then, to tease him with the very same words he'd uttered earlier that morning, I said, "We'll save it for later."

Then I told him how *Later!* would always remind me of him. He laughed and said, *"Later!"*—meaning exactly what I wanted it to mean for a change: not just goodbye, or be off with you, but afternoon lovemaking. I turned around and was instantly on my bike, speeding my way back downhill, smiling broadly, almost singing if I could.

Never in my life had I been so happy. Nothing could go wrong, everything was happening my way, all the doors were clicking open one by one, and life couldn't have been more radiant: it was shining right at me, and when I turned my bike left or right or tried to move away from its light, it followed me as limelight follows an actor onstage. I craved him but I could just as easily live without him, and either way was fine.

On my way, I decided to stop at Marzia's house. She was headed to the beach. I joined her, and we went down to the rocks together and lay in the sun. I loved her smell, loved her mouth. She took off her top and asked me to put some sunscreen on her back, knowing that my hands would inevitably cup her breasts. Her family owned a thatched cabana by the beach and she said we should go inside. No one would come. I locked the door from the inside, sat her on the table, took off her bathing suit, and put my mouth where she smelled of the sea. She leaned back, and lifted both legs over my shoulders. How strange, I thought, how each shadowed and screened the other, without precluding the other. Barely half an hour ago I was asking Oliver to fuck me and now here I was about to make love to Marzia, and yet neither had anything to do with the other except through Elio, who happened to be one and the same person.

After lunch Oliver said he had to go back to B. to hand Signora Milani his latest corrections. He cast an instant glance in my direction but, seeing I hadn't responded, was already on his way. After two glasses of wine, I couldn't wait to take a nap. I grabbed two huge peaches from the table and took them with me, and kissed my mother along the way. I'd eat them later, I said. In the dark bedroom, I deposited the fruit on the marble tabletop. And then undressed totally. Clean, cool, crisp-starched, sun-washed sheets drawn tight across my bed—God bless you, Mafalda. Did I want to be alone? Yes. One person last night; then again at dawn. Then in the morning, another. Now I lay on the sheets as happy as a stiff-grown, newly sprung sunflower filled with listless vigor on this sunniest of summer afternoons. Was I glad to be alone now that sleep was upon me? Yes. Well, no. Yes. But maybe not. Yes, yes, yes. I was happy, and this was all that mattered, with others, without others, I was happy.

Half an hour later, or maybe sooner, I was awakened by the rich brown cloistral scent of coffee wafting through the house. Even with the door closed I could smell it and I knew this wasn't my parents' coffee. Theirs had been brewed and served a while ago. This was the afternoon's second brew, made in the Neapolitan espresso coffeemaker in which Mafalda, her husband, and

Anchise made coffee after they too had lunched. Soon they would be resting as well. Already a heavy torpor hung in the air—the world was falling asleep. All I wanted was for him or Marzia to pass by my balcony door and, through the half-drawn shutters, make out my naked body sprawled on the bed. Him or Marzia—but I wanted someone to pass by and notice me, and up to them to decide what to do. I could go on sleeping or, if they should sidle up to me, I'd make room for them and we'd sleep together. I saw one of them enter my room and reach for the fruit, and with the fruit in hand, come to my bed and bring it to my hard cock. *I know you're not sleeping*, they'd say, and gently press the soft, overripe peach on my cock till I'd pierced the fruit along the crease that reminded me so much of Oliver's ass. The idea seized me and would not let go.

I got up and reached for one of the peaches, opened it halfway with my thumbs, pushed the pit out on my desk, and gently brought the fuzzy, blush-colored peach to my groin, and then began to press into it till the parted fruit slid down my cock. If Anchise only knew, if Anchise knew what I was doing to the fruit he cultivated with such slavish devotion every day, him and his large straw hat and his long, gnarled, callused fingers that were always ripping out weeds from the parched earth. His peaches were more apricots than peaches, except larger, juicier. I had already tried the animal kingdom. Now I was moving to the kingdom of plants. Next would come minerals. The idea almost made me chuckle. The fruit was leaking all over my cock. If Oliver walked in on me now, I'd let him suck me as he had this morning. If Marzia came, I'd let her help me finish the job. The peach was soft and firm, and when I finally succeeded in tearing it apart with my cock, I saw that its reddened core reminded me not just of an anus but of a vagina, so that holding each half in either hand firmly against my cock, I began to rub myself, thinking of no one and of everyone, including the poor peach, which had no idea what was being done to it except that it had to play along and probably in the end took some pleasure in the act as well, till I thought I heard it say to me, *Fuck me, Elio, fuck me harder,* and after a moment, *Harder, I said!* while I scanned my mind for images from Ovid—wasn't there a character who had turned into a peach and, if there wasn't, couldn't I make one up on the spot, say, an ill-fated young man and young girl who in their peachy beauty had spurned an envious deity who had turned them into a peach tree, and only now, after three thousand years, were being given what had been so unjustly taken away from them, as they murmured, *I'll die when you're done, and you mustn't be done, must never be done?* The story so aroused me that practically without warning the orgasm was almost upon me. I sensed I could just stop then and there or, with one more stroke, I could come, which I finally did, carefully, aiming the spurt into the reddened core of the open peach as if in a ritual of insemination.

What a crazy thing this was. I let myself hang back, holding the fruit in both hands, grateful that I hadn't gotten the sheet dirty with either juice or come. The bruised and damaged peach, like a rape victim, lay on its side on my desk, shamed, loyal, aching, and confused, struggling not to spill what I'd left inside. It reminded me that I had probably looked no different on his bed last night after he'd come inside me the first time.

I put on a tank top but decided to stay naked and get under the sheet.

I awoke to the sound of someone unhooking the latch of the shutters and then hooking it back behind him. As in my dream once, he was tiptoeing toward me, not in an effort to surprise me, but so as not to wake me up. I knew it was Oliver and, with my eyes still closed, raised my arm to him. He grabbed it and kissed it, then lifted the sheet and seemed surprised to find me naked.

He immediately brought his lips to where they'd promised to return this morning. He loved the sticky taste. What had I done?

I told him and pointed to the bruised evidence sitting on my desk.

"Let me see."

He stood up and asked if I'd left it for him.

Perhaps I had. Or had I simply put off thinking how to dispose of it?

"Is this what I think it is?"

I nodded naughtily in mock shame.

"Any idea how much work Anchise puts into each one of these?"

He was joking, but it felt as though he, or someone through him, was asking the same question about the work my parents had put into me.

He brought the half peach to bed, making certain not to spill its contents as he took his clothes off.

"I'm sick, aren't I?" I asked.

"No, you're not sick—I wish everyone were as sick as you. Want to see sick?"

What was he up to? I hesitated to say yes.

"Just think of the number of people who've come before you—you, your grandfather, your great-great-grandfather, and all the skipped generations of Elios before you, and those from places far away, all squeezed into this trickle that makes you who you are. Now may I taste it?"

I shook my head.

He dipped a finger into the core of the peach and brought it to his mouth.

"Please don't." This was more than I could bear.

"I never could stand my own. But this is yours. Please explain."

"It makes me feel terrible."

He simply shrugged my comment away.

"Look, you don't have to do this. I'm the one who came after you, I sought you out, everything that happened is because of me—you don't have to do this."

"Nonsense. I wanted you from day one. I just hid it better."

"Sure!"

I lunged out to grab the fruit from his hand, but with his other hand he caught hold of my wrist and squeezed it hard, as they do in movies, when one man forces another to let go of a knife.

"You're hurting me."

"Then let go."

I watched him put the peach in his mouth and slowly begin to eat it, staring at me so intensely that I thought even lovemaking didn't go so far.

"If you just want to spit it out, it's okay, it's really okay, I promise I won't be offended," I said to break the silence more than as a last plea.

He shook his head. I could tell he was tasting it at that very instant. Something that was mine was in his mouth, more his than mine now. I don't know what happened to me at that moment as I kept staring at him, but suddenly I had a fierce urge to cry. And rather than fight it, as with orgasm, I simply let myself go, if only to show him something equally private about me as well. I reached for him and muffled my sobs against his shoulder. I was crying because no stranger had ever been so kind or gone so far for me, even Anchise, who had cut open my foot once and sucked and spat out and sucked and spat out the scorpion's venom. I was crying because I'd never known so much gratitude and there was no other way to show it. And I was crying for the evil thoughts I'd nursed against him this morning. And for last night as well, because, for better or worse, I'd never be able to undo it, and now was as good a time as any to show him that he was right, that this wasn't easy, that fun and games had a way of skidding off course and that if we had rushed into things it was too late to step back from them now—crying because something was happening, and I had no idea what it was.

"Whatever happens between us, Elio, I just want you to know. Don't ever say you didn't know." He was still chewing. In the heat of passion it would have been one thing. But this was quite another. He was taking me away with him.

His words made no sense. But I knew exactly what they meant.

I rubbed his face with my palm. Then, without knowing why, I began to lick his eyelids.

"Kiss me now, before it's totally gone," I said. His mouth would taste of peaches and me.

I stayed in my room long after Oliver left. When I finally awoke, it was almost evening, which put me in a grumpy mood. The pain was gone, but I had a resurgence of the same malaise I'd experienced toward dawn. I didn't know now if this was the same feeling, resurfacing after a long hiatus, or if the earlier one had healed and this was a totally new one, resulting from the afternoon's lovemaking. Would I always experience such solitary guilt in the wake of our intoxicating moments together? Why didn't I experience the same thing after Marzia? Was this nature's way of reminding me that I would rather be with her?

I took a shower and put on clean clothes. Downstairs, everyone was having cocktails. Last night's two guests were there again, being entertained by my mother, while a newcomer, another reporter, was busily listening to Oliver's description of his book on Heraclitus. He had perfected the art of giving a stranger a five-sentence précis that seemed invented on the spur of the moment for the benefit of that particular listener. "Are you staying?" asked my mother.

"No, I'm going to see Marzia."

My mother gave me an apprehensive look, and ever so discreetly began to shake her head, meaning, *I don't approve, she's a good girl, you should be going out together as a group.* "Leave him alone, you and your groups," was my father's rebuttal, which set me free. "As it is, he's shut up in the house all day. Let him do as he pleases. *As he pleases!*"

If he only knew.

And what if he did know?

My father would never object. He might make a face at first, then take it back.

It never occurred to me to hide from Oliver what I was doing with Marzia. Bakers and butchers don't compete, I thought. Nor, in all likelihood, would he have given it another thought himself.

That night Marzia and I went to the movies. We had ice cream in the piazzetta. And again at her parents' home.

"I want to go to the bookstore again," she said when she walked me toward the gate to their garden. "But I don't like going to the movies with you."

"You want to go around closing time tomorrow?"

"Why not?" She wanted to repeat the other night.

She kissed me. What I wanted instead was to go to the bookstore when it had just opened in the morning, with the option of going there that same night.

When I returned home the guests were just about to leave. Oliver was not home.

Serves me right, I thought.

I went to my room and, for lack of anything else to do, opened my diary.

Last night's entry: *"I'll see you at midnight."* You watch. He won't even be there. *"Get lost"*—that's what *"Grow up"* means. *I wish I'd never said anything.*

On the nervous doodlings I had traced around these words before heading out to his room, I was trying to recover the memory of last night's jitters. Perhaps I wanted to relive the night's anxieties, both to mask tonight's and to remind myself that if my worst fears had suddenly been dispelled once I'd entered his room, perhaps they might end no differently tonight and be as easily subdued once I'd heard his footsteps.

But I couldn't even remember last night's anxieties. They were completely overshadowed by what followed them and seemed to belong to a segment of time to which I had no access whatsoever. Everything about last night had suddenly vanished. I remembered nothing. I tried to whisper "Get lost" to myself as a way of jump-starting my memory. The words had seemed so real last night. Now they were just two words struggling to make sense.

And then I realized it. What I was experiencing tonight was unlike anything I'd experienced in my life.

This was much worse. I didn't even know what to call this.

On second thought, I didn't even know what to call last night's jitters either.

I had taken a giant step last night. Yet here I was, no wiser and no more sure of things than I'd been before feeling him all over me. We might as well not even have slept together.

At least last night there was the fear of failing, the fear of being thrown out or called the very name I had used on others. Now that I had overcome that fear, had this anxiety been present all along, though latent, like a presage and a warning of killer reefs beyond the squall?

And why did I care where he was? Wasn't this what I wanted for both of us—butchers and bakers and all that? Why feel so unhinged just because he wasn't there or because he'd given me the slip, why sense that all I was doing now was waiting for him—waiting, waiting, waiting?

What was it about waiting that was beginning to feel like torture?

If you are with someone, Oliver, it is time to come home. No questions asked, I promise, just don't keep me waiting.

If he doesn't show up in ten minutes, I'll do something.

Ten minutes later, feeling helpless and hating myself for feeling helpless, I resolved to wait another *this-time-for-real* ten minutes.

Twenty minutes later, I couldn't stand it any longer. I put on a sweater, walked off the balcony, and came downstairs. I'd go to B., if I had to, and check for myself. I was on my way to the bike shed, already debating whether to head out to N. first, where people tended to stay up and party much later than in B., and was cursing myself for not putting air in the tires earlier this morning, when suddenly something told me I should stop dead in my tracks and try not to disturb Anchise, who slept in the hut nearby. Sinister Anchise—everyone said he was sinister. Had I suspected it all along? I must have. The fall from the bike, Anchise's peasant ointment, the kindness with which he took care of him and cleaned up the scrape.

But down below along the rocky shore, in the moonlight, I caught sight of him. He was sitting on one of the higher rocks, wearing his sailor's white-and-blue-striped sweater with the buttons always undone along his shoulder which he'd purchased in Sicily earlier in the summer. He was doing nothing, just hugging his knees, listening to the ripples lap against the rocks below him. Looking at him now from the balustrade, I felt something so tender for him that it reminded me how eagerly I had rushed to B. to catch him before he'd even made it into the post office. This was the best person I'd ever known in my life. I had chosen him well. I opened the gate and skipped down the several rocks and reached him.

"I was waiting for you," I said.

"I thought you'd gone to sleep. I even thought you didn't want to."

"No. Waiting. I just turned the lights off."

I looked up to our house. The window shutters were all closed. I bent down and kissed him on his neck. It was the first time I had kissed him with feeling, not just desire. He put his arm around me. Harmless, if anyone saw.

"What were you doing?" I asked.

"Thinking."

"About?"

"Things. Going back to the States. The courses I have to teach this fall. The book. You."

"Me?"

"Me?" He was mimicking my modesty.

"No one else?"

"No one else." He was silent for a while. "I come here every night and just sit here. Sometimes I spend hours."

"All by yourself?"

He nodded.

"I never knew. I thought—"

"I know what you thought."

The news couldn't have made me happier. It had obviously been shadowing everything between us. I decided not to press the matter.

"This spot is probably what I'll miss the most." Then, upon reflection: "I've been happy in B."

It sounded like a preamble to farewells.

"I was looking out towards there," he continued, pointing to the horizon, "and thinking that in two weeks I'll be back at Columbia."

He was right. I had made a point never to count the days. At first because I didn't want to think how long he'd stay with us; later because I didn't want to face how few were his remaining days.

"All this means is that in ten days when I look out to this spot, you won't be here. I don't know what I'll do then. At least you'll be elsewhere, where there are no memories."

He squeezed my shoulder to him. "The way you think sometimes . . . You'll be fine."

"I might. But then I might not. We wasted so many days—so many weeks."

"Wasted? I don't know. Perhaps we just needed time to figure out if this is what we wanted."

"Some of us made things purposely difficult."

"Me?"

I nodded. "You know what we were doing exactly one night ago."

He smiled. "I don't know how I feel about that."

"I'm not sure either. But I am glad we did."

"Will you be okay?"

"I'll be okay." I slipped a hand into his pants. "I do love being here with you."

It was my way of saying, I've been happy here as well. I tried to picture what *happy here* meant to him: happy once he got here after imagining what the place might look like, happy doing his work on those scorching mornings in *heaven*, happy biking back and forth from the translator, happy disappearing into town every night and coming back so late, happy with my parents and *dinner drudgery*, happy with his poker friends and all the other friends he had made in town and about whom I knew nothing whatsoever? One day he might tell me. I wondered what part I played in the overall happiness package.

Meanwhile, tomorrow, if we went for an early morning swim, I might be overcome again with this surfeit of self-loathing. I wondered if one got used to that. Or does one accrue a deficit of malaise so large that one learns to find ways to consolidate it in one lump feeling with its own amnesties and grace periods? Or does the presence of the other, who yesterday morning felt almost like an intruder, become ever more necessary because it shields us from our own hell—so that the very person who causes our torment by daybreak is the same who'll relieve it at night?

The next morning we went swimming together. It was scarcely past six o'clock, and the fact that it was so early gave an energized quality to our exercise. Later, as he performed his own version of the dead-man's float, I wanted to hold him, as swimming instructors do when they hold your body so lightly that they seem to keep you afloat with barely a touch of their fingers. Why did I feel older than he was at that moment? I wanted to protect him from everything this morning, from the rocks, from the jellyfish, now that jellyfish season was upon us, from Anchise, whose sinister leer, as he'd trundle into the garden to turn on the sprinklers, constantly pulling out weeds wherever he turned, even when it rained, even when he spoke to you, even when he threatened to leave us, seemed to tease out every secret you thought you'd neatly buried from his gaze.

"How are you?" I asked, mimicking his question to me yesterday morning.

"You should know."

At breakfast, I couldn't believe what seized me, but I found myself cutting the top of his soft-boiled egg before Mafalda intervened or before he had smashed it with his spoon. I had never done this for anyone else in my life, and yet here I was, making certain that not a speck of the shell fell into his egg. He was happy with his egg. When Mafalda brought him his daily *polpo*, I was happy for him. Domestic bliss. Just because he'd let me be his top last night.

I caught my father staring at me as I finished slicing off the tip of his second soft-boiled egg.

"Americans never know how to do it," I said.

"I am sure they have their way . . . ," he said.

The foot that came to rest on mine under the table told me that perhaps I should let it go and assume my father was onto something. "He's no fool," he said to me later that morning as he was getting ready to head up to B.

"Want me to come with?"

"No, better keep a low profile. You should work on your Haydn today. Later."

"Later."

Marzia called that morning while he was getting ready to leave. He almost winked when he handed me the telephone. There was no hint of irony, nothing that didn't remind me, unless I was mistaken—and I don't think I was—that what we had between us was the total transparency that exists among friends only.

Perhaps we were friends first and lovers second.

But then perhaps this is what lovers are.

———

When I think back to our last ten days together, I see an early-morning swim, our lazy breakfasts, the ride up to town, work in the garden, lunches, our afternoon naps, more work in the afternoon, tennis maybe, after-dinners in the piazzetta, and every night the kind of lovemaking that can run circles around time. Looking back to these days, I don't think there was ever a minute, other than the half hour or so he spent with his translator, or when I managed to steal a few hours with Marzia, when we weren't together.

"When did you know about me?" I asked him one day. I was hoping he'd say, *When I squeezed your shoulder and you almost wilted in my arms.* Or, *When you got wet under your bathing suit that one afternoon when we chatted in your room.* Something along those lines. "When you blushed," he said. "Me?" We had been talking about translating poetry; it was early in the morning, during his very first week with us. We had started working earlier than usual that day, probably because we already enjoyed our spontaneous conversations while the breakfast table was being laid out under the linden tree and were eager to spend some time together. He'd asked me if I'd ever translated poetry. I said I had. Why, had he? Yes. He was reading Leopardi and had landed on a few verses that were impossible to translate. We had been speaking back and forth, neither of us realizing how far a conversation started on the fly could go, because all the while delving deeper into Leopardi's world, we were also finding occasional side alleys where our natural sense of humor and our love for clowning were given free play. We translated the passage into English, then from English to ancient Greek, then back to gobbledygenglish to gobbledygitalian. Leopardi's closing lines of "To the Moon" were so warped that it brought bursts of laughter as we kept repeating the nonsense lines in Italian—when suddenly there was a moment of silence, and when I looked up at him he was staring at me point-blank, that icy, glassy look of his which always disconcerted me. I was struggling to say something, and when he asked how I knew so many things, I had the presence of mind to say something about being a professor's son. I was not always eager to show off my knowledge, especially with someone who could so easily intimidate me. I had nothing to fight back with, nothing to add, nothing to throw in to muddy the waters between us, nowhere to hide or run for cover. I felt as exposed as a stranded lamb on the dry, waterless plains of the Serengeti.

The staring was no longer part of the conversation, or even of the fooling around with translation; it had superseded it and become its own subject, except that neither dared nor wanted to bring it up. And yes, there was such a luster in his eyes that I had to look away, and when I looked back at him, his gaze hadn't moved and was still focused on my face, as if to say, *So you looked away and you've come back, will you be looking away again soon?*—which was why I had to look away once more, as if immersed in thought, yet all the while scrambling for something to say, the way a fish struggles for water in a muddied pond that's fast drying up in the heat. He must have known exactly what I was feeling. What made me blush in the end was not the natural embarrassment of the moment when I could tell he'd caught me trying to hold his gaze only then to let mine scamper to safety; what made me blush was the thrilling possibility, unbelievable as I wanted it to remain, that he might actually like me, and that he liked me in just the way I liked him.

For weeks I had mistaken his stare for barefaced hostility. I was wide of the mark. It was simply a shy man's way of holding someone else's gaze.

We were, it finally dawned on me, the two shyest persons in the world.

My father was the only one who had seen through him from the very start.

"Do you like Leopardi?" I asked, to break the silence, but also to suggest that it was the topic of Leopardi that had caused me to seem somewhat distracted during a pause in our conversation.

"Yes, very much."

"I like him very much too."

I'd always known I wasn't speaking about Leopardi. The question was, did he?

"I knew I was making you uncomfortable, but I just had to make sure."

"So you knew all this time?"

"Let's say I was pretty sure."

In other words, it had started just days after his arrival. Had everything since been pretense, then? And all these swings between friendship and indifference—what were they? His and my ways of keeping stealthy tabs on each other while disclaiming that we were? Or were they simply as cunning a way as any to stave each other off, hoping that what we felt was indeed genuine indifference?

"Why didn't you give me a sign?" I said.

"I did. At least I tried."

"When?"

"After tennis once. I touched you. Just as a way of showing I liked you. The way you reacted made me feel I'd almost molested you. I decided to keep my distance."

Our best moments were in the afternoon. After lunch, I'd go upstairs for a nap just when coffee was about to be served. Then, when the lunch guests had left, or slunk away to rest in the guest-house, my father would either retire to his study or steal a nap with my mother. By two in the afternoon, an intense silence would settle over the house, over the world it seemed, interrupted here and there either by the cooing of doves or by Anchise's hammer when he worked on his tools and was trying not to make too much noise. I liked hearing him at work in the afternoon, and even when his occasional banging or sawing woke me up, or when the knife grinder would start his whetstone running every Wednesday afternoon, it left me feeling as restful and at peace with the world as I would feel years later on hearing a distant foghorn off Cape Cod in the middle of the night. Oliver liked to keep the windows and shutters wide open in the afternoon, with just the swelling sheer curtains between us and life beyond, because it was a "crime" to block away so much sunlight and keep such a landscape from view, especially when you didn't have it all life long, he said. Then the rolling fields of the valley leading up to the hills seemed to sit in a rising mist of olive green: sunflowers, grapevines, swatches of lavender, and those squat and humble olive trees stooping like gnarled, aged scarecrows gawking through our window as we lay naked on my bed, the smell of his sweat, which was the smell of my sweat, and next to me my man-woman whose man-woman I was, and all around us Mafalda's chamomile-scented laundry detergent, which was the scent of the torrid afternoon world of our house.

I look back on those days and regret none of it, not the risks, not the shame, not the total lack of foresight. The lyric cast of the sun, the teeming fields with tall plants nodding away under the intense midafternoon heat, the squeak of our wooden floors, or the scrape of the clay ashtray pushed ever so lightly on the marble slab that used to sit on my nightstand. I knew that our minutes were numbered, but I didn't dare count them, just as I knew where all this was headed, but didn't care to read the mile-posts. This was a time when I intentionally failed to drop bread crumbs for my return journey; instead, I ate them. He could turn out to be a total creep; he could change me or ruin me forever, while time and gossip might ultimately disembowel everything we shared and trim the whole thing down till nothing but fish bones remained. I might miss this day, or I might do far better, but I'd always know that on those afternoons in my bedroom I had held my moment.

One morning, though, I awoke and saw the whole of B. overborne by dark, lowering clouds racing across the sky. I knew exactly what this spelled. Autumn was just around the corner.

A few hours later, the clouds totally cleared, and the weather, as though to make up for its little prank, seemed to erase every hint of fall from our lives and gave us one of the most temperate days of the season. But I had heeded the warning, and as is said of juries who have heard inadmissible evidence before it is stricken from the record, I suddenly realized that we were on borrowed time, that time is always borrowed, and that the lending agency exacts its premium precisely when we are least prepared to pay and need to borrow more. Suddenly, I began to take mental snap-shots of him, picked up the bread crumbs that fell off our table and collected them for my hideaway, and, to my shame, drew lists: the rock, the berm, the bed, the sound of the ashtray. The rock, the berm, the bed . . . I wished I were like those soldiers in films who run out of bullets and toss away their guns as though they would never again have any use for them, or like runaways in the desert who, rather than ration the water in the gourd, yield to thirst and swill away, then drop their gourd in their tracks. In-stead, I squirreled away small things so that in the lean days ahead glimmers from the past might bring back the warmth. I began, re-luctantly, to steal from the present to pay off debts I knew I'd incur in the future. This, I knew, was as much a crime as closing the shutters on sunny afternoons. But I also knew that in Mafalda's superstitious world, anticipating the worst was as sure a way of preventing it from happening.

When we went on a walk one night and he told me that he'd soon be heading back home, I realized how futile my alleged foresight had been. Bombs never fall on the same spot; this one, for all my premonitions, fell exactly in my hideaway.

Oliver was leaving for the States the second week of August. A few days into the month, he said he wanted to spend three days in Rome and use that time to work on the final draft of his manuscript with his Italian publisher. Then he'd fly directly home. Would I like to join him?

I said yes. Shouldn't I ask my parents first? No need, they never said no. Yes, but wouldn't they . . . ? They wouldn't. On hearing that Oliver was leaving earlier than anticipated and would spend a few days in Rome, my mother asked—with il cauboi's permission, of course—if I might accompany him. My father was not against it.

My mother helped me pack. Would I need a jacket, in case the publisher wished to take us out to dinner? There'd be no dinner. Besides, why would I be asked to join? I should still take a jacket, she thought. I wanted to take a backpack, travel as everyone my age did. Do as you please. Still, she helped me empty and repack the backpack when it was clear there wasn't room for everything I wanted to take along. You're only going for two to three days. Neither Oliver nor I had ever been precise about our last days together. Mother would never know how her "two to three days" cut me that morning. Did we know which hotel we were planning to stay in? Pensione something or other. Never heard of it, but then who was she to know, she said. My father would have none of it. He made the reservations himself. It's a gift, he said.

Oliver not only packed his own duffel bag but on the day we were to catch the *direttissimo* to Rome he managed to take out his suitcase and place it on the exact same spot in his bedroom where I had plopped it down the day of his arrival. On that day I had fast-forwarded to the moment when I'd have my room back. Now I wondered what I'd be willing to give up if only to rewind things back to the afternoon in late June when I took him on the de rigueur tour of our property and how, with one thing leading to the next, we'd found ourselves approaching the empty scorched lot by the abandoned train tracks where I received my first dose of so many *Later!*s. Anyone my age would much rather have taken a nap than trekked to the back reaches of our property on that day. Clearly, I already knew what I was doing.

The symmetry of it all, or was it the emptied, seemingly ransacked neatness of his room, tied a knot in my throat. It reminded me less of a hotel room when you wait for the porter to help you take your things downstairs after a glorious stay that was ending too soon, than of a hospital room after all your belongings have been packed away, while the next patient, who hasn't been admitted yet, still waits in the emergency room exactly as you waited there yourself a week earlier.

This was a test run for our final separation. Like looking at someone on a respirator before it's finally turned off days later.

I was happy that the room would revert to me. In my/his room, it would be easier to remember our nights.

No, better keep my current room. Then, at least, I could pretend he was still in his, and if he wasn't there, that he was still out as he so frequently used to be on those nights when I counted the minutes, the hours, the sounds.

When I opened his closet I noticed that he had left a bathing suit, a pair of underwear, his chinos, and a clean shirt on a few hangers. I recognized the shirt. Billowy. And I recognized the suit. Red. This for when he'd go swimming one last time this morning.

"I must tell you about this bathing suit," I said when I closed his closet door.

"Tell me what?"

"I'll tell you on the train."

But I told him all the same. "Just promise to let me keep it after you're gone."

"That's all?"

"Well, wear it a lot today—and don't swim in it."

"Sick and twisted."

"Sick and twisted and very, very sad."

"I've never seen you like this."

"I want Billowy too. And the espadrilles. And the sunglasses. And you."

On the train I told him about the day we thought he'd drowned and how I was determined to ask my father to round up as many fishermen as he could to go look for him, and when they found him, to light a pyre on our shore, while I grabbed Mafalda's knife from the kitchen and ripped out his heart, because that heart and his shirt were all I'd ever have to show for my life. A heart and a shirt. His heart wrapped in a damp shirt—like Anchise's fish.

PART 3

The San Clemente Syndrome

We arrived at Stazione Termini around 7 p.m. on a Wednesday evening. The air was thick and muggy, as if Rome had been awash in a rainstorm that had come and gone and relieved none of the dampness. With dusk scarcely an hour away, the streetlights glistened through dense halos, while the lighted storefronts seemed doused in gleaming colors of their own invention. Dampness clung to every forehead and every face. I wanted to caress his face. I couldn't wait to get to our hotel and shower and throw myself on the bed, knowing all the while that, unless we had good air-conditioning, I'd be no better off after the shower. But I also loved the languor that sat upon the city, like a lover's tired, unsteady arm resting on your shoulders.

Maybe we'd have a balcony. I could use a balcony. Sit on its cool marble steps and watch the sun set over Rome. Mineral water. Or beer. And tiny snacks to munch on. My father had booked us one of the most luxurious hotels in Rome.

Oliver wanted to take the first taxi. I wanted to take a bus instead. I longed for crowded buses. I wanted to go into a bus, wedge my way into the sweating mass of people, with him pushing his way behind me. But seconds after hopping on the bus, we decided to get out. This was too *real*, we joked. I backed out through the

incoming press of infuriated home-goers who couldn't understand
what we were doing. I managed to step on a woman's foot. "*E non
chiede manco scusa*, doesn't even say he's sorry," she hissed to
those around her who had just jostled their way into the bus and
were not letting us squeeze out.

Finally, we hailed a cab. Noting the name of our hotel and
hearing us speak English, the cabby proceeded to make several
unexplained turns. "*Inutile prendere tante scorciatoie*, no need
for so many shortcuts. We're in no rush!" I said in Roman dialect.

To our delight the larger of our adjoining bedrooms had both
a balcony and a window, and when we opened the French windows, the glistening domes of numberless churches reflected the
setting sun in the vast, unencumbered vista below us. Someone
had sent us a bunch of flowers and a bowl filled with fruit. The
note came from Oliver's Italian publisher: "*Come to the bookstore around eight-thirty. Bring your manuscript. There's a party
for one of our authors.* Ti aspettiamo, *we're awaiting you.*"

We had not planned on doing anything except go for dinner and wander the streets afterward. "Am I invited, though?" I
asked, feeling a tad uncomfortable. "You are now," he replied.

We picked at the bowl of fruit sitting by the television cabinet and peeled figs for each other.

He said he was going to take a shower. When I saw him
naked I immediately got undressed as well. "Just for a second," I
said as our bodies touched, for I loved the dampness that clung
all over his. "I wish you didn't have to wash." His smell reminded
me of Marzia's, and how she too always seemed to exude that
brine of the seashore on those days when there isn't a breeze on
the beaches and all you smell is the raw, ashen scent of scalding
sand. I loved the salt of his arms, of his shoulders, along the
ridges of his spine. They were still new to me. "If we lie down
now, there'll be no book party," he said.

CALL ME BY YOUR NAME

These words, spoken from a height of bliss it seemed no one could steal from us, would take me back to this hotel room and to this damp *ferragosto* evening as both of us leaned stark-naked with our arms on the windowsill, overlooking an unbearably hot Roman late-late afternoon, both of us still smelling of the stuffy compartment on the southbound train that was probably nearing Naples by now and on which we'd slept, my head resting on his in full view of the other passengers. Leaning out into the evening air, I knew that this might never be given to us again, and yet I couldn't bring myself to believe it. He too must have had the same thought as we surveyed the magnificent cityscape, smoking and eating fresh figs, shoulder to shoulder, each wanting to do something to mark the moment, which was why, yielding to an impulse that couldn't have felt more natural at the time, I let my left hand rub his buttocks and then began to stick my middle finger into him as he replied, "You keep doing this, and there's definitely no party." I told him to do me a favor and keep staring out the window but to lean forward a bit, until I had a brainstorm once my entire finger was inside him: we might start but under no condition would we finish. Then we'd shower and go out and feel like two exposed, live wires giving off sparks each time they so much as flicked each other. Look at old houses and want to hug each one, spot a lamppost on a street corner and, like a dog, want to spray it, pass an art gallery and look for the hole in the nude, cross a face that did no more than smile our way and already initiate moves to undress the whole person and ask her, or him, or both, if they were more than one, to join us first for drinks, for dinner, anything. Find Cupid everywhere in Rome because we'd clipped one of his wings and he was forced to fly in circles.

We had never taken a shower together. We had never even been in the same bathroom together. "Don't flush," I'd said, "I want to look." What I saw brought out strains of compassion, for him, for his body, for his life, which suddenly seemed so frail and vulnerable. "Our bodies won't have secrets now," I said as I took my turn and sat down. He had hopped into the bathtub and was just about to turn on the shower. "I want you to see mine," I said. He did more. He stepped out, kissed me on the mouth, and, pressing and massaging my tummy with the flat of his palm, watched the whole thing happen.

I wanted no secrets, no screens, nothing between us. Little did I know that if I relished the gust of candor that bound us tighter each time we swore *my body is your body*, it was also because I enjoyed rekindling the tiny lantern of unsuspected shame. It cast a spare glow precisely where part of me would have preferred the dark. Shame trailed instant intimacy. Could intimacy endure once indecency was spent and our bodies had run out of tricks?

I don't know that I asked the question, just as I am not sure I am able to answer it today. Was our intimacy paid for in the wrong currency?

Or is intimacy the desired product no matter where you find it, how you acquire it, what you pay for it—black market, gray market, taxed, untaxed, under the table, over the counter?

All I knew was that I had nothing left to hide from him. I had never felt freer or safer in my life.

We were alone together for three days, we knew no one in the city, I could be anyone, say anything, do anything. I felt like a war prisoner who's suddenly been released by an invading army and told that he can start heading home now, no forms to fill out, no debriefing, no questions asked, no buses, no gate passes, no clean clothes to stand in line for—just start walking.

We showered. We wore each other's clothes. We wore each other's underwear. It was my idea.

Perhaps all this gave him a second wind of silliness, of youth.

Perhaps he had already been "there" years earlier and was stopping for a short stay on his return journey home.

Perhaps he was playing along, watching me.

Perhaps he had never done it with anyone and I'd showed up in the nick of time.

He took his manuscript, his sunglasses, and we shut the door to our hotel room. Like two live wires. We stepped outside the elevator door. Broad smiles for everyone. To the hotel personnel. To the flower vendor in the street. To the girl in the newspaper kiosk.

Smile, and the world smiles back. "Oliver, I'm happy," I said.

He looked at me in wonderment. "You're just horny."

"No, happy."

Along the way we caught sight of a human statue of Dante cloaked in red with an exaggerated aquiline nose and the most scornful frown limned on all his features. The red toga and the red bell cap and the thick-rimmed wooden spectacles gave his already stern face the wizened look of an implacable father confessor. A crowd had gathered around the great bard, who stood motionless on the pavement, his arms crossed defiantly, the whole body standing erect, like a man waiting for Virgil or for an overdue bus. As soon as a tourist threw a coin into a hollowed-out, antique book, he simulated the besotted air of a Dante who's just spied his Beatrice ambling across the Ponte Vecchio and, craning his cobralike neck, would right away moan out, like a street performer spitting fire,

Guido, vorrei che tu e Lapo ed io
fossimo presi per incantamento,
e messi ad un vascel, ch'ad ogni vento
per mare andasse a voler vostro e mio.

Guido, I would that Lapo, thou, and I
Led by some strong enchantment, might ascend
A magic ship, whose charmed sails should fly
With winds at will, where'er our thoughts might wend.

How very true, I thought. Oliver, I wish that you and I and
all those we've held dear might live forever in one house . . .
Having muttered his sotto voce verses, he would slowly resume his glaring, misanthropic stance until another tourist
tossed him a coin.

E io, quando 'l suo braccio a me distese,
ficcaï li occhi per lo cotto aspetto,
sì che 'l viso abbrusciato non difese
la conoscenza süa al mio 'ntelletto;
e chinando la mano a la sua faccia,
rispuosi: "Siete voi qui, ser Brunetto?"

Soon as he touched me, I could no more avert
Mine eyes, but on his visage scorched and sered
Fixed them, until beneath the mask of hurt
Did the remembered lineaments appear.
And to his face my hand inclining down,
I answered, "Ser Brunetto, are you here?"

Same scornful look. Same rictus. The crowd dispersed.
No one seemed to recognize the passage from the Fifteenth
Canto of the *Inferno* where Dante meets his former teacher,
Brunetto Latini. Two Americans, who had finally managed
to fish out a few coins from their knapsack, tossed Dante a
hail of tiny coins. Same glowering, pissed-off stare:

Ma che ciarifrega, che ciarimporta,
se l'oste ar vino cia messo l'acqua:
e noi je dimo, e noi je famo,
"ciai messo l'acqua
e nun te pagamo."

What do we care, why do we give a damn
If the innkeeper watered down our wine.
We'll just tell him, and we'll just say:
"You've added water, and we won't pay."

Oliver couldn't understand why everyone had burst out laughing at the hapless tourists. Because he's reciting a Roman drinking song, and, unless you know it, it's not funny.

I told him I'd show him a shortcut to the bookstore. He didn't mind the long way. Maybe we should take the long way, what's the rush? he said. Mine was better. Oliver seemed on edge and insisted. "Is there something I should know?" I finally asked. I thought it was a tactful way of giving him a chance to voice whatever was bothering him. Something he was uncomfortable with? Something having to do with his publisher? Someone else? My presence, perhaps? I can take perfectly good care of myself if you prefer to go alone. It suddenly hit me what was bothering him. I'll be the professor's son tagging along.

"That's not it at all, you goose."

"Then what is it?"

As we walked he put an arm around my waist.

"I don't want anything to change or to come between us tonight."

"Who's the goose?"

He took a long look at me.

We decided to proceed my way, crossing over from Piazza Montecitorio to the Corso. Then up via Belsiana. "This is around where it started," I said.

"What?"

"It."

"That's why you wanted to come by here?"

"With you."

I had already told him the story. A young man on a bicycle three years ago, probably a grocer's helper or errand boy, riding down a narrow path with his apron on, staring me straight in the face, as I stared back, no smile, just a troubled look, till he passed me by. And then I did what I always hope others might do in such cases. I waited a few seconds, then turned around. He had done the exact same thing. I don't come from a family where you speak to strangers. He clearly did. He whisked the bicycle around and pedaled until he caught up with me. A few insignificant words uttered to make light conversation. How easily it came to him. Questions, questions, questions—just to keep the words flowing—while I didn't even have breath to utter "yes" or "no." He shook my hand but clearly as an excuse to hold it. Then put his arm around me and pressed me to him, as if we were sharing a joke that had made us laugh and drawn us closer. Did I want to get together in a nearby movie house, perhaps? I shook my head. Did I want to follow him to the store—boss was most likely gone by this time in the evening. Shook my head again. Are you shy? I nodded. All this without letting go of my hand, squeezing my hand, squeezing my shoulder, rubbing the nape of my neck with a patronizing and forgiving smile, as if he'd already given up but wasn't willing to call it quits just yet. Why not? he kept asking. I could have—easily—I didn't.

"I turned down so many. Never went after anyone."

"You went after me."

"You let me."

Via Frattina, via Borgognona, via Condotti, via delle Carrozze, della Croce, via Vittoria. Suddenly I loved them all. As we approached the bookstore, Oliver said I should go along, he'd just make a quick local phone call. He could have called from the hotel. Or perhaps he needed privacy. So I kept walking, stopping at a local bar to buy cigarettes. When I reached the bookstore with its large glass door and two clay Roman busts sitting on two seemingly antique stumps, I suddenly got nervous. The place was packed, and through the thick glass door, with spare bronze trimming around it, you could make out a throng of adults, all of them eating what appeared to be petits fours. Someone inside saw me peering into the store and signaled me to come in. I shook my head, indicating with a hesitant index finger that I was waiting for someone who was just coming up this road here. But the owner, or his assistant, like a club manager, without stepping down on the sidewalk, pushed the glass door wide open with his arm totally extended and held it there, almost ordering me to come in. "Venga, su, venga!" he said, the sleeves of his shirt rakishly rolled up to his shoulders. The reading had not started yet but the bookstore was filled to capacity, everyone smoking, chatting loudly, leafing through new books, each holding a tiny plastic cup with what looked like scotch whiskey. Even the upstairs gallery, whose banister was lined with the bare elbows and forearms of women, was tightly packed. I recognized the author right away. He was the same man who had signed both Marzia's and my copy of his book of poems, *Se l'amore*. He was shaking several hands.

When he walked by me, I couldn't help but extend my hand and shake his and tell him how much I had enjoyed reading his poems. How could I have read his poems, if the book wasn't even out yet? Someone else overheard his question—were they going to throw me out of the store like an impostor?

"I purchased it in the bookstore in B. a few weeks ago, and you were kind enough to sign it for me."

He remembered the evening, so he said. "*Un vero fan*, a real fan, then," he added loudly, so that the others within hearing distance might hear. In fact, they all turned around. "Maybe not a fan—at his age they're more likely to be called groupies," added an elderly woman with a goiter and loud colors that made her look like a toucan.

"Which poem did you like best?"

"Alfredo, you're behaving like a teacher at an oral exam," jibed a thirty-something woman.

"I just wanted to know which poem he liked best. There's no harm in asking, is there?" he whined with quivering mock exasperation in his voice.

For a moment I believed that the woman who had stood up for me had gotten me off the hook. I was mistaken.

"So tell me," he resumed, "which one."

"The one comparing life to San Clemente."

"The one comparing *love* to San Clemente," he corrected, as though meditating the profundity of both our statements. " 'The San Clemente Syndrome.' " The poet stared at me. "And why?"

"My God, just leave the poor boy alone, will you? Here," interrupted another woman who had overheard my other advocate. She grabbed hold of my hand. "I'll lead you to the food so that you can get away from this monster with an ego the size of his feet—have you seen how big his shoes are? Alfredo, you should really do something about your shoes," she said from across the crowded bookstore.

"My shoes? What's wrong with my shoes?" asked the poet.

"*They. Are. Too. Big.* Don't they look huge?" she was asking me. "Poets can't have such big feet."

"Leave my feet alone."

Someone else took pity on the poet. "Don't mock his feet, Lucia. There's nothing wrong with his feet."

"A pauper's feet. Walked barefoot all his life, and still buys shoes a size bigger, in case he grows before next Christmas when the family stocks up for the holidays!" Playing the embittered or forsaken shrew.

But I did not let go of her hand. Nor she of mine. City camaraderie. How nice to hold a woman's hand, especially when you don't know a thing about her. *Se l'amore,* I thought. And all these tanned arms and elbows that belonged to all these women looking down from the gallery. *Se l'amore.*

The bookstore owner interrupted what could just as easily have been a staged tiff between husband and wife. "*Se l'amore,*" he shouted. Everyone laughed. It was not clear whether laughter was a sign of relief in having the marital spat broken up or because the use of the words *Se l'amore* implied, *If this is love, then* . . .

But people understood that this was also a signal for the reading to start and everyone found a comfortable corner or a wall against which to lean. Our corner was the best, right on the spiral staircase, each of us sitting on a tread. Still holding hands. The publisher was about to introduce the poet when the door squeaked open. Oliver was trying to squeeze his way in accompanied by two stunning girls who were either flashy models or movie actresses. It felt as though he had snatched them along the way to the bookstore and was bringing one for him and one for me. *Se l'amore.*

"Oliver! Finally!" shouted the publisher, holding up his glass of scotch. "Welcome, welcome."

Everyone turned around.

"One of the youngest, most talented American philoso-phers," he said, "accompanied by my lovely daughters, without whom *Se l'amore* would never have seen the light of day."

The poet agreed. His wife turned to me and whispered, "Such babes, aren't they?" The publisher came down the little stepladder and hugged Oliver. He took hold of the large X-ray envelope in which Oliver had stuffed his pages. "Manuscript?" "Manuscript," replied Oliver. In exchange, the publisher handed him tonight's book. "You gave me one already." "That's right." But Oliver politely admired the cover, then looked around and fi-nally spotted me sitting next to Lucia. He walked up to me, put an arm around my shoulder, and leaned over to kiss her. She looked at me again, looked at Oliver, sized up the situation: "Oliver, *sei un dissoluto*, you're debauched."

"*Se l'amore,*" he replied, displaying a copy of the book, as if to say that whatever he did in life was already in her husband's book, and therefore quite permissible.

"*Se l'amore* yourself."

I couldn't tell whether he was being called dissolute because of the two babes he had wandered in with or because of me. Or both.

Oliver introduced me to both girls. Obviously he knew them well, and both cared for him. "*Sei l'amico di Oliver, vero?* You're Oliver's friend, right?" one of them asked. "He spoke about you."

"Saying?"

"Good things."

She leaned against the wall next to where I was now standing by the poet's wife. "He's never going to let go of my hand, is he?" said Lucia, as though speaking to an absent third party. Perhaps she wanted the two babes to notice.

I did not want to let go of her hand immediately but knew that I must. So I held it in both hands, brought it to my lips, kissed its edge close to the palm, then let it go. It was, I felt, as though I'd had her for an entire afternoon and was now releasing her to her husband as one releases a bird whose broken wing had taken forever to mend.

"*Se l'amore,*" she said, all the while shaking her head to simulate a reprimand. "No less dissolute than the other, just sweeter. I leave him to you."

One of the daughters gave a forced giggle. "We'll see what we can do with him."

I was in heaven.

She knew my name. Hers was Amanda. Her sister's Adele. "There's a third one too," said Amanda, making light of their number. "She should already be around here somewhere."

The poet cleared his throat. The usual words of thanks to everyone. Last but not least, to the light of his eyes, Lucia. Why she puts up with him? Why ever does she? hissed the wife with a loving smile aimed at the poet.

"Because of his shoes," he said.

"There."

"Get on with it, Alfredo," said the goitered toucan.

"*Se l'amore. Se l'amore* is a collection of poems based on a season in Thailand teaching Dante. As many of you know, I loved Thailand before going and hated it as soon as I arrived. Let me rephrase: I hated it once I was there and loved it as soon as I left."

Laughter.

Drinks were being passed around.

"In Bangkok I kept thinking of Rome—what else?—of this little roadside shop here, and of the surrounding streets just before sunset, and of the sound of church bells on Easter Sunday, and on rainy days, which last forever in Bangkok, I could almost cry. Lucia, Lucia, Lucia, why didn't you ever say no when you knew how much I'd miss you on these days that made me feel more hollow than Ovid when they sent him to that misbegotten outpost where he died? I left a fool and came back no wiser. The people of Thailand are beautiful—so loneliness can be a cruel thing when you've had a bit to drink and are on the verge of touching the first stranger that comes your way—they're all beautiful there, but you pay for a smile by the shot glass." He stopped as though to collect his thoughts. "I called these poems 'Tristia.'"

"Tristia" took up the better part of twenty minutes. Then came the applause. The word one of the two girls used was *forte*. *Molto forte*. The goitered toucan turned to another woman who had never stopped nodding at almost every syllable spoken by the poet and who now kept repeating, *Straordinario-fantastico*. The poet stepped down, took a glass of water, and held his breath for a while—to get rid of a bad case of hiccups. I had mistaken his hiccups for suppressed sobs. The poet, looking into all the pockets of his sports jacket and coming out empty, joined his index and middle fingers tightly together and, waving both fingers next to his mouth, signaled to the bookstore owner that he wanted to smoke and maybe mingle for a couple of minutes. Straordinario-fantastico, who intercepted his signal, instantly produced her cigarette case. "*Stasera non dormo*, tonight I won't be able to sleep, the wages of poetry," she said, blaming his poetry for what was sure to be a night of throbbing insomnia.

By now everyone was sweating, and the greenhouse atmosphere both inside and outside the bookstore had become unbearably sticky.

"For the love of God, open the door," cried the poet to the owner of the bookstore. "We're suffocating in here." Mr. Venga took out a tiny wedge of wood, opened the door, and prodded it in between the wall and the bronze frame.

"Better?" he asked deferentially.

"No. But at least we know the door is open."

Oliver looked at me, meaning, *Did you like it?* I shrugged my shoulders, like someone reserving judgment for later. But I was not being sincere; I liked it a lot.

Perhaps what I liked far more was the evening. Everything about it thrilled me. Every glance that crossed my own came like a compliment, or like an asking and a promise that simply lingered in midair between me and the world around me. I was electrified—by the chaffing, the irony, the glances, the smiles that seemed pleased I existed, by the buoyant air in the shop that graced everything from the glass door to the petits fours, to the golden ochre spell of plastic glasses filled with scotch whiskey, to Mr. Venga's rolled-up sleeves, to the poet himself, down to the spiral staircase where we had congregated with the babe sisters—all seemed to glow with a luster at once spellbound and aroused.

I envied these lives and thought back to the thoroughly delibidinized lives of my parents with their stultifying lunches and dinner drudges, our dollhouse lives in our dollhouse home, and of my senior year looming ahead. Everything appeared like child's play compared to this. Why go away to America in a year when I could just as easily spend the rest of my four years away coming to readings like this and sit and talk as some were already doing right now? There was more to learn in this tiny crammed bookstore than in any of the mighty institutions across the Atlantic.

An older man with a scraggly large beard and Falstaff's paunch brought me a glass of scotch.

"Ecco."

"For me?"

"Of course for you. Did you like the poems?"

"Very much," I said, trying to look ironic and insincere, I don't know why.

"I'm his godfather and I respect your opinion," he said, as though he'd seen through my first bluff and gone no further. "But I respect your youth more."

"In a few years I promise you there won't be much youth left," I said, trying to assume the resigned irony of men who've been around and know themselves.

"Yes, but by then I won't be around to notice."

Was he hitting on me?

"So take it," he said, offering me the plastic cup. I hesitated before accepting. It was the same brand of scotch my father drank at home.

Lucia, who had caught the exchange, said: "*Tanto*, one scotch more or less won't make you any less dissolute than you already are."

"I wish I were dissolute," I said, turning to her and ignoring Falstaff.

"Why, what's missing in your life?"

"What's missing in my life?" I was going to say *Everything*, but corrected myself. "Friends—the way everyone seems to be fast friends in this place—I wish I had friends like yours, like you."

"There'll be plenty of time for these friendships. Would friends save you from being *dissoluto*?" The word kept coming back like an accusation of a deep and ugly fault in my character.

"I wish I had one friend I wasn't destined to lose."

She looked at me with a pensive smile.

"You're speaking volumes, my friend, and tonight we're doing short poems only."

She kept looking at me. "I feel for you." She brought her

palm in a sad and lingering caress to my face, as if I had suddenly become her child.

I loved that too.

"You're too young to know what I'm saying—but one day soon, I hope we'll speak again, and then we'll see if I'm big enough to take back the word I used tonight. *Scherzavo*, I was only joking." A kiss to my cheek.

What a world this was. She was more than twice my age but I could have made love to her this minute and wept with her.

"Are we toasting or what?" shouted someone in another corner of the shop.

There was a mêlée of sounds.

And then it came. A hand on my shoulder. It was Amanda's. And another on my waist. Oh, I knew that other hand so well. May it never let go of me tonight. I worship every finger on that hand, every nail you bite on every one of your fingers, my dear, dear Oliver—don't let go of me yet, for I need that hand there. A shudder ran down my spine.

"And I'm Ada," someone said almost by way of apology, as though aware she'd taken far too long to work her way to our end of the store and was now making it up to us by letting everyone in our corner know that she was the Ada everyone had surely been speaking about. Something raucous and rakish in her voice, or in the way she took her time saying Ada, or in the way she seemed to make light of everything—book parties, introductions, even friendship—suddenly told me that, without a doubt, this evening I'd stepped into a spellbound world indeed.

I'd never traveled in this world. But I loved this world. And I would love it even more once I learned how to speak its language—for it was my language, a form of address where our deepest longings are smuggled in banter, not because it is safer to put a smile on what we fear may shock, but because the inflections of desire, of all desire in this new world I'd stepped into, could only be conveyed in play.

Everyone was available, lived *availably*—like the city—and assumed everyone else wished to be so as well. I longed to be like them.

The bookstore owner chimed a bell by the cash register and everyone was quiet.

The poet spoke. "I was not going to read this poem tonight, but because *someone*"—here, he altered his voice—"*someone* mentioned it, I could not resist. It's entitled 'The San Clemente Syndrome.' It is, I must admit, i.e., if a versifier is allowed to say this about his own work, my favorite." (I later found out that he never referred to himself as a poet or his work as poetry.) "Because it was the most difficult, because it made me terribly, terribly homesick, because it saved me in Thailand, because it explained my entire life to me. I counted my days, my nights, with San Clemente in mind. The idea of coming back to Rome without finishing this long poem scared me more than being stranded at Bangkok's airport for another week. And yet, it was in Rome, where we live not two hundred meters away from the Basilica of San Clemente, that I put the finishing touches to a poem which, ironically enough, I had started eons ago in Bangkok precisely because Rome felt galaxies away."

As he read the long poem, I began thinking that, unlike him, I had always found a way to avoid counting the days. We were leaving in three days—and then whatever I had with Oliver was destined to go up in thin air. We had talked about meeting in the States, and we had talked of writing and speaking by phone— but the whole thing had a mysteriously surreal quality kept intentionally opaque by both of us—not because we wanted to allow events to catch us unprepared so that we might blame circumstances and not ourselves, but because by not planning to keep things alive, we were avoiding the prospect that they might ever die. We had come to Rome in the same spirit of avoidance: Rome was a final bash before school and travel took us away, just a way of putting things off and extending the party long past closing time. Perhaps, without thinking, we had taken more than a brief vacation; we were eloping together with return-trip tickets to separate destinations.

Perhaps it was his gift to me.

Perhaps it was my father's gift to the two of us.

Would I be able to live without his hand on my tummy or around my hips? Without kissing and licking a wound on his hip that would take weeks to heal, but away from me now? Whom else would I ever be able to call by my name?

There would be others, of course, and others after others, but calling them by my name in a moment of passion would feel like a derived thrill, an affectation.

I remembered the emptied closet and the packed suitcase next to his bed. Soon I'd sleep in Oliver's room. I'd sleep with his shirt, lie with it next to me, wear it in my sleep.

After the reading, more applause, more conviviality, more drinks. Soon it was time to close the store. I remembered Marzia when the bookstore in B. was closing. How far, how different. How thoroughly unreal she'd become.

Someone said we should all head out to dinner together. There were about thirty of us. Someone else suggested a restaurant on Lake Albano. A restaurant overlooking a starlit night sprang to my imagination like something out of an illuminated manuscript from the late Middle Ages. No, too far, someone said. Yes, but the lights on the lake at night . . . The lights on the lake at night will have to wait for another time. Why not some-

where on via Cassia? Yes, but that didn't solve the problem of the
cars: there weren't enough of them. Sure there were enough cars.
And if we had to sit on top of each other for a little while, would
anyone mind? Of course not. Especially if I get to sit in between
these two beauties. Yes, but what if Falstaff were to sit on the
beauties?

There were only five cars, and all were parked in different
tiny side alleys not far from the bookstore. Because we could not
depart en masse, we were to reconvene somewhere by Ponte Milvio. From there up via Cassia to the trattoria whose precise
whereabouts someone, but no one else, knew.

We arrived more than forty-five minutes later—less than the
time needed to reach distant Albano, where the lights on the lake
at night . . . The place was a large al fresco trattoria with check-
ered tablecloths and mosquito candles spread out sparely among
the diners. By now it must have been eleven o'clock. The air was
still very damp. You could see it on our faces, and on our clothes,
we looked limp and soggy. Even the tablecloths felt limp and soggy.
But the restaurant was on a hill and occasionally a breathless draft
would sough through the trees, signifying that tomorrow it would
rain again but that the mugginess would remain unchanged.

The waitress, a woman nearing her sixties, made a quick
count of how many we were and asked the help to set the tables
in a double-sided horseshoe, which was instantly done. Then she
told us what we were going to eat and drink. Thank God we
don't have to decide, because with him deciding what to eat—
said the poet's wife—we'd be here for another hour and by then
they'd be out of food in the kitchen. She ran down a long list of
antipasti, which materialized no sooner than invoked, followed
by bread, wine, mineral water, *frizzante* and *naturale*. Simple
fare, she explained. Simple is what we want, echoed the publisher. "This year, we're in the red again."

Once again a toast to the poet. To the publisher. To the store owner. To the wife, the daughters, who else?

Laughter and good fellowship. Ada made a small improvised speech—well, not so improvised, she conceded. Falstaff and Toucan admitted having had a hand in it.

The tortellini in cream sauce arrived more than half an hour later. By then I had decided not to drink wine because the two scotch whiskeys gulped down in a rush were only now starting to have their full effect. The three sisters were sitting between us and everyone on our bench was sitting pressed together. Heaven.

Second course much later: Pot roast, peas. Salad.

Then cheeses.

One thing led to another, and we began speaking of Bangkok. "Everyone is beautiful, but beautiful in an exceptionally hybrid, crossbred manner, which is why I wanted to go there," said the poet. "They're not Asiatic, not Caucasian, and Eurasian is too simple a term. They're exotic in the purest sense of the word, and yet not alien. We instantly recognize them though we've never seen them before, and have no words either for what they stir in us or for what they seem to want from us.

"At first I thought that they thought differently. Then I realized they felt things differently. Then that they were unspeakably sweet, sweet as you can't imagine anyone being sweet here. Oh, we can be kind and we can be caring and we can be very, very warm in our sunny, passionate Mediterranean way, but they were sweet, selflessly sweet, sweet in their hearts, sweet in their bodies, sweet without a touch of sorrow or malice, sweet like children, without irony or shame. I was ashamed of what I felt for them. This could be paradise, just as I'd fantasized. The twenty-four-year-old night clerk of my rinky-dink hotel, who's wearing a visorless cap and has seen all types come and go, stares and I stare back. His features are a girl's. But he looks like a girl who looks like a boy. The girl at the American Express desk stares and I stare back. She looks like a boy who looks like a girl and who's therefore just a boy. The younger ones, men and women, always giggle when I give them the look. Even the girl at the consulate who speaks fluent Milanese, and the undergraduates who wait at the same hour of each and every morning for the same bus to pick us up, stare at me and I stare back—does all this staring add up to what I think it means, because, like it or not, when it comes to the senses all humans speak the same beastly tongue."

A second round of grappa and sambuca.

"I wanted to sleep with all of Thailand. And all of Thailand, it turns out, was flirting with me. You couldn't take a step without almost lurching into someone."

"Here, take a sip of this grappa and tell me it's not the work of a witch," interrupted the bookstore owner. The poet allowed the waiter to pour another glass. This time he sipped it slowly. Falstaff downed it in one gulp. Straordinario-fantastico growled it down her gullet. Oliver smacked his lips. The poet said it made you young again. "I like grappa at night, it reinvigorates me. But you"—he was looking to me now—"wouldn't understand. At your age, God knows, invigoration is the last thing you need."

He watched me down part of the glass. "Do you feel it?"

"Feel what?" I asked.

"The invigoration."

I swilled the drink again. "Not really."

"Not really," he repeated with a puzzled, disappointed look.

"That's because, at his age, it's already there, the invigoration," added Lucia.

"True," said someone, "your 'invigoration' works only on those who no longer have it."

The poet: "Invigoration is not hard to come by in Bangkok. One warm night in my hotel room I thought I would go out of my mind. It was either loneliness, or the sounds of people out-side, or the work of the devil. But this is when I began to think of San Clemente. It came to me like an undefined, nebulous feeling, part arousal, part homesickness, part metaphor. You travel to a place because you have this picture of it and you want to couple with the whole country. Then you find that you and its natives haven't a thing in common. You don't understand the basic sig-nals which you'd always assumed all humanity shared. You de-cide it was all a mistake, that it was all in your head. Then you dig a bit deeper and you find that, despite your reasonable suspi-cions, you still desire them all, but you don't know what it is ex-actly you want from them, or what they seem to want from you, because they too, it turns out, are all looking at you with what could only be one thing on their mind. But you tell yourself you're imagining things. And you're ready to pack up and go back to Rome because all of these touch-and-go signals are driv-ing you mad. But then something suddenly clicks, like a secret underground passageway, and you realize that, just like you, they are desperate and aching for you as well. And the worst thing is that, with all your experience and your sense of irony and your ability to overcome shyness wherever it threatens to crop up, you feel totally stranded. I didn't know their language, didn't know the language of their hearts, didn't even know my own. I saw veils everywhere: what I wanted, what I didn't know I wanted, what I didn't want to know I wanted, what I'd always known I wanted. This is either a miracle. Or it is hell.

"Like every experience that marks us for a lifetime, I found myself turned inside out, drawn and quartered. This was the sum of everything I'd been in my life—and more: who I am when I sing and stir-fry vegetables for my family and friends on Sunday afternoons; who I am when I wake up on freezing nights and want nothing more than to throw on a sweater, rush to my desk, and write about the person I know no one knows I am; who I am when I crave to be naked with another naked body, or when I crave to be alone in the world; who I am when every part of me seems miles and centuries apart and each swears it bears my name.

"I called it the San Clemente Syndrome. Today's Basilica of San Clemente is built on the site of what once was a refuge for persecuted Christians. The home of the Roman consul Titus Flavius Clemens, it was burnt down during Emperor Nero's reign. Next to its charred remains, in what must have been a large, cavernous vault, the Romans built an underground pagan temple dedicated to Mithras, God of the Morning, Light of the World, over whose temple the early Christians built another church, dedicated—coincidentally or not, this is a matter to be further excavated—to another Clement, Pope St. Clement, on top of which came yet another church that burnt down and on the site of which stands today's basilica. And the digging could go on and on. Like the subconscious, like love, like memory, like time itself, like every single one of us, the church is built on the ruins of subsequent restorations, there is no rock bottom, there is no first anything, no last anything, just layers and secret passageways and interlocking chambers, like the Christian Catacombs, and right along these, even a Jewish Catacomb.

"But, as Nietzsche says, my friends, I have given you the moral before the tale."

"Alfredo, my love, please, make it brief."

By then the management of the restaurant had figured that we weren't about to leave yet, and so, once again, served grappa and sambuca for everyone.

"So on that warm night when I thought I was losing my mind, I'm sitting in the rinky-dink bar of my rinky-dink hotel, and who should be seated at the table right next to mine but our night clerk, wearing that strange visorless cap. Off duty? I ask. Off duty, he replies. Why don't you head home, then? I live here. Just having a drink before turning in.

"I stare at him. And he stares at me.

"Without letting another moment go by, he picks up his drink with one hand, the decanter with the other—I thought I'd intruded and offended him and that he wanted to be alone and was moving to a table farther away from mine—when lo and behold, he comes right to my table and sits right in front of me. Want to try some of this? he asks. Sure, why not, I think, when in Rome, when in Thailand . . . Of course, I've heard all manner of stories, so I figure there's something fishy and unsavory in all this, but let's play along.

"He snaps his fingers and peremptorily orders a tiny cup for me. No sooner said than done.

"Have a sip.

"I may not like it, I say.

"Have one anyway. He pours some for me and some for him.

"The brew is quite delicious. The glass is scarcely bigger than my grandmother's thimble, with which she used to darn socks.

"Have another sip—just to make sure.

"I down this one as well. No question about it. It's a little like grappa, only stronger but less tart.

"Meanwhile, the night clerk keeps staring at me. I don't like being stared at so intensely. His glance is almost unbearable. I can almost detect the beginnings of a giggle.

"You're staring at me, I finally say.

"I know.

"Why are you staring?

"He leans over to my side of the table: Because I like you.

"Look—, I begin.

"Have another. Pours himself one, one for me.

"Let me put it this way: I'm not—

"But he won't let me finish.

"All the more reason why you should have another.

"My mind is flashing red signals all over the place. They get you drunk, they take you somewhere, they rob you clean, and when you complain to the police, who are no less corrupt than the thieves themselves, they make all manner of allegations about you, and have pictures to prove it. Another worry sweeps over me: the bill from the bar could turn out to be astronomical while the one doing the ordering downs dyed tea and pretends to get drunk. Oldest trick in the book—what am I, born yesterday?

"I don't think I'm really interested. Please, let's just—

"Have another.

"Smiles.

"I'm about to repeat my tired protestation, but I can already hear him say, Have another. I'm almost on the point of laughing.

"He sees my laugh, doesn't care where it's coming from, all he cares is I'm smiling.

"Now he's pouring himself one.

"Look, amigo, I hope you don't think I'm paying for these drinks.

"Little bourgeois me has finally spoken out. I know all about these mincing niceties that always, always end up taking advantage of foreigners.

"I didn't ask you to pay for the drinks. Or, for that matter, to pay me.

"Ironically, he is not offended. He must have known this was coming. Must have done it a million times—comes with the job, probably.

"Here, have another—in the name of friendship.

"Friendship?

"You have nothing to fear from me.

"I'm not sleeping with you.

"Maybe you won't. Maybe you will. The night is young. And I haven't given up.

"At which point he removes his cap and lets down so much hair that I couldn't understand how such a huge tumble could have been wrapped and tucked under so small a bonnet. He was a woman.

"Disappointed?

"No, on the contrary.

"The tiny wrists, the bashful air, the softest skin under the sun, tenderness that seemed to spill out of her eyes, not with the smirking boldness of those who've been around but with the most heartrending promises of utter sweetness and chastity in bed. Was I disappointed? Perhaps—because the sting of the situation had been dispelled.

"Out came a hand that touched my cheek and stayed there, as if to soothe away the shock and surprise. Better now?

"I nodded.

"You need another.

"And you do too, I said, pouring her a drink this time.

"I asked her why she purposely misled people into thinking she was a man. I was expecting, *It's safer for business*—or something a bit more rakish, like: *For moments such as these.*

"Then came the giggle, this time for real, as if she had committed a naughty prank but was not in the least bit displeased or surprised by the result. But I am a man, she said.

"She was nodding away at my disbelief, as if the nod itself were part of the same prank.

"You're a man? I asked, no less disappointed than when I discovered she was a woman.

"I'm afraid so.

"With both elbows on the table he leaned forward and almost touched my nose with the tip of his and said: I like you very, very much, Signor Alfredo. And you like me too, very, very much—and the beautiful thing is we both know it.

"I stared at him, at her, who knows. Let's have another, I said.

"I was going to suggest it, said my impish friend.

"Do you want me man or woman? she/he asked, as if one could scale one's way back up our phylogenetic tree.

"I didn't know what answer to give. I wanted to say, I want you as intermezzo. So I said, I want you as both, or as in between.

"He seemed taken aback.

"Naughty, naughty, he said, as though for the first time that night I'd actually managed to shock him with something thoroughly debauched.

"When he stood up to go to the bathroom, I noticed she was indeed a woman wearing a dress and high-heeled shoes. I couldn't help staring at the most lovely skin on her most lovely ankles.

"She knew she had caught me yet once more and started to giggle in earnest.

"Will you watch my purse? she asked. She must have sensed that if she hadn't asked me to watch something of hers, I would probably have paid the bill and left the bar.

"This, in a nutshell, is what I call the San Clemente Syndrome."

There was applause, and it was affectionate applause. We not only liked the story but the man telling the story.

"Evviva il sindromo di San Clemente," said Straordinario-fantastico.

"*Sindromo* is not masculine, it's feminine, *la sindrome*," corrected someone sitting next to her.

"Evviva la sindrome di San Clemente," hailed someone who was clearly aching to shout something. He, along with a few others, had arrived very late for dinner, crying in good Roman di-

alect *Lassatece passà*, let us through, to the restaurant owners as
a way of announcing his arrival to the company. Everyone had
long since started eating. His car had taken a wrong turn around
Ponte Milvio. Then he couldn't find the restaurant, etc. As a result he missed the first two courses. He was now sitting at the
very end of the table and he as well as those he had brought with
him from the bookstore had been given the last of the cheeses remaining in the house. This plus two flans for each, because this
was all that was left. He made up for the missing food with too
much wine. He had heard most of the poet's speech on San
Clemente.

"I think that all this *clementizing*," he said, "is quite charm-
ing, though I've no idea how your metaphor will help us see who
we are, what we want, where we're headed, any more than the
wine we've been drinking. But if the job of poetry, like that
of wine, is to help us see double, then I propose another toast until we've drunk enough to see the world with four eyes—and,
if we're not careful, with eight."

"*Evviva!*" interrupted Amanda, toasting to the latecomer, in
a desperate effort to shut him up.

"*Evviva!*" everyone else toasted.

"Better write another book of poems—and soon," said
Straordinario-fantastico.

Someone suggested an ice cream place not far from the
restaurant. No, skip the ice cream, let's go for coffee. We all
massed into cars and headed along the Lungotevere, toward the
Pantheon.

In the car, I was happy. But I kept thinking of the basilica and
how similar to our evening, one thing leading to the next, to the
next, to something totally unforeseen, and just when you thought
the cycle had ended, something new cropped up and after it
something else as well, until you realized you could easily be

back where you started, in the center of old Rome. A day ago we had gone swimming by the light of the moon. Now we were here. In a few days he'd be gone. If only he'd be back exactly a year from now. I slipped my arm around Oliver's and leaned against Ada. I fell asleep.

It was well past one in the morning when the party arrived at Caffè Sant'Eustachio. We ordered coffees for everyone. I thought I understood why everyone swears by Sant'Eustachio's coffee; or perhaps I wanted to think I understood, but I wasn't sure. I wasn't even sure I liked it. Perhaps no one else did but felt obliged to fall in with the general opinion and claimed that they too couldn't live without it. There was a large crowd of coffee drinkers standing and sitting around the famed Roman coffeehouse. I loved watching all these lightly dressed people standing so close to me, all of them sharing the same basic thing: love for the night, love for the city, love for its people, and an ardent desire to couple—with anyone. Love for anything that would prevent the tiny groups of people who had come together here from disbanding. After coffee, when the group considered separating, someone said, "No, we can't say goodbye yet." Someone suggested a pub nearby. Best beer in Rome. Why not? So we headed down a long and narrow side alley leading in the direction of Campo de' Fiori. Lucia walked between me and the poet. Oliver, talking with two of the sisters, was behind us. The old man had made friends with Straordinario-fantastico and they were both confabulating about San Clemente. "What a metaphor for life!" said Straordinario-fantastico. "Please! No need to overdo things either with *clementification* this and *clementization* that. It was just a figure of speech, you know," said Falstaff, who probably had had his fill of his godson's glory for the night. Noticing that Ada was walking by herself, I walked back and held her by the hand. She was dressed in white and her tanned skin had a sheen that made me want to touch every pore in her body. We did not speak. I could hear her high heels tapping the slate pavement. In the dark she seemed an apparition.

I wanted this walk never to end. The silent and deserted alley was altogether murky and its ancient, pockmarked cobblestones glistened in the damp air, as though an ancient carrier had spilled the viscous contents of his amphora before disappearing underground in the ancient city. Everyone had left Rome. And the emptied city, which had seen too many and seen them all, now belonged to us alone and to the poet who had cast it, if only for one night, in his own image. The mugginess was not going to break tonight. We could, if we wished, have walked in circles and no one would have known and none would have minded.

As we ambled down an emptied labyrinth of sparely lit streets, I began to wonder what all this talk of San Clemente had to do with us—how we move through time, how time moves through us, how we change and keep changing and come back to the same. One could even grow old and not learn a thing but this. That was the poet's lesson, I presume. In a month or so from now, when I'd revisit Rome, being here tonight with Oliver would seem totally unreal, as though it had happened to an entirely different me. And the wish born three years ago here when an errand boy offered to take me to a cheap movie theater known for what went on there would seem no less unfulfilled to me three months from now than it was three years ago. He came. He left. Nothing else had changed. I had not changed. The world hadn't changed. Yet nothing would be the same. All that remains is dreammaking and strange remembrance.

The bar was closing when we arrived. "We close at two." "Well, we still have time for drinks." Oliver wanted a martini, an American martini. What a beautiful idea, said the poet. "Me too," chimed in someone else. On the large jukebox you could

hear the same summer hit we'd heard during the entire month of
July. On hearing the word "martini," the old man and the publisher also dittoed the order. "Ehi! Taverniere!" shouted Falstaff.
The waiter told us that we could either have wine or beer; the
bartender had left earlier that evening, on account of because
his mother was taken gravely ill to the hospital where she had
to be taken. Everyone smothered a laugh at the waiter's garbled
speech. Oliver asked what they charged for martinis. The waiter
yelled the question to the girl at the cash register. She told him
how much. "Well, what if I make the drinks and you charge us
your price on account of because we can mix the drinks we are
mixing?"

There was hesitation on the part of the waiter and of the
cashier. The owner had long since left. "Why not?" said the girl.
"If you know how to make them, *faccia pure*, go right ahead."

Round of applause for Oliver, who sauntered his way behind
the bar and, in a matter of seconds, after adding ice to the gin and
a bit of vermouth, was vigorously shaking the cocktail mixer.
Olives couldn't be found in the tiny refrigerator by the bar. The
cashier came and checked and produced a bowl. "Olives," she
said, staring Oliver straight in the face, as if to mean, *It was under your very nose—had you looked? And what else?* "Maybe I
could entice you to accept a martini from us," he said. "This has
been a crazy evening. A drink could not possibly make it any crazier. Make it a small one."

"Want me to teach you?"

And he proceeded to explain the intricacies of a straight-up
dry martini. He was okay being a bartender to the bar's help.

"Where did you learn this?" I asked.

"Mixology 101. Courtesy Harvard. Weekends, I made a living as a bartender all through college. Then I became a chef, then
a caterer. But always a poker player."

His undergraduate years, each time he spoke of them, acquired a limelit, incandescent magic, as if they belonged to another life, a life to which I had no access since it already belonged to the past. Proof of its existence trickled, as it did now, in his ability to mix drinks, or to tell arcane grappas apart, or to speak to all women, or in the mysterious square envelopes addressed to him that arrived at our house from all over the world.

I had never envied him the past, nor felt threatened by it. All these facets of his life had the mysterious character of incidents that had occurred in my father's life long before my birth but which continued to resonate into the present. I didn't envy life before me, nor did I ache to travel back to the time when he had been my age.

There were at least fifteen of us now, and we occupied one of the large wooden rustic tables. The waiter announced last call a second time. Within ten minutes, the other customers had left. The waiter had already started lowering the metal gate, on account of because it was the closing hour of the *chiusura*. The jukebox was summarily unplugged. If each of us kept talking, we might be here till daybreak.

"Did I shock you?" asked the poet.

"Me?" I asked, not certain why, of all people at the table, he should have addressed me.

Lucia stared at us. "Alfredo, I'm afraid he knows more than you know about corrupting youth. E un dissoluto assoluto," she intoned, as always now, her hand to my cheek.

"This poem is about one thing and one thing only," said Straordinario-fantastico.

"San Clemente is really about four—at the very least!" retorted the poet.

Third last call.

"Listen," interrupted the owner of the bookstore to the

waiter, "why don't you let us stay? We'll put the young lady in a cab when we're done. And we'll pay. Another round of martinis?"

"Do as you please," said the waiter, removing his apron. He'd given up on us. "I'm going home."

Oliver came up to me and asked me to play something on the piano.

"What would you like?" I asked.

"Anything."

This would be my thanks for the most beautiful evening of my life. I took a sip from my second martini, feeling as decadent as one of those jazz piano players who smoke a lot and drink a lot and are found dead in a gutter at the end of every film.

I wanted to play Brahms. But an instinct told me to play something very quiet and contemplative. So I played one of the Goldberg Variations, which made me quiet and contemplative. There was a sigh among the fifteen or so, which pleased me, since this was my only way of repaying for this magical evening.

When I was asked to play something else, I proposed a capriccio by Brahms. They all agreed it was a wonderful idea, until the devil took hold of me and, after playing the opening bars of the capriccio, out of nowhere I started to play a *stornello*. The contrast caught them all by surprise and all began to sing, though not in unison, for each sang the stornello he or she knew. Each time we came to the refrain, we agreed we'd all sing the same words, which earlier that evening Oliver and I had heard Dante the statue recite. Everyone was ecstatic, and I was asked to play another, then another. Roman *stornelli* are usually bawdy, lilting songs, not the lacerating, heart-wrenching arias from Naples. After the third, I looked over at Oliver and said I wanted to go out to take a breath of fresh air.

"What is it, doesn't he feel well?" the poet asked Oliver.

"No, just needs some air. Please don't move."

The cashier leaned all the way down, and with one arm lifted up the rolling shutter. I got out from under the partly lowered shutter and suddenly felt a fresh gust of wind on the empty alley. "Can we walk a bit?" I asked Oliver.

We sauntered down the dark alley, exactly like two shades in Dante, the younger and the older. It was still very hot and I caught the light from a streetlamp glistening on Oliver's forehead. We made our way deeper into an extremely quiet alley, then through another, as if drawn through these unreal and sticky goblin lanes that seemed to lead to a different, nether realm you entered in a state of stupor and wonderment. All I heard were the alley cats and the splashing of running water nearby. Either a marble fountain or one of those numberless municipal *fontanelle* found everywhere in Rome. "Water," I gasped. "I'm not made for martinis. I'm so drunk."

"You shouldn't have had any. You had scotch, then wine, grappa, now gin."

"So much for the evening's sexual buildup."

He snickered. "You look pale."

"I think I'm going to be sick."

"Best remedy is to make it happen."

"How?"

"Bend down and stick your finger all the way inside your mouth."

I shook my head. No way.

We found a garbage bin on the sidewalk. "Do it inside here."

I normally resisted throwing up. But I was too ashamed to be childish now. I was also uncomfortable puking in front of him. I wasn't even sure that Amanda had not followed us.

"Here, bend down, I'll hold your head."

I was resisting. "It will pass. I'm sure it will."

"Open your mouth."

I opened my mouth. Before I knew it I was sick as soon as he touched my uvula.

But what a solace to have my head held, what selfless courage to hold someone's head while he's vomiting. Would I have had it in me to do the same for him?

"I think I'm done," I said.

"Let's see if more doesn't come out."

Sure enough, another heave brought out more of tonight's food and drink.

"Don't you chew your peas?" he asked, smiling at me.

How I loved being made fun of that way.

"I just hope I didn't get your shoes dirty," I said.

"They're not shoes, they're sandals."

Both of us almost burst out laughing.

When I looked around, I saw that I had vomited right next to the statue of the Pasquino. How like me to vomit right in front of Rome's most venerable lampoonist.

"I swear, there were peas there that hadn't even been bitten into and could have fed the children of India."

More laughter. I washed my face and rinsed my mouth with the water of a fountain we found on our way back.

Right before us we caught sight of the human statue of Dante again. He had removed his cape and his long black hair was all undone. He must have sweated five pounds in that costume. He was now brawling with the statue of Queen Nefertiti, also with her mask off and her long hair matted together by sweat. "I'm picking up my things tonight and good night and good riddance." "Good riddance to you too, and vaffanculo." "Fancúlo yourself, e poi t'inculo." And so saying, Nefertiti threw a handful of coins at Dante, who ducked the coins, though one hit him on the face. "Aiiiio," he yelped. For a moment I thought they were going to come to blows.

We returned by another equally dark, deserted, glistening side alley, then onto via Santa Maria dell'Anima. Above us was a weak square streetlight mounted to the wall of a tiny old corner building. In the old days, they probably had a gas jet in its place. I stopped and he stopped. "The most beautiful day of my life and I end up vomiting." He wasn't listening. He pressed me against the wall and started to kiss me, his hips pushing into mine, his arms about to lift me off the ground. My eyes were shut, but I knew he had stopped kissing me to look around him; people could be walking by. I didn't want to look. Let him be the one to worry. Then we kissed again. And, with my eyes still shut, I think I did hear two voices, old men's voices, grumbling something about taking a good look at these two, wondering if in the old days you'd ever see such a sight. But I didn't want to think about them. I didn't worry. If he wasn't worried, I wasn't worried. I could spend the rest of my life like this: with him, at night, in Rome, my eyes totally shut, one leg coiled around his. I thought of coming back here in the weeks or months to come— for this was our spot.

We returned to the bar to find everyone had already left. By then it must have been three in the morning, or even later. Except for a few cars, the city was dead quiet. When, by mistake, we reached the normally crowded Piazza Rotonda around the Pantheon, it too was unusually empty. There were a few tourists lugging huge knapsacks, a few drunks, and the usual drug dealers. Oliver stopped a street vendor and bought me a Lemonsoda. The taste of bitter lemons was refreshing and made me feel better. Oliver bought a bitter orange drink and a slice of watermelon. He offered me a bite, but I said no. How wonderful, to walk half drunk with a Lemonsoda on a muggy night like this around the gleaming slate cobblestones of Rome with someone's arm around me. We turned left and, heading toward Piazza Febo, suddenly, from nowhere, made out someone strumming a guitar, singing not a rock song, but as we got closer, an old, old Neapolitan tune. "Fenesta ca lucive." It took me a moment to recognize it. Then I remembered.

Mafalda had taught me that song years ago when I was a boy. It was her lullaby. I hardly knew Naples, and, other than for her and her immediate entourage, and a few casual visits to Naples with my parents, had never had contact with Neapolitans. But the strains of the doleful song stirred such powerful nostalgia for lost loves and for things lost over the course of one's life and for lives, like my grandfather's, that had come long before mine that I was suddenly taken back to a poor, disconsolate universe of simple folk like Mafalda's ancestors, fretting and scurrying in the tiny *vicoli* of an old Naples whose memory I wanted to share word for word with Oliver now, as if he too, like Mafalda and Manfredi and Anchise and me, were a fellow southerner whom I'd met in a foreign port city and who'd instantly understand why the sound of this old song, like an ancient prayer for the dead in the deadest of languages, could bring tears even in those who couldn't understand a syllable.

The song reminded him of the Israeli national anthem, he said. Or was it inspired by the *Moldau*? On second thought, it might have been an aria from Bellini's *Sonnambula*. Warm, but still off, I said, though the song has often been attributed to Bellini. We're *clementizing*, he said.

I translated the words from Neapolitan to Italian to English. It's about a young man who passes by his beloved's window only to be told by her sister that Nennélla has died. *From the mouth where flowers once blossomed only worms emerge. Farewell, window, for my Nenna can no longer look out again.*

A German tourist, who seemed all alone and quite drunk himself that night, had overheard me translating the song into

English and approached us, begging in halting English to know if I could be so kind as to translate the words into German as well. Along the way to our hotel, I taught Oliver and the German how to sing the refrain, which all three of us repeated again and again, our voices reverberating in the narrow, damp alleys of Rome as each mangled his own version of Neapolitan. Finally we said goodbye to the German on Piazza Navona. On our way to our hotel, Oliver and I began to sing the refrain again, softly,

> *Chiagneva sempe ca durmeva sola,*
> *mo dorme co' li muorte accompagnata.*

> She always wept because she slept alone,
> Now she sleeps among the dead.

I can, from the distance of years now, still think I'm hearing the voices of two young men singing these words in Neapolitan toward daybreak, neither realizing, as they held each other and kissed again and again on the dark lanes of old Rome, that this was the last night they would ever make love again.

"Tomorrow let's go to San Clemente," I said.

"Tomorrow is today," he replied.

PART 4

Ghost Spots

Anchise was waiting for me at the station. I spotted him as soon as the train made its prolonged curve around the bay, slowing down and almost grazing the tall cypresses that I loved so much and through which I always caught an ever-welcoming preview of the glaring midafternoon sea. I lowered the window and let the wind fan my face, catching a glimpse of our lumbering engine car far, far ahead. Arriving in B. always made me happy. It reminded me of arrivals in early June at the end of every school year. The wind, the heat, the glinting gray platform with the ancient stationmaster's hut permanently shuttered since the First World War, the dead silence, all spelled my favorite season at this deserted and beloved time of day. Summer was just about to start, it seemed, things hadn't happened yet, my head was still buzzing with last-minute cramming before exams, this was the first time I was sighting the sea this year. Oliver who?

The train stopped for a few seconds, let off about five passengers. There was the usual rumble, followed by the loud hydraulic rattle of the engine. Then, as easily as they had stopped, the cars squeaked out of the station, one by one, and slithered away. Total silence.

I stood for a moment under the dried wooden cantilever. The

whole place, including the boarded hut, exuded a strong odor of petrol, tar, chipped paint, and piss.

And as always: blackbirds, pine trees, cicadas.

Summer.

I had seldom thought of the approaching school year. Now I was grateful that, with so much heat and so much summer around me, it still seemed months away.

Within minutes of my arrival, the direttissimo to Rome swished in on the opposite track—always punctual, that train. Three days ago, we had taken the exact same one. I remembered now staring from its windows and thinking: In a few days, you'll be back, and you'll be alone, and you'll hate it, so don't let anything catch you unprepared. Be warned. I had rehearsed losing him not just to ward off suffering by taking it in small doses beforehand, but, as all superstitious people do, to see if my willingness to accept the very worst might not induce fate to soften its blow. Like soldiers trained to fight by night, I lived in the dark so as not to be blinded when darkness came. Rehearse the pain to dull the pain. Homeopathically.

Once again, then. View of the bay: check.

Scent of the pine trees: check.

Stationmaster's hut: check.

Sight of the hills in the distance to recall the morning we rode back to B. and came speeding downhill, almost running over a gypsy girl: check.

Smell of piss, petrol, tar, enamel paint: check, check, check, and check.

Anchise grabbed my backpack and offered to carry it for me. I told him not to; backpacks were not made to be carried except by their owners. He didn't understand why exactly and handed it back to me.

He asked if the Signor Ulliva had left.

Yes, this morning.

"Triste," he remarked.

"Yes, a bit."

"*Anche a me duole*, I too am saddened."

I avoided his eyes. I did not want to encourage him to say anything or even to bring up the subject.

My mother, when I arrived, wanted to know everything about our trip. I told her we had done nothing special, just seen the Capitol and Villa Borghese, San Clemente. Otherwise we'd just walked around a lot. Lots of fountains. Lots of strange places at night. Two dinners. "Dinners?" my mother asked, with an understated triumphant *see-I-was-right-wasn't-I?* "And with whom?" "People." "What people?" "Writers, publishers, friends of Oliver's. We stayed up every night." "Not even eighteen years old, and already he leads la dolce vita," came Mafalda's acid satire. My mother agreed.

"We've fixed up your room the way it was. We thought you'd like finally to have it back."

I was instantly saddened and infuriated. Who had given them the right? They'd clearly been prying, together or separately.

I always knew I'd eventually have my room back. But I had hoped for a slower, more extended transition to the way things used to be before Oliver. I'd pictured lying in bed struggling to work up the courage to make it across to his room. What I had failed to anticipate was that Mafalda would have already changed his sheets—our sheets. Luckily I'd asked him again to give me Billowy that morning, after I'd made sure he wore it all through our stay in Rome. I had put it in a plastic laundry bag in our hotel room and would in all likelihood have to hide it from anyone's prying reach for the rest of my life. On certain nights, I'd remove Billowy from its bag, make sure it hadn't acquired the scent of plastic or of my clothes, and hold it next to me, flap its long sleeves around me, and breathe out his name in the dark. *Ulliva, Ulliva, Ulliva*—it was Oliver calling me by his name when he'd imitate its transmogrified sound as spoken by Mafalda and Anchise; but it'd also be me calling him by his name as well, hoping he'd call me back by mine, which I'd speak for him to me, and back to him: *Elio, Elio, Elio.*

To avoid entering my bedroom from the balcony and finding him missing, I used the inner stairwell. I opened the door to my room, dropped my backpack on the floor, and threw myself on my warm, sunlit bed. Thank goodness for that. They had not washed the bedspread. Suddenly I was happy to be back. I could have fallen asleep right then and there, forgetting all about Billowy and the smell, and about Oliver himself. Who can resist sleep at two or three in the afternoon in these sunlit parts of the Mediterranean?

In my exhaustion, I resolved to take out my scorebook later in the afternoon and pick up the Haydn exactly where I'd left off. Either this or I'd head over to the tennis courts and sit in the sun on one of those warm benches that were sure to send a shiver of well-being through my body, and see who was available for a game. There was always someone.

I had never welcomed sleep so serenely in my life. There'd be plenty of time for mourning, I thought. It will come, probably on the sly, as I've heard these things always do, and there won't be any getting off lightly, either. Anticipating sorrow to neutralize sorrow—that's paltry, cowardly stuff, I told myself, knowing I was an ace practitioner of the craft. And what if it came fiercely? What if it came and didn't let go, a sorrow that had come to stay, and did to me what longing for him had done on those nights when it seemed there was something so essential missing from my life that it might as well have been missing from my body, so that losing him now would be like losing a hand you could spot in every picture of yourself around the house, but without which you couldn't possibly be you again. You lose it, as you always knew you would, and were even prepared to; but you can't bring yourself to live with the loss. And hoping not to think of it, like praying not to dream of it, hurts just the same.

Then a strange idea got hold of me: What if my body—just my body, my heart—cried out for his? What to do then?

What if at night I wouldn't be able to live with myself unless I had him by me, inside me? What then?

Think of the pain before the pain.

I knew what I was doing. Even in my sleep, I knew what I was doing. Trying to immunize yourself, that's what you're doing— you'll end up killing the whole thing this way—sneaky, cunning boy, that's what you are, sneaky, heartless, cunning boy. I smiled at the voice. The sun was right on me now, and I loved the sun with a near-pagan love for the things of earth. Pagan, that's what you are. I had never known how much I loved the earth, the sun, the sea—people, things, even art seemed to come second. Or was I fooling myself?

In the middle of the afternoon, I became aware that I was enjoying sleep, and not just seeking refuge in it—sleep within sleep, like dreams within dreams, could anything be better? An access of something as exquisite as pure bliss began to take hold of me. This must be Wednesday, I thought, and indeed it was Wednesday, when the cutlery grinder sets up shop in our courtyard and begins to hone every blade in the household, Mafalda always chatting him up as she stands next to him, holding a glass of lemonade for him while he plies away at the whetstone. The raspy, fricative sound of his wheel crackling and hissing in the midafternoon heat, sending sound waves of bliss up my way to my bedroom. I had never been able to admit to myself how happy Oliver had made me the day he'd swallowed my peach. Of course it had moved me, but it had flattered me as well, as though his gesture had said, *I believe with every cell in my body that every cell in yours must not, must never, die, and if it does have to die, let it die inside my body.* He'd unlatched the partly opened door to the balcony from the outside, stepped in—we weren't quite on speaking terms that day; he didn't ask if he could come in. What was I going to do? Say, You can't come in? This was when I raised my arm to greet him and tell him I was done pouting, no more pouting, ever, and let him lift the sheets and get into my bed. Now, no sooner had I heard the sound of the whetstone amid the cicadas than I knew I'd either wake up or go on sleeping, and both were good, dreaming or sleeping, one and the same, I'd take either or both.

When I awoke it was nearing five o'clock. I no longer wanted to play tennis, just as I had absolutely no desire to work on the Haydn. Time for a swim, I thought. I put on my bathing suit and walked down the stairway. Vimini was sitting on the short wall next to her parents' house.

"How come you're going for a swim?" she asked.

"I don't know. I just felt like it. Want to come?"

"Not today. They're forcing me to wear this ridiculous hat if I want to stay outside. I look like a Mexican bandit."

"Pancho Vimini. What will you do if I go swimming?"

"I'll watch. Unless you can help me get onto one of those rocks, then I'll sit there, wet my feet, and keep my hat on."

"Let's go, then."

You never needed to ask for Vimini's hand. It was given naturally, the way blind people automatically take your elbow. "Just don't walk too fast," she said.

We went down the stairway and when we reached the rocks I found the one she liked best and sat next to her. This was her favorite spot with Oliver. The rock was warm and I loved the way the sun felt on my skin at this time of the afternoon. "Am I glad I'm back," I said.

"Did you have a good time in Rome?"

I nodded.

"We missed you."

"We who?"

"Me. Marzia. She came looking for you the other day."

"Ah," I said.

"I told her where you went."

"Ah," I repeated.

I could tell the child was scanning my face. "I think she knows you don't like her very much."

There was no point debating the issue.

"And?" I asked.

"And nothing. I just felt sorry for her. I said you'd left in a great rush."

Vimini was obviously quite pleased with her guile.

"Did she believe you?"

"I think so. It wasn't exactly a lie, you know."

"What do you mean?"

"Well, you both left without saying goodbye."

"You're right, we did. We didn't mean anything by it."

"Oh, with you, I don't mind. But him I do. Very much."

"Why?"

"Why, Elio? You must forgive me for saying so, but you've never been very intelligent."

It took me a while to see where she was headed with this. Then it hit me.

"I may never see him again either," I said.

"No, you still might. But I don't know about me."

I could feel my throat tightening, so I left her on the rock and began to edge my way into the water. This was exactly what I'd predicted might happen. I'd stare at the water that evening and for a split second forget that he wasn't here any longer, that there was no point in turning back and looking up to the balcony, where his image hadn't quite vanished. And yet, scarcely hours ago, his body and my body . . . Now he had probably already had his second meal on the plane and was preparing to land at JFK. I knew that he was filled with grief when he finally kissed me one last time in one of the bathroom stalls at Fiumicino Airport and that, even if on the plane the drinks and the movie had distracted him, once alone in his room in New York, he too would be sad again, and I hated thinking of him sad, just as I knew he'd hate to see me sad in our bedroom, which had all too soon become my bedroom.

Someone was coming toward the rocks. I tried to think of something to dispel my sorrow and fell upon the ironic fact that the distance separating Vimini from me was exactly the same that separated me from Oliver. Seven years. In seven years, I began thinking, and suddenly felt something almost burst in my throat. I dove into the water.

It was after dinner when the phone rang. Oliver had arrived safely. Yes, in New York. Yes, same apartment, same people, same noise—unfortunately the same music streaming from outside the window—you could hear it now. He put the receiver out the window and allowed us to get a flavor of the Hispanic rhythms of New York. One Hundred and Fourteenth Street, he said. Going out to a late lunch with friends. My mother and father were both talking to him from separate phones in the living room. I was on the phone in the kitchen. Here? Well, you know. The usual dinner guests. Just left. Yes, very, very hot here too. My father hoped this had been productive. This? Staying with us, explained my father. Best thing in my life. If I could, I'd hop on the same plane and

come with the shirt on my back, an extra bathing suit, a toothbrush. Everyone laughed. With open arms, *caro*. Jokes were being
bandied back and forth. You know our tradition, explained my
mother, you must always come back, even for a few days. *Even for
a few days* meant for no more than a few days—but she'd meant
what she said, and he knew it. "Allora ciao, Oliver, e a presto," she
said. My father more or less repeated the same words, then
added, "Dunque, ti passo Elio—vi lascio." I heard the clicks of
both extension phones signal that no one else was on the line.
How tactful of my father. But the all-too-sudden freedom to be
alone across what seemed a time barrier froze me. Did he have a
good trip? Yes. Did he hate the meal? Yes. Did he think of me? I
had run out of questions and should have thought better than to
keep pounding him with more. "What do you think?" was his
vague answer—as if fearing someone might accidentally pick up
the receiver? Vimini sends her love. Very upset. I'll go out and buy
her something tomorrow and send it by express mail. I'll never
forget Rome so long as I live. Me neither. Do you like your room?
Sort of. Window facing noisy courtyard, never any sun, hardly
any room for anything, didn't know I owned so many books, bed
way too small now. Wish we could start all over in that room, I
said. Both leaning out the window in the evening, rubbing shoulders, as we did in Rome—every day of my life, I said. Every day
of mine too. Shirt, toothbrush, scorebook, and I'm flying over, so
don't tempt me either. I took something from your room, he said.
What? You'll never guess. What? Find out for yourself. And then
I said it, not because it was what I wanted to say to him but because the silence was weighing on us, and this was the easiest
thing to smuggle in during a pause—and at least I would have
said it: I don't want to lose you. We would write. I'd call from the
post office—more private that way. There was talk of Christmas,
of Thanksgiving even. Yes, Christmas. But his world, which until

then seemed no more distant from mine than by the thickness of the skin Chiara had once picked from his shoulders, had suddenly drifted light-years away. By Christmas it might not matter. Let me hear the noise from your window one last time. I heard crackle. Let me hear the sound you made when . . . A faint, timid sound— on account of because there were others in the house, he said. It made us laugh. Besides, they're waiting for me to go out with them. I wished he had never called. I had wanted to hear him say my name again. I had meant to ask him, now that we were far apart, what ever had happened between him and Chiara. I had also forgotten to ask where he'd put his red bathing suit. Probably he had forgotten and taken it away with him.

The first thing I did after our telephone conversation was go up to my room and see what he could possibly have taken that would remind him of me. Then I saw the unyellowed blank spot on the wall. Bless him. He had taken a framed, antique postcard of Monet's berm dating back to 1905 or so. One of our previous American summer residents had fished it out in a flee market in Paris two years ago and had mailed it to me as a souvenir. The faded colored postcard had originally been mailed in 1914— there were a few hasty, sepia-toned scribbles in German script on the back, addressed to a doctor in England, next to which the American student had inscribed his own greetings to me in black ink—*Think of me someday*. The picture would remind Oliver of the morning when I first spoke out. Or of the day when we rode by the berm pretending not to notice it. Or of that day we'd decided to picnic there and had vowed not to touch each other, the better to enjoy lying in bed together the same afternoon. I wanted him to have the picture before his eyes for all time, his whole life, in front of his desk, of his bed, everywhere. Nail it everywhere you go, I thought.

The mystery was resolved, as such things always are with

me, in my sleep that night. It had never struck me until then. And yet it had been staring me in the face for two whole years. His name was Maynard. Early one afternoon, while he must have known everyone was resting, he had knocked at my window to see if I had black ink—he had run out, he said, and only used black ink, as he knew I did. He stepped in. I was wearing only a bathing suit and went to my desk and handed him the bottle. He stared at me, stood there for an awkward moment, and then took the bottle. That same evening he left the flask right outside my balcony door. Any other person would have knocked again and handed it back to me. I was fifteen then. But I wouldn't have said no. In the course of one of our conversations I had told him about my favorite spot in the hills.

I had never thought of him until Oliver had lifted his picture.

A while after supper, I saw my father sitting at his usual place at the breakfast table. His chair was turned out and facing the sea, and on his lap were the proofs of his latest book. He was drinking his usual chamomile tea, enjoying the night. Next to him, three large citronella candles. The mosquitoes were out with a vengeance tonight. I went downstairs to join him. This was our usual time to sit together, and I had neglected him over the past month.

"Tell me about Rome," he said as soon as he saw me ready to sit next to him. This was also the moment when he would allow himself his last smoke of the day. He put away his manuscript with something of a tired toss that suggested an eager *now-we-come-to-the-good-part* and proceeded to light his cigarette with a roguish gesture, using one of the citronella candles. "So?"

There was nothing to tell. I repeated what I'd told my mother: the hotel, the Capitol, Villa Borghese, San Clemente, restaurants.

"Eat well too?"

I nodded.

"And drank well too?"

Nodded again.

"Done things your grandfather would have approved of?" I laughed. No, not this time. I told him about the incident near the Pasquino. "What an idea, to vomit in front of the talking statue!

"Movies? Concerts?"

It began to creep over me that he might be leading somewhere, perhaps without quite knowing it himself. I became aware of this because, as he kept asking questions remotely approaching the subject, I began to sense that I was already applying evasive maneuvers well before what was awaiting us around the corner was even visible. I spoke about the perennially dirty, run-down conditions of Rome's piazzas. The heat, the weather, traffic, too many nuns. Such-and-such a church closed down. Debris everywhere. Seedy renovations. And I complained about the people, and the tourists, and about the minibuses loading and unloading numberless hordes bearing cameras and baseball hats.

"Seen any of the inner, private courtyards I told you about?"

I guess we had failed to visit the inner, private courtyards he had told us about.

"Paid my respects to Giordano Bruno's statue?" he asked.

We certainly did. Almost vomited there too that night.

We laughed.

Tiny pause. Another drag from his cigarette.

Now.

"You two had a nice friendship."

This was far bolder than anything I anticipated.

"Yes," I replied, trying to leave my "yes" hanging in midair as though buoyed by the rise of a negative qualifier that was ultimately suppressed. I just hoped he hadn't caught the mildly hostile, evasive, seemingly fatigued *Yes, and so?* in my voice.

I also hoped, though, that he'd seize the opportunity of the unstated *Yes, and so?* in my answer to chide me, as he so often did, for being harsh or indifferent or way too critical of people who had every reason to consider themselves my friends. He might then add his usual bromide about how rare good friendships were and that, even if people proved difficult to be with after a while, still, most meant well and each had something good to impart. No man is an island, can't shut yourself away from others, people need people, blah, blah.

But I had guessed wrong.

"You're too smart not to know how rare, how special, what you two had was."

"Oliver was Oliver," I said, as if that summed things up.

"Parce que c'était lui, parce que c'était moi," my father added, quoting Montaigne's all-encompassing explanation for his friendship with Etienne de la Boétie.

I was thinking, instead, of Emily Brontë's words: because "he's more myself than I am."

"Oliver may be very intelligent—," I began. Once again, the disingenuous rise in intonation announced a damning *but* hanging invisibly between us. Anything not to let my father lead me any further down this road.

"Intelligent? He was more than intelligent. What you two had had everything and nothing to do with intelligence. He was good, and you were both lucky to have found each other, because you too are good."

My father had never spoken of goodness this way before. It disarmed me.

"I think he was better than me, Papa."

"I am sure he'd say the same about you, which flatters the two of you."

He was about to tap his cigarette and, in leaning toward the ashtray, he reached out and touched my hand.

"What lies ahead is going to be very difficult," he started to say, altering his voice. His tone said: *We don't have to speak about it, but let's not pretend we don't know what I'm saying.*

Speaking abstractly was the only way to speak the truth to him.

"Fear not. It will come. At least I hope it does. And when you least expect it. Nature has cunning ways of finding our weakest spot. Just remember: I am here. Right now you may not want to feel anything. Perhaps you never wished to feel anything. And perhaps it's not with me that you'll want to speak about these things. But feel something you did."

I looked at him. This was the moment when I should lie and tell him he was totally off course. I was about to.

"Look," he interrupted. "You had a beautiful friendship. Maybe more than a friendship. And I envy you. In my place, most parents would hope the whole thing goes away, or pray that their sons land on their feet soon enough. But I am not such a parent. In your place, if there is pain, nurse it, and if there is a flame, don't snuff it out, don't be brutal with it. Withdrawal can be a terrible thing when it keeps us awake at night, and watching others forget us sooner than we'd want to be forgotten is no better. We rip out so much of ourselves to be cured of things faster than we should that we go bankrupt by the age of thirty and have less to offer each time we start with someone new. But to feel nothing so as not to feel anything—what a waste!"

I couldn't begin to take all this in. I was dumbstruck.

"Have I spoken out of turn?" he asked.

I shook my head.

"Then let me say one more thing. It will clear the air. I may have come close, but I never had what you had. Something always held me back or stood in the way. How you live your life is your business. But remember, our hearts and our bodies are given to us only once. Most of us can't help but live as though we've got two lives to live, one is the mockup, the other the finished version, and then there are all those versions in between. But there's only one, and before you know it, your heart is worn out, and, as for your body, there comes a point when no one looks at it, much less wants to come near it. Right now there's sorrow. I don't envy the pain. But I envy you the pain."

He took a breath.

"We may never speak about this again. But I hope you'll never hold it against me that we did. I will have been a terrible father if, one day, you'd want to speak to me and felt that the door was shut or not sufficiently open."

I wanted to ask him how he knew. But then how could he not have known? How could anyone not have known? "Does Mother know?" I asked. I was going to say *suspect* but corrected myself. "I don't think she does." His voice meant, *But even if she did, I am sure her attitude would be no different than mine.*

We said good night. On my way upstairs I vowed to ask him about his life. We'd all heard about his women when he was young, but I'd never even had an inkling of anything else.

Was my father someone else? And if he was someone else, who was I?

Oliver kept his promise. He came back just before Christmas and stayed till New Year's. At first he was totally jet-lagged. He needs time, I thought. But so did I. He whiled away the hours with my parents mostly, then with Vimini, who was overjoyed to feel that

nothing had changed between them. I was starting to fear we'd
slip back to our early days when, but for patio pleasantries,
avoidance and indifference were the norm. Why had his phone
calls not prepared me for this? Was I the one responsible for the
new tenor of our friendship? Had my parents said something?
Had he come back for me? Or for them, for the house, to get
away? He had come back for his book, which had already been
published in England, in France, in Germany, and was finally due
to come out in Italy. It was an elegant volume, and we were all
very happy for him, including the bookseller in B., who promised
a book party the following summer. "Maybe. We'll see," said
Oliver after we'd stopped there on our bikes. The ice cream vendor was closed for the season. As were the flower shop and the
pharmacy where we'd stopped on leaving the berm that very first
time when he showed me how badly he'd scraped himself. They
all belonged to a lifetime ago. The town felt empty, the sky was
gray. One night he had a long talk with my father. In all likelihood they were discussing me, or my prospects for college, or
last summer, or his new book. When they opened the door, I
heard laughter in the hallway downstairs, my mother kissing
him. A while later there was a knock at my bedroom door, not
the French windows—that entrance was to remain permanently
shut, then. "Want to talk?" I was already in bed. He had a
sweater on and seemed dressed to go out for a walk. He sat on
the edge of my bed, looking as uneasy as I must have seemed the
first time when this room used to be his. "I might be getting married this spring," he said. I was dumbfounded. "But you never
said anything." "Well, it's been on and off for more than two
years." "I think it's wonderful news," I said. People getting
married was always wonderful news, I was happy for them,
marriages were good, and the broad smile on my face was genuine enough, even if it occurred to me a while later that such

news couldn't possibly bode well for us. Did I mind? he asked. "You're being silly," I said. Long silence. "Will you be getting in bed now?" I asked. He looked at me gingerly. "For a short while. But I don't want to do anything." It sounded like an updated and far more polished version of *Later, maybe*. So we were back to that, were we? I had an impulse to mimic him but held back. He lay beside me on top of the blanket with his sweater on. All he had taken off was his loafers. "How long do you think this will go on?" he asked wryly. "Not long, I hope." He kissed me on the mouth, but it wasn't the kiss after the Pasquino, when he'd pressed me hard against the wall on via Santa Maria dell'Anima. I recognized the taste instantly. I'd never realized how much I liked it or how long I'd missed it. One more item to log on that checklist of things I'd miss before losing him for good. I was about to get out from under the blankets. "I can't do this," he said, and sprang away. "I can," I replied. "Yes, but I can't." I must have had iced razor blades in my eyes, for he suddenly realized how angry I was. "I'd love nothing better than to take your clothes off and at the very least hold you. But I can't." I put my arms around his head and held it. "Then maybe you shouldn't stay. They know about us." "I figured," he said. "How?" "By the way your father spoke. You're lucky. My father would have carted me off to a correctional facility." I looked at him: I want one more kiss.

I should, could, have seized him.

By the next morning, things became officially chilly.

One small thing did occur that week. We were sitting in the living room after lunch having coffee when my father brought out a large manila folder in which were stacked six applications accompanied with the passport photo of each applicant. Next summer's candidates. My father wanted Oliver's opinion, then passed around the folder to my mother, me, and another professor who had stopped by for lunch with his wife, also a university colleague who had come for the same reason the year before. "My successor," said Oliver, picking one application above the rest and passing it around. My father instinctively darted a glance in my direction, then immediately withdrew it.

The exact same thing had occurred almost a year, to the day, before. Pavel, Maynard's successor, had come to visit that Christmas and on looking over the files had strongly recommended one from Chicago—in fact, he knew him very well. Pavel and everyone else in the room felt quite tepid about a young postdoc teaching at Columbia who specialized in, of all things, the pre-Socratics. I had taken longer than needed to look at his picture and was relieved to notice that I felt nothing.

In thinking back now, I couldn't be more certain that everything between us had started in this very room during Christmas break.

"Is this how I was selected?" he asked with a sort of earnest, awkward candor, which my mother always found disarming.

"I wanted it to be you," I told Oliver later that evening when I helped him load his things in the car minutes before Manfredi drove him to the station. "I made sure they picked you."

That night I riffled through my father's cabinet and found the file containing last year's applicants. I found his picture. Open shirt collar, Billowy, long hair, the dash of a movie star unwillingly snapped by a paparazzo. No wonder I'd stared at it. I wished I could remember what I'd felt on that afternoon exactly a year ago—that burst of desire followed by its instant antidote, fear. The real Oliver, and each successive Oliver wearing a different-colored bathing suit every day, or the Oliver who lay naked in bed, or who leaned on the window ledge of our hotel in Rome, stood in the way of the troubled and confused image I had drawn of him on first seeing his snapshot.

I looked at the faces of the other applicants. This one wasn't so bad. I began to wonder what turn my life would have taken had someone else shown up instead. I wouldn't have gone to Rome. But I might have gone elsewhere. Wouldn't have known the first thing about San Clemente. But I might have discovered something else which I'd missed out on and might never know about. Wouldn't have changed, would never be who I am today, would have become someone else.

I wonder now who that someone else is today. Is he happier? Couldn't I dip into his life for a few hours, a few days, and see for myself—not just to test if this other life is better, or to measure how our lives couldn't be further apart because of Oliver, but also to consider what I would say to this other me were I to pay him a short visit one day. Would I like him, would he like me, would either of us understand why the other became who he is, would either be surprised to learn that each of us had in fact run into an Oliver of one sort or another, man or woman, and that we were very possibly, regardless of who came to stay with us that summer, one and the same person still?

It was my mother, who hated Pavel and would have forced my father to turn down anyone Pavel recommended, who finally twisted the arm of fate. We may be Jews of discretion, she'd said, but this Pavel is an anti-Semite and I won't have another anti-Semite in my house.

I remembered that conversation. It too was imprinted on the photo of his face. So he's Jewish too, I thought.

And then I did what I'd been meaning to do all along that night in my father's study. I pretended not to know who this chap Oliver was. This was last Christmas. Pavel was still trying to persuade us to host his friend. Summer hadn't happened yet. Oliver would probably arrive by cab. I'd carry his luggage, show him to his room, take him to the beach by way of the stairway down to

the rocks, and then, time allowing, show him around the property as far back as the old railway stop and say something about
the gypsies living in the abandoned train cars bearing the insignia of the royal House of Savoy. Weeks later, if we had time,
we might take a bike ride to B. We'd stop for refreshments. I'd
show him the bookstore. Then I'd show him Monet's berm.
None of it had happened yet.

We heard of his wedding the following summer. We sent gifts
and I included a little mot. The summer came and went. I was often tempted to tell him about his "successor" and embroider all
manner of stories about my new neighbor down the balcony. But
I never sent him anything. The only letter I did send the year after was to tell him that Vimini had died. He wrote to all of us
saying how sorry he was. He was traveling in Asia, so that by the
time his letter reached us, his reaction to Vimini's death, rather
than soothe an open sore, seemed to graze one that had healed
on its own. Writing to him about her was like crossing the last
footbridge between us, especially after it became clear we weren't
ever going to mention what had once existed between us, or, for
that matter, that we weren't even mentioning it. Writing had also
been my way of telling him what college I was attending in the
States, in case my father, who kept an active correspondence
with all of our previous residents, hadn't already told him. Ironically, Oliver wrote back to my address in Italy—another reason
for the delay.

    Then came the blank years. If I were to punctuate my life
with the people whose bed I shared, and if these could be divided
in two categories—those before and those after Oliver—then the
greatest gift life could bestow on me was to move this divider forward in time. Many helped me part life into Before X and After

X segments, many brought joy and sorrow, many threw my life off course, while others made no difference whatsoever, so that Oliver, who for so long had loomed like a fulcrum on the scale of life, eventually acquired successors who either eclipsed him or reduced him to an early milepost, a minor fork in the road, a small, fiery Mercury on a voyage out to Pluto and beyond. Fancy this, I might say: at the time I knew Oliver, I still hadn't met so-and-so. Yet life without so-and-so was simply unthinkable.

One summer, nine years after his last letter, I received a phone call in the States from my parents. "You'll never guess who is staying with us for two days. In your old bedroom. And standing right in front of me now." I had already guessed, of course, but pretended I couldn't. "The fact that you refuse to say you've already guessed says a great deal," my father said with a snicker before saying goodbye. There was a tussle between my parents over who was to hand their phone over. Finally his voice came through. "Elio," he said. I could hear my parents and the voices of children in the background. No one could say my name that way. "Elio," I repeated, to say it was I speaking but also to spark our old game and show I'd forgotten nothing. "It's Oliver," he said. He had forgotten.

"They showed me pictures, you haven't changed," he said. He spoke about his two boys who were right now playing in the living room with my mother, eight and six, I should meet his wife, I am so happy to be here, you have no idea, no idea. It's the most beautiful spot in the world, I said, pretending to infer that he was happy because of the place. You can't understand how happy I am to be here. His words were breaking up, he passed the phone back to my mother, who, before turning to me, was still speaking to him with endearing words. "*Ma s'è tutto commosso*, he's all choked up," she finally said to me. "I wish I could be with you all," I responded, getting all worked up myself over someone I had almost entirely stopped thinking about. Time makes us sentimental. Perhaps, in the end, it is because of time that we suffer.

Four years later, while passing through his college town, I did the unusual. I decided to show up. I sat in his afternoon lecture hall and, after class, as he was putting away his books and packing loose sheets into a folder, I walked up to him. I wasn't going to make him guess who I was, but I wasn't going to make it easy either.

There was a student who wanted to ask him a question. So I waited my turn. The student eventually left. "You probably don't remember me," I began, as he squinted somewhat, trying to place me. He was suddenly distant, as if stricken by the fear that we had met in a place he didn't care to remember. He put on a tentative, ironic, questioning look, an uncomfortable, puckered smile, as if rehearsing something like, *I'm afraid you're mistaking me for somebody else.* Then he paused. "Good God—Elio!" It was my beard that had thrown him off, he said. He embraced me, and then patted my furry face several times as if I were younger than I'd even been that summer so long ago. He hugged me the way he couldn't bring himself to do on the night when he stepped into my room to tell me he was getting married. "How many years has it been?"

"Fifteen. I counted them last night on my way here." Then I added: "Actually, that's not true. I've always known."

"Fifteen it is. Just look at you!

"Look," he added, "come for a drink, come for dinner, tonight, now, meet my wife, my boys. Please, please, please."

"I'd love to—"

"I have to drop something in my office, and off we go. It's a lovely walk along to the parking lot."

"You don't understand. I'd love to. But I can't."

The "can't" did not mean I wasn't free to visit him but that I couldn't bring myself to do it.

He looked at me as he was still putting away his papers in the leather bag.

"You never did forgive me, did you?"

"Forgive? There was nothing to forgive. If anything, I'm grateful for everything. I remember good things only."

I had heard people say this in the movies. They seemed to believe it.

"Then what is it?" he asked.

We were leaving his classroom and stepped into the commons where one of those long, languorous autumnal sunsets on the East Coast threw luminous shades of orange over the adjoining hills.

How was I ever going to explain to him, or to myself, why I couldn't go to his home and meet his family, though every part of me was dying to? Oliver wife. Oliver sons. Oliver pets. Oliver study, desk, books, world, life. What had I expected? A hug, a handshake, a perfunctory hail-fellow-well-met, and then the unavoidable *Later!*?

The very possibility of meeting his family suddenly alarmed me—too real, too sudden, too in-my-face, not rehearsed enough. Over the years I'd lodged him in the permanent past, my pluperfect lover, put him on ice, stuffed him with memories and mothballs like a hunted ornament confabulating with the ghost of all my evenings. I'd dust him off from time to time and then put him back on the mantelpiece. He no longer belonged to earth or to life. All I was likely to discover at this point wasn't just how distant were the paths we'd taken, it was the measure of loss that was going to strike me—a loss I didn't mind thinking about in abstract terms but which would hurt when stared at in the face,

the way nostalgia hurts long after we've stopped thinking of
things we've lost and may never have cared for.

Or was it that I was jealous of his family, of the life he'd made
for himself, of the things I never shared and couldn't possibly
have known about? Things he had longed for, loved, and lost, and
whose loss had crushed him, but whose presence in his life, when
he had them, I wasn't there to witness and wouldn't know the
first thing about. I wasn't there when he'd acquired them, wasn't
there when he'd given them up. Or was it much, much simpler? I
had come to see if I felt something, if something was still alive.
The trouble was I didn't want anything to be alive either.

All these years, whenever I thought of him, I'd think either of
B. or of our last days in Rome, the whole thing leading up to two
scenes: the balcony with its attendant agonies and via Santa
Maria dell'Anima, where he'd pushed me against the old wall
and kissed me and in the end let me put one leg around his. Every
time I go back to Rome, I go back to that one spot. It is still alive
for me, still resounds with something totally present, as though
a heart stolen from a tale by Poe still throbbed under the ancient
slate pavement to remind me that, here, I had finally encountered
the life that was right for me but had failed to have. I could never
think of him in New England. When I lived in New England for
a while and was separated from him by no more than fifty miles,
I continued to imagine him as stuck in Italy somewhere, unreal
and spectral. The places where he'd lived also felt inanimate, and
as soon as I tried thinking of them, they too would float and drift
away, no less unreal and spectral. Now, it turned out, not only
were New England towns very much alive, but so was he. I could
easily have thrust myself on him years ago, married or unmar-
ried—unless it was I who, despite all appearances, had all along
been unreal and spectral myself.

Or had I come with a far more menial purpose? To find him

living alone, waiting for me, craving to be taken back to B.? Yes, both our lives on the same artificial respirator, waiting for that time when we'd finally meet and scale our way back to the Piave memorial.

And then it came out of me: "The truth is I'm not sure I can feel nothing. And if I am to meet your family, I would prefer not to feel anything." Followed by a dramatic silence. "Perhaps it never went away."

Was I speaking the truth? Or was the moment, tense and delicate as it was, making me say things I'd never quite admitted to myself and could still not wager were entirely true? "I don't think it went away," I repeated.

"So," he said. His *so* was the only word that could sum up my uncertainties. But perhaps he had also meant *So?* as though to question what could possibly have been so shocking about still wanting him after so many years.

"So," I repeated, as though referring to the capricious aches and sorrows of a fussy third party who happened to be me.

"So, that's why you can't come over for drinks?"

"So, that's why I can't come over for drinks."

"What a goose!"

I had altogether forgotten his word.

We reached his office. He introduced me to two or three colleagues who happened to be in the department, surprising me with his total familiarity with every aspect of my career. He knew everything, had kept abreast of the most insignificant details. In some cases, he must have dug out information about me that could only be obtained by surfing the Web. It moved me. I'd assumed he'd totally forgotten me.

"I want to show you something," he said. His office had a large leather sofa. Oliver sofa, I thought. So this is where he sits and reads. Papers were strewn about the sofa and on the floor, except for the corner seat, which was under an alabaster lamp. Oliver lamp. I remembered sheets lining the floor in his room in B. "Recognize it?" he asked. On the wall was a framed colored reproduction of a poorly preserved fresco of a bearded Mithraic figure. Each of us had bought one on the morning of our visit to San Clemente. I hadn't seen mine in ages. Next to it on the wall was a framed postcard of Monet's berm. I recognized it immediately.

"It used to be mine, but you've owned it far, far longer than I have." We belonged to each other, but had lived so far apart that we belonged to others now. Squatters, and only squatters, were the true claimants to our lives.

"It has a long history," I said.

"I know. When I had it reframed I saw the inscriptions on the back, which is why you can also read the back of the card now. I've often thought about this Maynard guy. *Think of me someday.*"

"Your predecessor," I said to tease him. "No, nothing like that. Whom will you give it to one day?"

"I had hoped one day to let one of my sons bring it in person when he comes for his residency. I've already added my inscription—but you can't see it. Are you staying in town?" he asked to change the subject as he was putting on his raincoat.

"Yes. For one night. I'm seeing some people at the university tomorrow morning, then I'm off."

He looked at me. I knew he was thinking of that night during Christmas break, and he knew I knew it. "So I'm forgiven."

He pressed his lips in muted apology.

"Let's have a drink at my hotel."

I felt his discomfort.

"I said a drink, not a fuck."

He looked at me and literally blushed. I was staring at him. He was amazingly handsome still, no loss of hair, no fat, still jogged every morning, he said, skin still as smooth as then. Only a few sunspots on his hands. Sunspots, I thought, and I couldn't put the thought away. "What are these?" I asked, pointing at his hand and then touching it. "I have them all over." Sunspots. They broke my heart, and I wanted to kiss each and every one away. "Too much sun in my salad days. Besides, it shouldn't be so surprising. I'm getting on. In three years, my elder son will be as old as you were then—in fact, he's closer to the person you were when we were together than you are to the Elio I knew then. Talk about uncanny."

Is that what you call it, *when we were together*? I thought.

In the bar of the old New England hotel, we found a quiet spot overlooking the river and a large flower garden that was very much in bloom that month. We ordered two martinis—Sapphire gin, he specified—and sat close together in the horseshoe-shaped booth, like two husbands who are forced to sit uncomfortably close while their wives are in the powder room.

"In another eight years, I'll be forty-seven and you forty. Five years from then, I'll be fifty-two and you forty-five. Will you come for dinner then?"

"Yes. I promise."

"So what you're really saying is you'll come only when you think you'll be too old to care. When my kids have left. Or when I'm a grandfather. I can just see us—and on that evening, we'll sit together and drink a strong eau-de-vie, like the grappa your father used to serve at night sometimes."

"And like the old men who sat around the piazzetta facing the Piave memorial, we'll speak about two young men who found much happiness for a few weeks and lived the remainder of their lives dipping cotton swabs into that bowl of happiness, fearing they'd use it up, without daring to drink more than a thimbleful on ritual anniversaries." But this thing that almost never was still beckons, I wanted to tell him. They can never undo it, never unwrite it, never unlive it, or relive it—it's just stuck there like a vision of fireflies on a summer field toward evening that keeps saying, *You could have had this instead*. But going back is false. Moving ahead is false. Looking the other way is false. Trying to redress all that is false turns out to be just as false.

Their life is like a garbled echo buried for all time in a sealed Mithraic chamber.

Silence.

"God, the way they envied us from across the dinner table that first night in Rome," he said. "Staring at us, the young, the old, men, women—every single one of them at that dinner table—gaping at us, because we were so happy.

"And on that evening when we grow older still we'll speak about these two young men as though they were two strangers we met on the train and whom we admire and want to help along. And we'll want to call it envy, because to call it regret would break our hearts."

Silence again.

"Perhaps I am not yet ready to speak of them as strangers," I said.

"If it makes you feel any better, I don't think either of us ever will be."

"I think we should have another."

He conceded even before putting up a weak argument about getting back home.

We got the preliminaries out of the way. His life, my life, what did he do, what did I do, what's good, what's bad. Where did he hope to be, where did I. We avoided my parents. I assumed he knew. By not asking he told me that he did.

An hour.

"Your best moment?" he finally interrupted.

I thought awhile.

"The first night is the one I remember best—perhaps because I fumbled so much. But also Rome. There is a spot on via Santa Maria dell'Anima that I revisit every time I'm in Rome. I'll stare at it for a second, and suddenly it'll all come back to me. I had just thrown up that night and on the way back to the bar you kissed me. People kept walking by but I didn't care, nor did you. That kiss is still imprinted there, thank goodness. It's all I have from you. This and your shirt."

He remembered.

"And you," I asked, "what moment?"

"Rome too. Singing together till dawn on Piazza Navona."

I had totally forgotten. It wasn't just a Neapolitan song we ended up singing that night. A group of young Dutchmen had taken out their guitars and were singing one Beatles song after the other, and everyone by the main fountain had joined in, and so did we. Even Dante showed up again and he too sang along in his warped English. "Did they serenade us, or am I making it up?"

He looked at me in bewilderment.

"They serenaded *you*—and you were drunk out of your mind. In the end you borrowed the guitar from one of them and you started playing, and then, out of nowhere, singing. Gaping, they all were. All the druggies of the world listening like sheep to Handel. One of the Dutch girls had lost it. You wanted to bring her to the hotel. She wanted to come too. What a night. We ended up sitting in the emptied terrace of a closed caffè behind the piazza, just you and I and the girl, watching dawn, each of us slumped on a chair."

He looked at me. "Am I glad you came."

"I'm glad I came too."

"Can I ask you a question?"

Why was this suddenly making me nervous? "Shoot."

"Would you start again if you could?"

I looked at him. "Why are you asking?"

"Because. Just answer."

"Would I start again if I could? In a second. But I've had two of these, and I'm about to order a third."

He smiled. It was obviously my turn to ask the same question, but I didn't want to embarrass him. This was my favorite Oliver: the one who thought exactly like me.

"Seeing you here is like waking from a twenty-year coma. You look around you and you find that your wife has left you, your children, whose childhood you totally missed out on, are grown men, some are married, your parents have died long ago, you have no friends, and that tiny face staring at you through goggles belongs to none other than your grandson, who's been brought along to welcome Gramps from his long sleep. Your face in the mirror is as white as Rip Van Winkle's. But here's the catch: you're still twenty years younger than those gathered around you, which is why I can be twenty-four in a second—I am twenty-four. And if you pushed the parable a few years further up, I could wake up and be younger than my elder son."

"What does this say about the life you've lived, then?"

"Part of it—just part of it—was a coma, but I prefer to call it a parallel life. It sounds better. Problem is that most of us have—live, that is—more than two parallel lives."

Maybe it was the alcohol, maybe it was the truth, maybe I didn't want things to turn abstract, but I felt I should say it, because this was the moment to say it, because it suddenly dawned on me that this was why I had come, to tell him "You are the only person I'd like to say goodbye to when I die, because only then will this thing I call my life make any sense. And if I should hear that you died, my life as I know it, the me who is speaking with you now, will cease to exist. Sometimes I have this awful picture of waking up in our house in B. and, looking out to the sea, hearing the news from the waves themselves, *He died last night*. We missed out on so much. It was a coma. Tomorrow I go back to my coma, and you to yours. Pardon, I didn't mean to offend—I am sure yours is no coma."

"No, a parallel life."

Maybe every other sorrow I'd known in life suddenly decided to converge on this very one. I had to fight it off. And if he didn't see, it's probably because he himself was not immune to it.

On a whim, I asked him if he'd ever read a novel by Thomas Hardy called *The Well-Beloved*. No, he hadn't. About a man who falls in love with a woman who, years after leaving him, dies. He visits her house and ends up meeting her daughter, with whom he falls in love, and after losing her as well, many years later, runs into her daughter, with whom he falls in love. "Do these things die out on their own or do some things need generations and lifetimes to sort themselves out?"

"I wouldn't want one of my sons in your bed, any more than I'd like yours, if you were to have one, in my son's."

We chuckled. "I wonder about our fathers, though."

He thought for a while, then smiled.

"What I don't want is to receive a letter from your son with the bad news: *And by the way, enclosed please find a framed postcard my father asked me to return to you*. Nor do I want to answer with something like: *You can come whenever you please, I am sure he would have wanted you to stay in his room*. Promise me it won't happen."

"Promise."

"What did you write on the back of the postcard?"

"It was going to be a surprise."

"I'm too old for surprises. Besides, surprises always come

with a sharp edge that is meant to hurt. I don't want to be hurt—
not by you. Tell me."

"Just two words."

"Let me guess: *If not later, when?*"

"Two words, I said. Besides, that would be cruel."

I thought for a while.

"I give up."

"*Cor cordium*, heart of hearts, I've never said anything truer
in my life to anyone."

I stared at him.

It was good we were in a public place.

"We should go." He reached for his raincoat, which was
folded next to his seat, and began to make motions of standing up.

I was going to walk him outside the hotel lobby and then
stand and watch him go. Any moment now we were going to say
goodbye. Suddenly part of my life was going to be taken away
from me now and would never be given back.

"Suppose I walk you to your car," I said.

"Suppose you came for dinner."

"Suppose I did."

Outside, the night was settling fast. I liked the peace and the
silence of the countryside, with its fading alpenglow and dark-
ling view of the river. Oliver country, I thought. The mottled
lights from across the other bank beamed on the water, reminding me of Van Gogh's *Starlight Over the Rhone*. Very autumnal,
very beginning of school year, very Indian summer, and as always at Indian summer twilight, that lingering mix of unfinished
summer business and unfinished homework and always the illusion of summer months ahead, which wears itself out no sooner
than the sun has set.

I tried to picture his happy family, boys immersed in homework, or lumbering back from late practice, surly, ill-tempered

thumping with muddied boots, every cliché racing through my mind. *This is the man whose house I stayed in when I lived in Italy*, he'd say, followed by grumpy harrumphs from two adolescents who couldn't be bothered by the man from Italy or the house in Italy, but who'd reel in shock if told, *Oh, and by the way, this man who was almost your age back then and who spent most of his days quietly transcribing* The Seven Last Words of Christ *each morning would sneak into my room at night and we'd fuck our brains out. So shake hands and be nice.*

Then I thought of the drive back, late at night, along the starlit river to this rickety antique New England hotel on a shoreline that I hoped would remind us both of the bay of B., and of Van Gogh's starry nights, and of the night I joined him on the rock and kissed him on the neck, and of the last night when we walked together on the coast road, sensing we'd run out of last-minute miracles to put off his leaving. I imagined being in his car asking myself, Who knows, would I want to, would he want to, perhaps a nightcap at the bar would decide, knowing that, all through dinner that evening, he and I would be worrying about the same exact thing, hoping it might happen, praying it might not, perhaps a nightcap would decide—I could just read it on his face as I pictured him looking away while uncorking a bottle of wine or while changing the music, because he too would catch the thought racing through my mind and want me to know he was debating the exact same thing, because, as he'd pour the wine for his wife, for me, for himself, it would finally dawn on us both that he was more me than I had ever been myself, because when he became me and I became him in bed so many years ago, he was and would forever remain, long after every forked road in life had done its work, my brother, my friend, my father, my son, my husband, my lover, myself. In the weeks we'd been thrown together that summer, our lives had scarcely touched, but we had

crossed to the other bank, where time stops and heaven reaches
down to earth and gives us that ration of what is from birth di-
vinely ours. We looked the other way. We spoke about everything
but. But we've always known, and not saying anything now confirmed it all the more. We had found the stars, you and I. And
this is given once only.

Last summer he finally did come back. It was for an overnight
visit, on his way from Rome to Menton. He arrived by cab down
the tree-lined driveway, where the car stopped more or less where
it had stopped twenty years before. He sprang out with his lap-
top, a huge athletic duffel bag, and a large gift-wrapped box, obviously a present. "For your mother," he said when he caught my
glance. "Better tell her what's in it," I said as soon as I helped put
his things down in the foyer. "She suspects everyone." He understood. It saddened him.

"Old room?" I asked.

"Old room," he confirmed, even though we'd arranged everything by e-mail already.

"Old room it is, then."

I wasn't eager to go upstairs with him and was relieved to see
Manfredi and Mafalda shuffle out of the kitchen to greet him as
soon as they'd heard his taxi. Their giddy hugs and kisses de-
fused some of the uneasiness I knew I'd feel as soon as he'd settled down in our house. I wanted their overexcited welcome to
last well into the first hour of his stay. Anything to prevent us
from sitting face-to-face over coffee and finally speaking the unavoidable two words: twenty years.

Instead, we'd leave his things in the foyer and hope Manfredi
would bring them upstairs while Oliver and I took a quick walk
around the house. "I'm sure you're dying to see," I'd say, meaning

the garden, the balustrade, and the view of the sea. We'd work our way behind the pool, back into the living room where the old piano stood next to the French windows, and finally we would return to the foyer and find that his things had indeed already been carried upstairs. Part of me might want him to realize that nothing had changed since he'd been here last, that the *orle of paradise* was still there, and that the tilting gate to the beach still squeaked, that the world was exactly as he'd left it, minus Vimini, Anchise, and my father. This was the welcoming gesture I meant to extend. But another part of me wanted him to sense there was no point trying to catch up now—we'd traveled and been through too much without each other for there to be any common ground between us. Perhaps I wanted him to feel the sting of loss, and grieve. But in the end, and by way of compromise, perhaps, I decided that the easiest way was to show I'd forgotten none of it. I made a motion to take him to the empty lot that remained as scorched and fallow as when I'd shown it to him two decades before. I had barely finished my offer—"Been there, done that," he replied. It was his way of telling me he hadn't forgotten either. "Maybe you'd prefer to make a quick stop at the bank." He burst out laughing. "I'll bet you they never closed my account." "If we have time, and if you care to, I'll take you to the belfry. I know you've never been up there."

"To-die-for?"

I smiled back. He remembered our name for it.

As we toured the patio overlooking the huge expanse of blue before us, I stood by and watched him lean on the balustrade overlooking the bay.

Beneath us was his rock, where he sat at night, where he and Vimini had whiled away entire afternoons together.

"She'd be thirty today," he said.

"I know."

"She wrote to me every day. Every single day."

He was staring at their spot. I remembered how they'd hold hands and scamper together all the way down to the shore.

"Then one day she stopped writing. And I knew. I just knew. I've kept all her letters, you know."

I looked at him wistfully.

"I've kept yours too," he immediately added, to reassure me, though vaguely, not knowing whether this was something I wanted to hear.

It was my turn. "I have all of yours too. And something else as well. Which I may show you. Later."

Did he not remember Billowy, or was he too modest, too cautious, to show he knew exactly what I was referring to? He resumed staring into the offing.

He had come on the right day. Not a cloud, not a ripple, not a stir in the wind. "I'd forgotten how much I loved this place. But this is exactly how I remember it. At noon it's paradise."

I let him talk. It was good to see his eyes drift into the offing. Perhaps he too wanted to avoid the face-to-face.

"And Anchise?" he finally asked.

"We lost him to cancer, poor man. I used to think he was so old. He wasn't even fifty."

"He too loved it here—him and his grafts and his orchard."

"He died in my grandfather's bedroom."

Silence again. I was going to say My old room, but I changed my mind.

"Are you happy you're back?"

He saw through my question before I did.

"Are *you* happy I'm back?" he retorted.

I looked at him, feeling quite disarmed, though not threatened. Like people who blush easily but aren't ashamed of it, I knew better than to stifle this feeling, and let myself be swayed by it.

"You know I am. More than I ought to be, perhaps."

"Me too."

That said it all.

"Come, I'll show you where we buried some of my father's ashes."

We walked down the back stairwell into the garden where the old breakfast table used to be. "This was my father's spot. I call it his ghost spot. My spot used to be over there, if you remember." I pointed to where my old table used to stand by the pool.

"Did I have a spot?" he asked with a half grin.

"You'll always have a spot."

I wanted to tell him that the pool, the garden, the house, the tennis court, the *orle of paradise*, the whole place, would always be his ghost spot. Instead, I pointed upstairs to the French windows of his room. Your eyes are forever there, I wanted to say, trapped in the sheer curtains, staring out from my bedroom upstairs where no one sleeps these days. When there's a breeze and they swell and I look up from down here or stand outside on the balcony, I'll catch myself thinking that you're in there, staring out from your world to my world, saying, as you did on that one night when I found you on the rock, *I've been happy here.* You're thousands of miles away but no sooner do I look at this window than I'll think of a bathing suit, a shirt thrown on on the fly, arms resting on the banister, and you're suddenly there, lighting up your first cigarette of the day—twenty years ago today. For as long as the house stands, this will be your ghost spot—and mine too, I wanted to say.

We stood there for a few seconds where my father and I had spoken of Oliver once. Now he and I were speaking of my father. Tomorrow, I'll think back on this moment and let the ghosts of their absence maunder in the twilit hour of the day.

"I know he would have wanted something like this to happen, especially on such a gorgeous summer day."

"I am sure he would have. Where did you bury the rest of his ashes?" he asked.

"Oh, all over. In the Hudson, the Aegean, the Dead Sea. But this is where I come to be with him."

He said nothing. There was nothing to say.

"Come, I'll take you to San Giacomo before you change your mind," I finally said. "There is still time before lunch. Remember the way?"

"I remember the way."

"You remember the way," I echoed.

He looked at me and smiled. It cheered me. Perhaps because I knew he was taunting me.

Twenty years was yesterday, and yesterday was just earlier this morning, and morning seemed light-years away.

"I'm like you," he said. "I remember everything."

I stopped for a second. If you remember everything, I wanted to say, and if you are really like me, then before you leave tomorrow, or when you're just ready to shut the door of the taxi and have already said goodbye to everyone else and there's not a thing left to say in this life, then, just this once, turn to me, even in jest, or as an afterthought, which would have meant everything to me when we were together, and, as you did back then, look me in the face, hold my gaze, and call me by your name.

Date
Due →

Books returned after due date
are subject to a fine.

Fairleigh Dickinson University Library
Teaneck, New Jersey

T001-15M
11-8-02